first verse

A PERFECT SONG DUET: PART ONE

L.M. HALLORAN

Copyright © 2025 by L.M. Halloran

Cover design by Laura Halloran. No generative AI.

ISBN 979-8-9922707-2-3

Editing by *Lawrence Editing*

lmhalloran.com

dedication

For Brit and her love of Harry Styles...

*If Harry were a 6'5" walking red flag with
even more tattoos and a pierced dick.*

Your mental health matters, so please review the following content warning. If you have no triggers, skip this to avoid spoilers.

This novel contains the following mature themes: heavy emotional angst, anxiety disorder rep, depression rep, neurodivergence rep, other woman drama (no cheating/open relationship), explicit MF sex, degradation/praise kink, nyctophobia (fear of the dark), on-page drug use (pills/opioids), and the mental/emotional effects of addiction on both the addict and their loved ones. Please be aware, there may be additional triggering content that is not listed.

Buckle up, lovely. You're in for a wild ride.

first verse

"It is by going down into the abyss that we recover the treasure of life. Where you stumble, there lies your treasure."

JOSEPH CAMPBELL

NIGHT ☆ THEORY
BABY THIS IS DESTINY
I'LL FOLLOW YOU INTO THE SEA
I'LL COME FOR YOU, YOU'LL SEE
SET US FREE — YOU AND ME
DEAD OR ALIVE

PART ONE

intro

intro : the opening piece of a song that establishes
key, tempo, and rhythm

prologue

EVA 15 | WILDER 17

Late afternoon sunlight dances among leaves in the giant sycamore tree, polka-dotting Wilder's dark, messy hair and broad shoulders with flares of gold. His face is downturned, his focus on the open notebook in his lap. As I watch, he pulls a pencil from between his teeth, scratches a few words onto a page, then tucks it back in his mouth.

This has been going on for ten minutes. Write-chew-write-chew. The anxiety of not knowing what he's writing, coupled with the fact I can't seem to look away, makes me feel like I'm being sunburned in the shade.

I can't take it anymore.

"Stop chewing on my pencil. What are you, five?"

"Better than chewing my nails," he mutters without looking up.

I tuck my hands discreetly under my crossed legs. "Whatever. Are you done yet?"

Speckled green eyes lift from the notebook. He pulls the pencil from between his teeth, the wet eraser briefly depressing his lower lip. My breath catches and my thoughts turn hazy.

"Why do you care what I do with my mouth, Evangeline?" he asks teasingly.

Snapped out of my trance, I glower at him. "I care about my pencil, dumbass."

He wipes it off on his chest, then offers it to me.

I make a face. "Forget it. It's yours now."

His grin is a sunrise that begins in his eyes and spreads across his face, so bright it scorches my cheeks.

"I'm done," he says lightly, tossing the notebook into my lap.

Seizing the distraction, I flip to the page of lyrics we're working on. He left most of them untouched but rewrote the chorus. When I read his messy words in the margin, my stomach flips.

I look up to find him smirking, his eyes narrowed as he waits for my reaction.

"No way. I'm not singing this."

His brows lift. "Why not? Besides, we'd sing it together."

A breeze skips around us, rustling leaves and shifting the paths of sunbeams. My gaze bounces between the words and him. He's not looking at me anymore, his face upturned to the lush, arterial beauty above us.

"It's..." *Incredible,* I think. But what comes out instead is, "Cheesy."

His eyes cut to me sharply. "You think it's cheesy?"

Instant regret fills me. I clear my throat, shaking my head. "No," I say softly. "I don't know why I said that."

But I do.

The words are unlike any he's written before. I don't know how to feel about them—or maybe they make me feel too much. I'm surprised. Flustered. Curious. My heart is racing. There's a knot in stomach I can't explain.

I read the lyrics again.

BABY, THIS IS DESTINY
I'LL FOLLOW YOU INTO THE SEA
I'LL COME FOR YOU, YOU'LL SEE
SET US FREE — YOU AND ME
DEAD OR ALIVE

Someone definitely inspired this. Does he have a crush on a girl at his school? Is he going to ask her out? Has he already? Is that why he canceled last weekend?

Normally, the fact we go to different high schools is annoying, but I'm suddenly grateful for the distance between our houses and everyday lives. I don't want to see his sunrise smile aimed at someone else.

I refuse to analyze why.

Swallowing the questions clogging my throat, I remind myself that Wilder and I aren't the kind of friends who share every little detail of our lives. Our bond is music, and it transcends the trivial and mundane.

After reading his words a few more times, I close the notebook and drop it to the grass.

"I still like my chorus better."

He scoffs, his gaze drifting past me. Around me. Never landing directly. Silence falls between us, vibrating with words in a language neither of us knows.

I stretch out my legs, then recross them. Chew on a hangnail. Rip out my ponytail and redo it. Pick up my guitar, tune it halfheartedly for a minute, then lay it back in its case. I look at my phone to check the time and am bummed to see my parents aren't picking me up for another half-hour. I can't even text them to come sooner because they're probably already on their way.

Wilder's exaggerated sigh snaps my head up. Frowning, he studies my face. "Are you going to tell me what's wrong?"

I blurt, "Who are the lyrics about?"

His eyes widen. "*That's* why you're being weird?"

My body boils with embarrassment, but I shrug like I don't care about his answer.

Wilder shakes his head slowly. Then he laughs, a burst of disbelief. "I was thinking about *you*, Evangeline."

My ears ring. "W-what?"

He drags a hand through his hair, shoulders twitching in agitation. "Why is that a big deal? You know you're my muse. It's always been this way. It will always *be* this way."

When I don't say anything—I can't even breathe—he huffs and glares at me.

"It doesn't mean I want to see you naked, so stop freaking out."

"I'm not freaking out."

I'm definitely freaking out.

A cloud eclipses the sun, dimming the world. Darkening his eyes from a sunlit glade to a shadowed forest. Despite the warmth of the air, the next gust of wind lifts goosebumps on my arms.

"We aren't a love story." His voice is low. I feel it beneath my skin. In my bones.

"I know," I whisper.

His head tilts. "Do you? Girlfriends and boyfriends are temporary. Background noise. We're neither. We're *more*."

I nod, but it's a reflex, my mind disconnected from the action. The ground suddenly doesn't feel solid under my hands. My *hands* don't feel solid.

Wilder leans forward, one finger connecting with the cover of the notebook. His eyes are maelstroms sucking me into depths unknown.

"Tell me you understand. Swear to me that no matter what happens, we'll stay the same. You and me— forever, Evangeline."

After a second that lasts a lifetime, I echo, "Forever."

♫

That afternoon, in the dappled shade beneath the sycamore, I swore to Wilder we'd always stay the same. That background noise would never come between us. Never infect our art.

We both lied that day.

It wasn't the first time. Or the last.

Maybe the lies started earlier that summer, when we accidentally brushed against each other in the pool, then jerked away like we'd been electrocuted.

Or maybe they started six years before, when he held my hand as my dad dug a grave in our backyard for our family cat, Pickle. As I soaked Wilder's shoulder with my tears, I asked him to swear he'd never leave me.

Maybe it's my fault for setting the precedent for impossible promises. Or his fault for believing we could fight gravity by pretending it didn't exist.

Wilder was right about one thing, though. We weren't a love story. We were something better and immeasurably worse.

A perfect song.

- Journal of Eva Sullivan

evangeline

EVA 20 | WILDER 22

The voices around me melt together, pooling into a backdrop of discordant static. Words drift like debris through my exhausted mind, knocking together, drifting apart. Shapes and sounds. Rhythms and melodies. I can't hold any of them for more than a second before they, too, fade into obscurity.

I don't want to be here. I should be in my backyard, relaxing in my hot tub. Cocooned by silence and reveling in solitude. Instead, the very people I'm most sick of surround me: musicians, the people who work with them, make money off them, and drool over them.

A familiar laugh pulls my gaze across the crowded living room to Wilder, who towers over a cluster of sycophants. Four out of five are displaying too much cleavage; the one man in the bunch has the same look on his face as the women, though. They all want a shot at being the lucky one tonight.

The giant potted plant I'm tucked behind partially obscures Wilder's face, but I can see half of his smile. Straight white teeth. A dimple made more pronounced by the scruff on his face. Dark hair that's too long after the last leg of our tour—so long it skims his broad shoulders and frames his poster-worthy face with haphazard waves.

Eddie offered to buzz it for him a few weeks ago, but Wilder declined and instead started using one of my hair ties to make a ridiculous, tiny topknot to keep it out of his eyes onstage. His flippant excuse was he didn't trust our drummer not to make him bleed. An obvious lie; no one has steadier hands than Eddie.

The real reason is that our fanbase is obsessed with his hair. It has its own hashtag: #wildmane. And after the explosion of concert photos on Instagram in the last few weeks, his topknot has a hashtag, too: #knotmewilder.

Cue eye roll.

"What or who are we hiding from?" asks Rye, sidling

up beside me. My best friend's blue eyes sparkle at me from his handsome, freckled face, and for the first time in weeks, my smile is genuine.

"The blob mind," I whisper.

He laughs, clinking his half-empty beer bottle to my full one. We're both underage, but no one here cares. I don't even know whose house this is, only that it belongs to someone from our record label.

"It's good to have you guys home," Rye says, hooking a muscled arm around my neck and smacking a loud kiss on the top of my head. "Life is boring without you."

"It's good to be home, Riley Piley."

He pretends to gag. "You don't call Wilder Why-Why anymore. Stop torturing me. It's not my fault my parents gave me a girl's name."

I smirk. "It was your grandfather's name."

"That was like a hundred years ago."

I concede with a laugh. "Fine. I'll give it a rest."

"Thank fuck."

He rubs his bearded cheek over the top of my head. He may only be nineteen, but he's built like a tank and has been growing beards since puberty. Probably why no one has blinked an eye at the fact he's drinking.

"Did you stop by your parents'?" he asks.

"Not yet." I wince, remembering the disappointment Mom tried and failed to conceal when I told her I needed to decompress for a day. "I'll see them at the barbecue tomorrow. I wouldn't even be here if it weren't for..." I trail off, my gaze moving across the room at the exact moment a woman strokes her hand suggestively down Wilder's chest. He smiles indulgently at her.

Rye sighs heavily. "He guilt tripped you, huh?"

I tear my gaze from Wilder and shrug at Rye. "He had a point. It would have been weird if I didn't show up at our tour wrap party."

He hums. "It's okay to say no to him sometimes, Eva."

I don't bother responding; the argument is ancient and I agree with him. Closing my eyes, I relax into my best friend's solid frame, his wintergreen and moss scent as familiar to me as hugs from my parents.

Looking at us from the outside, we're a mismatched pair. A redheaded behemoth and his lanky blond sidekick. But the bond between Rye and me began when we were in diapers and solidified into something unbreakable over the years.

We've known Wilder just as long, but he's always been a few steps outside our circle. And not because he's two years older than me and three years older than Rye, or because we never invited him in. It's just who he is. No one gets too close to Wilder. Not even me, despite my reputation in our families as being the only one he listens to.

If only they knew.

It surprised no one when the three of us formed our first band at ages ten, eleven, and thirteen respectively. We have music in our blood. Our dads are legends, members of the insanely popular indie rock band, Breaking Giants. Wilder's dad, Julian Ashburn, is the lead singer and songwriter. Rye's dad, Nick Henderson, plays drums. And my dad, Matt Sullivan, handles lead guitar and backup vocals. Suffice to say, our families have been enmeshed since before our births.

Nine years later, Wilder and I are still making music —music being about the only thing we agree on. Rye caught the bug, too, but realized early on he preferred to be behind the scenes. He found his niche in mixing and production, and his talents scored him an internship right out of high school at Icon Studios, one of Seattle's oldest and most revered recording studios. He even submitted his application with a fake name to ensure he was granted an interview on his own merits and not the power of his father's fame.

"Have you figured out what you're going to do?" he asks softly, gaze roaming the spacious living room and the throngs of people before snapping back to me.

A lump forms in my throat. "I think so."

Hearing what I'm not saying, he gives me a sympathetic squeeze. "No one is going to judge you." He pauses, wincing. "Except maybe You Know Who. But he'll get over it."

I doubt that.

My gaze slides across the room right as Wilder looks our way. He smiles when he sees Rye—his real smile, not the one he uses on the public—but it freezes when he sees me tucked under his arm. Our eyes meet. His glisten with an apology I don't want to hear again.

"Whoa," Rye whispers. "Why is he looking at you like he thinks you hate him? What happened?"

My mouth opens, then closes. There's no polite way to say a girl my age almost OD'd in Wilder's hotel room last week while he was screwing her friend a few feet away.

He finally realized what was happening and called our manager, Mack Martinez, who called me. The two of us cleaned up the mess like we always do, and afterward, I hung back like an idiot to ask Wilder if he was okay. Still wasted, he invited me to give him a blowjob— like he was doing *me* a favor—because he hadn't finished earlier.

Shoving the memory away, I lie to my best friend's face. "Nothing. He just knows I don't want to be here." I hand him my unfinished beer. "On that note, I've done my time. We'll catch up tomorrow, okay? Don't let Wilder suck you into any craziness tonight."

Rye's eyes scan mine before he nods. "See you tomorrow. Love you."

"Love you, too."

I make it halfway to the front door before a familiar figure intercepts me. Eddie's eyes have a telltale glaze as he grins at me.

"Don't tell me you're leaving!"

I force a chuckle. "I have an overdue date with my mattress. We've missed each other very much."

He laughs, then clears his throat and runs a hand over his short blond hair. "Well, I'm glad I caught you. I was wondering... now that we're home, do you want to go on a date? With me?"

For the twenty-millionth time, I regret the night a month into our tour when I found myself drunkenly making out with Eddie in a hotel hallway. The shittiest part is I hadn't even known it was him at first—even though he and our bassist, Jax, are a year apart in age, the brothers look like twins. They have similar haircuts and both had been wearing black T-shirts and jeans that night.

As embarrassing as Wilder's interruption was, I'm grateful he showed up. I wasn't in my right mind.

I *should* say yes to a date with Eddie. He's objectively

attractive, talented, and kind. Despite the fact I essentially threw myself at him that night—I might have also begged him to take my virginity—he's never made me feel uncomfortable or brought it up since.

In a perfect world, I'd be smitten with him. But my world is chaos.

"Sorry, Eddie. I don't think it's a good idea to mess with our working dynamic."

To my relief, he lives up to my opinion of him when I see disappointment but no anger in his eyes. "I figured. No hard feelings, Eva. See you next week?"

Probably not.

I nod and give him a hug, aware that the next time he and Jax hear my name, they'll probably curse it.

Over Eddie's shoulder, I spot Wilder and Rye chatting. The groupies have been dismissed, which shouldn't please me but does.

Like he can feel my gaze, Wilder turns his head. Before our stares can connect, I jerk away from Eddie and make a beeline for the door.

evangeline

If I had a dollar for every time

You almost touched me

I'd give my fortune to the wind

Cause unlike me she can move

Move against your skin

Curls of steam lift from the glowing surface of the hot tub. Water ripples decadently around my bare shoulders. Above me, strands of string lights bisect a sky framed by evergreens. The neighborhood is quiet at 2:00 a.m., so quiet that if I close my eyes, I can almost believe I'm in a peaceful, remote forest.

My peace shatters as the back slider on my two-bedroom bungalow slams open and Wilder storms onto my deck.

I sit up fast, my stomach somersaulting as I quickly cross my arms over my naked chest. "What the hell! What are you doing here? I gave you a key for emergencies only!"

"This is a fucking emergency," he growls. Both hands clenched in his hair, he paces back and forth across the deck, each footstep a resounding *thud*. "Tell me it's bullshit. Tell me you're not thinking about quitting."

My breath stills, a near-crushing weight settling on my chest. *Goddammit, Rye.* I shouldn't have left him at the party unsupervised, not with Wilder there. Rye is shit at keeping secrets, and Wilder is a master at spotting and extracting them.

I open my mouth with no idea what I'm going to say, but Wilder continues, "Is this about what happened in Vegas? I already said I was sorry. I was drunk, okay? It's not an excuse, just an explanation. I fucked up. Simple as that. You said you forgave me."

He stops suddenly, his chest heaving. Two steps bring him to the edge of the sunken hot tub. "What do I have to do? Do you want me to beg?"

My jaw drops as he lowers to his knees and clasps his hands over his chest.

"Wilder—stop. Get up."

His eyes veer downward, then widen and jerk back up. "You're naked."

"No shit," I snap. "I thought I was home alone."

Sagging backward so his weight rests on his feet, he whispers, "Please don't do this."

None of this is going how I wanted it to, but on the heels of that thought is the realization that it was never going to happen according to any plan I made—nothing with this man ever does.

"Grab my robe," I tell him. "Behind you on the chair."

He drags himself to his feet and fetches my robe, then holds it open and averts his eyes from my body. Bitterness makes my teeth grind as I step out of the water and snatch it from him, then slip into it. Once the belt is tied, I push past him and walk into the house.

He follows me inside, yanking the slider behind him. The frame is a little warped, and he mutters obscenities under his breath as he wrestles the door closed.

"I'll never understand why you live here."

I flop onto my second-hand couch in my tiny living room, ignoring the barb. Wilder, despite being obsessed with making a name for himself separate from his father's, has zero problems using his family's wealth to erase every inconvenience from his life.

He thinks Rye and I are idiots for not taking advantage of our parents' money; we think he's a hypocrite and a snob. If he was only that, maybe this would be easier. But he's also the most complex, beautiful, insanely talented person I know.

Dropping onto the couch beside me, he cradles his head in his hands. I steel my heart against the dejected curve of his shoulders. The sad fact is I can't be certain if it's an act or not.

At least he doesn't seem to be drunk or high.

"I *have* forgiven you for what happened in Vegas," I say hesitantly. "But forgiving isn't the same as forgetting. I can't do it anymore. I'm tired of being your babysitter, of making sure you don't run out of condoms, disappear for hours at a time, or choke on vomit—"

"I get it," he interrupts, hands falling as he straightens and faces me. "I got caught up in the bullshit. I'll slow down. I promise."

My heart pounds so hard my mouth tastes like pennies. I want to believe him—so, so badly—but it's too late. If all we did was write songs and perform together, it might be another story. But that's only a small part of the life we've chosen, and the insanity of the last two years has sucked the joy from it. From me.

Now that the rollercoaster of signing to a label, recording our debut album, and our first official tour has finally slowed, I want off the ride. Even if it means blowing up the most intimate, maddening, ecstatic partnership I've ever known and probably ever will. Even if I'm passing up a once-in-a-lifetime opportunity to have my music in millions of ears. Those are risks I'm willing to take—that I *have* to take.

It's a simple matter of survival. Thanks to the magic we make in the studio, the line between my head and heart is already blurred where he's concerned. I have to get away from him before I cross the point of no return.

Falling in love with Wilder Ashburn will destroy me.

"I hope you do slow down," I say carefully, "but I can't be your conscience anymore. I want a life that's mine, not one that's an extension of yours. You and I both know the label will bend over backward to find you another keyboardist and backup vocalist. The album is taking off, and the tour created a ton of buzz. Besides, Night Theory is your baby, not mine. You'll be fine without me."

Desperation twists his features. The hand closest to me twitches like he wants to reach for me. But he won't. He never does—sober, at least.

"Is this about the attention I'm getting? The spotlight? I wanted you to do lead vocals on half the album, but you refused! Fuck it—let's rerecord. Take my guitar, take my mic. You can have whatever you want!"

"No." Pain claws at my chest, propelled by the real

agony on his face. "They don't want me, Wilder. They never have. The label, the fans, they want you. Your voice, your presence. They need you."

"But I need *you*," he grinds out, his unique, spotted irises flashing with fury. "You're my fucking muse, and you know damn well I'm yours. Nothing will ever compare to us, to what we make together. You and me— we're musical destiny. So you can't leave me. You can't. We're endgame, Evangeline. We're forever. You *promised*."

I suck in a breath, heat blooming in my chest and face. Tears prick my eyes, my heart breaking and over-flowing at the same time.

Those words... they're weapons and he knows it. He knows all about my confusing feelings and he's using them against me. There's no mercy in his eyes. No remorse. Only anger and calculation.

"Fuck you," I choke out.

His gaze sharpens and darkens. "If that's what it takes, then let's go." He reaches for the hem of his shirt, lifting it enough for me to see a swath of taut, golden skin and a trail of dark hair.

"You're unbelievable," I snarl, leaping off the couch and knocking my shin against the coffee table in my effort to put space between us. I stalk to the front door and pull it open, ignoring the throb in my leg, the throb in my chest.

"I'm leaving the band. I'd really hoped we could handle this like adults, but I should have known better."

He rises and moves around the couch, his eyes tracking me like a predator. I stand my ground even when he veers toward me instead of the door. Even when he towers over me and his intoxicating scent surrounds me. It's not bodywash. Not cologne. Just *him*, like he was born with a midnight rainstorm in his cells.

The heat from his body breaches my robe, sinking into my still-drying skin. His gaze drops to my mouth and my breath hitches. Ribbons of heat curl and twist in my belly and lower.

I hate that after everything I've seen, everything I know about him, my body still betrays me like it's done for the last four years. Ever since I walked in on him getting a blowjob from Christine Buchanan, a girl he went to high school with. Until that moment, I'd been able to *mostly* separate his physical allure from my attraction to his mind, his soul. But when he'd looked at me standing frozen in his bedroom doorway, Christine's head bobbing in his lap, and his eyes flared with something I'd never seen directed at me before, that boundary was erased.

I've been fighting a losing battle since.

"I hate you," I whisper.

"No, you don't," he says huskily. "And that's the problem, isn't it? You want me so fucking bad and you can't handle the fact I haven't taken you."

He steps even closer, his chest grazing my robe as his other hand pushes the front door closed. The soft click makes me flinch.

I scream at myself to move, but I can't. Right now, I hate us both. Hate what we've become. But most of all, I hate that he's right. I want him, and I can't handle that he doesn't want me back.

I'm powerless to protest when he grabs ahold of my messy bun and jerks it so that my head falls back. He doesn't touch my skin—his unspoken rule—but he doesn't have to. He's all around me, his nearness caressing every inch of my body. A hot, prickling sensation shoots from my scalp, pulsing down my back to settle between my legs. I squeeze my thighs together, but it only makes the ache worse.

All I can do is stare up at him, silent tears of anger and misery pooling in my eyes as he lowers his mouth toward mine.

"We made a pact," he murmurs, his breath tickling my lips. "Are you asking me to break it?"

I swallow hard, remembering the night we swore to never cross the physical line. It wasn't long after I caught him with Christine. We were sitting on his bedroom floor with our guitars. We'd just written our best song to date—the same song that would eventually get us noticed by a scout from Indigo Records. We hadn't known it then, of course, but we still had that feeling of achieving something impossible. Capturing lightning in a bottle.

We were grinning at each other. I don't know who kissed who first, but I do remember him jerking away seconds after our lips touched. I remember the panic in his face as he jumped to his feet and started pacing, his voice shredding all the joy of the last moments.

"We can't. No. That didn't happen. We're not going out like that, Evangeline. How many incredible bands have broken up because they couldn't keep sex separate from the art? Too many. We can't risk it."

Reeling from his tirade, I hadn't protested when he made me swear we'd never kiss again. Never touch. Never, ever fall in love.

One more promise made.

One more nail in our coffin.

Now, I summon the fraying threads of my dignity and snap, "I don't want anything to do with you. You disgust me."

His lips curl mockingly. "Oh yeah? That's not what your pupils are telling me, or that pulse in your pretty neck." His gaze drops over my chest, dragging along the sliver of skin between the robe's lapels. When his eyes lift back to mine, they're blazing with derision. "If you're so horny, why didn't you go home with Eddie? Or did he not pop that sweet little cherry yet?"

A flash of shock gives way to rage. "He did," I lie. "My first time was perfect."

His nostrils flare, his jaw flexing, eyebrows drawing together.

Lost in the chaos of us, I laugh bitterly. "What—you thought I was going to stay a virgin forever while you screwed every groupie over eighteen?"

His fingers tighten in my hair, sending more fiery bolts across my scalp. "He doesn't deserve you," he growls. "I don't, either. But if you need me to fuck you, Evangeline, I will—if that's what it takes to prevent you from throwing away our future. But I'll never be your boyfriend. I'm more than that stupid label, and you're more than that, too. *We* are more than meaningless physical release."

Something inside me breaks—the final piece of me that was holding onto impossible hope. A fresh swell of tears makes tracks on my face as I look up into eyes that no longer feel like a safe haven.

"Get out," I whisper, my voice thin but unyielding.

His lips part as he sucks in a breath. His fingers spasm, releasing my hair, and I take a swift step back.

"Evangeline." My name trembles in the air. "Please. I'm sorry. Just tell me what you want."

"Get out of my house, Wilder. And leave the key." My voice is strong now, as cold and hard as my newly fossilized heart. "Whatever we were is done. We broke it. It's time to move on."

With sluggish movements, he dips a hand in his back pocket and holds up a silver key. I snatch it from his fingers, then wrench open the front door. He walks past me, stalling on the threshold.

Not looking back, he says softly, "Maybe you're right —maybe we're broken. But we'll never be done, Evangeline. Never."

The second his foot is out of the way, I close and lock the door, then throw the key into a nearby bowl. Then I walk to the kitchen where my phone is charging on the counter. Adrenaline makes my fingers shake as I type a text and send it.

> Fuck you Rye. I can't believe you told him

My phone rings in my hand, a picture of Rye on the screen that normally makes me smile. His eyes are crossed, his tongue out. I jab the red X to decline the call. Seconds later, the device buzzes with a series of texts.

> I'm so fucking sorry
>
> Did you talk to him? What did he say?
>
> Are you okay?
>
> I suck. I'm sorry

After an internal war that lasts close to a minute, I sigh and text him back.

> I'm fine. It's done. I'll see you at the barbecue tomorrow

I throw my phone back on the counter and drag myself to the couch, where I collapse and finally, finally let the last two years pour out of me in sobs.

wilder

From behind dark sunglasses, I watch Evangeline and Rye chatting on the other side of my parents' backyard. They're standing not ten feet from the sycamore tree.

Our tree.

My fingers squeeze the neck of the bottle in my hand, my knuckles cracking from the force. If it weren't for the bruises beneath Evangeline's eyes and the furtive glances she's been sending me since she got here, I'd think she was unaffected by blowing up our lives last night.

"Whatever we were is done. We broke it. It's time to move on."

She didn't break it, though. I did. And like an absolute asshole, last night I took what was broken, lit it on fire, and kicked the ashes into our eyes.

But it wouldn't have mattered if I'd been a saint. From the second Rye told me she was leaving the band, I knew there was nothing I could do to stop her. Once Evangeline makes up her mind about something—from a lyric to what she wants for dinner—there's no arguing with her. No changing her mind.

And she's done with me.

Distracted by the heaviness in my chest and the way the sunlight glints off her pale hair, I startle when someone sits in the Adirondack chair beside mine. My dad stretches his tattooed legs over the grass, crossing his ankles. I don't look at him, instead letting my gaze wander over the backyard and the dozen or so people I've known most or all my life.

My dad's bandmates—Nick Henderson, Matt Sullivan, and Jackson Everett—are playing some weirdly complicated frisbee game. For dudes in their fifties, they're pretty fit. I hope I'm half as active as they are when I'm their age. Their wives, including my mom, are sprawled on lounge chairs near the giant pool where six kids between the ages of eleven and seventeen are currently competing for the biggest cannonball.

The younger kids periodically call for Eva and Rye

to join them in the water. They won't ask me, though. Even if I wasn't basically hiding on the far side of the yard, everyone knows I'm not much for group activities. Sometimes—today, as a prime example—I wonder why I still come to these things.

"You've been avoiding me all day."

My dad's voice is mellow, but I feel the pressure of his stare on the side of my face. I take a sip of lukewarm root beer, wishing it were alcohol, then look at him—at the famous, handsome face that still gets photographed and drooled over, the dark hair without a single gray, and the bronze eyes that are currently filled with concern.

"Don't take it personally. I avoid most people." I tip the bottle his way. "I am, after all, the son of Julian Ashburn."

I hate the worry creasing his brow. Right now, I hate pretty much everything, including the fact I look so much like him. My hair is curlier and my eyes are my mom's, but the tabloids aren't wrong—I'm basically my father's clone.

He opens his mouth, but I speak first.

"Please don't spout some AA slogan about how we're only as sick as our secrets. I told Mom what happened when she cornered me right as I walked in the door, and I know she told you."

"Fair enough." His gaze veers away as he settles deeper in the chair. Thinking he's done grilling me, I relax a little. Then he says, "There are times I wish you weren't, you know."

I frown. "Weren't what?"

"So much like me."

Yeah, same.

Only my reasons are different than his. I detest the constant comparisons between my music and his, but he's talking about the similarities in our temperaments. My moodiness and isolation, especially when I'm working on songs. My tendency to horde my private thoughts and mask myself with a false persona in public. All of which makes him and my mom worry that in addition to following in his musical footsteps, I'll walk his darker roads, too.

I'm not stupid; the concern is valid. Addiction and music are intertwined in our family tree. Mom was spared the genetic bullet that took her own mother when she was a kid, but Dad was a crazy alcoholic during his teens. Thankfully, he straightened his life out when he was twenty and has been sober longer than I've been alive. He's told me enough stories over the years to make me both appreciate the fact I've never seen him drink and have a healthy wariness of my own habits.

But he's wrong—they're wrong. I'm not him. I can handle my shit.

Memories of that night in Vegas arise, but I shove them down. I know I made mistakes on tour. I overindulged. We all did, even Evangeline. I'd never seen her as drunk as she was the night I found her and Eddie in a hotel hallway dry humping each other.

The thought of them sneaking away on a different night, of him taking her virginity, makes me want to kill someone.

Preferably Eddie.

My eyes find Evangeline again, but I look away before she can feel me watching her.

"I know you're angry at her, Wild," murmurs my dad, "but I'm sure she has good reasons for stepping away. Give it a little time. Don't let this end your friendship."

I bite my tongue.

Evangeline and I aren't *friends*. We never have been. Most of our childhood, she was my unwanted shadow, following me around and poking her nose into my business. I could never escape her and by extension Rye, who trailed in her wake.

It all changed when I was thirteen and she was eleven and she handed me a sheet of lined paper covered in short verses. As I read them, I heard a melody. Halting and imperfect but still shockingly clear.

I grabbed my guitar and a pencil. We spent three hours perfecting our first song, and it didn't matter that the song itself was crap.

Those hours changed us. We traded parts of our souls, and since that day, when she writes, I hear, and when I write, she hears.

We're not friends. We're *entangled*. She's inside me just like I'm inside her.

And now she wants the pieces of her soul back? *My* pieces?

Never fucking happening.

"Anyway, I'm here if you want to talk."

I nod. "Thanks, Dad."

He squeezes my shoulder and walks toward the pool where the kids are now waging war on each other with foam noodles. My eleven-year-old twin sisters, Olive and Ivy, are currently trying to drown Eva's fifteen-year-old brother, Hunter. Normally their antics would make me smile, or at least take the edge off my bad mood.

Not today.

My mood sours even further as Eva and Rye approach the pool. They're still talking. Always fucking talking. Rye's mouth moves nonstop as he peels off his T-shirt, leaving him in black swim trunks. He winds up the fabric and whips it at Eva, who dodges and laughs. A forced laugh, but still a laugh. I'm sure she's pissed at

Rye for spilling her secret to me last night. But him, she'll forgive. Even though I didn't say a damn thing to prompt Rye's confession, I have no doubt I've been cast in the role of the villain.

Eva pulls her tank top over her head and steps out of her shorts, revealing a blue bikini. My stomach tightens at the sight of her full breasts in the tiny top. Her long, lean legs. Small waist. Subtly flaring hips.

The house could explode right now and I wouldn't even notice.

My parents' biggest worry is that I'll become an addict. They don't know I already am one, that I've been heroically abstaining from my drug of choice for years, fighting its hold over me with everything I am.

Like an alcoholic with booze, one sip of Evangeline will be too many and a million not enough. It's why I don't touch her. Ever. Last night was the closest I've been to succumbing. Even contact between my fingers and the silky strands of her hair was a risk, one I'm paying for now as I watch her wind the heavy, white-gold mass into a bun on the top of her head and remember the way her pupils dilated as I yanked that hair last night.

Given the pointedness of my stare, I'm unsurprised when her head turns in my direction. I've long chalked up our weird awareness of each other's regard as a symptom of our souls' entanglement. I know she can't see my eyes through my sunglasses, and she's too far away for me to see her mismatched irises—one hazel, one pale blue-gray—but it doesn't matter. For five long seconds, we're alone in the universe.

Then Rye picks her up and throws her into the pool. I hate that he can touch her without consequence. I hate that she lets him.

Dropping my head back, I close my eyes and take long, slow breaths until my balls stop aching and my dick deflates. The discomfort eventually fades—at least the physical one. Mentally I'm still a fucking wreck.

An indeterminable length of time later, a shadow falls over me. I blink up at my mom. Her dark curls are haloed by sunlight, her expressive face wearing a soft smile.

She holds out a small black notebook and a pencil.

"No," I rasp.

"Yes."

If anyone on Earth can come close to understanding me, it's my mom. Maybe because she understands my dad so well. Or maybe because everyone's wrong and I'm actually more like her than him. At least on the inside.

"I can't," I whisper, but I still take her offering.

She clasps my face in her graceful hands and stares at me with eyes I see in the mirror every day.

"We don't back away from pain," she says gently but firmly. "We seek out the cracks in our hearts and dive inside. It's okay to be afraid of the unknown, but we have to take the dive. It's the only way to keep the darkness at bay. Scoop it out with words, Wild. With music. Don't let it rise over your head."

My voice cracks as I confess, "I don't know if I can do it without her."

Her eyes burn with understanding and compassion. "You can, and you will."

evangeline

The palatial home Wilder grew up in is shadowed and quiet as I walk up carpeted stairs and down a hallway.

Sounds from the backyard drift through open windows: squeals from the kids still in the pool, laughter and shouts from adults. My stomach grumbles at the scent of smoking wood chips. I should be outside helping my dad with the grill—it's been a Sullivan tradition since I was a kid. But when he started prepping burgers, I decided to avoid the questions in his laser-like blue eyes and hid in a chair on the outskirts of the women.

Unfortunately, where I sat put me in Rose's direct line of sight, and her concerned glances made my skin itch with guilt. Or maybe the itching was due to all the sun and chlorine in combination with my lack of sleep last night. Either way, when Wilder's brother, River, walked over to ask Rose where he went and she said he was taking a nap, I slipped away with a mumbled excuse of needing the bathroom.

I just want to make sure he's okay.

In the light of a new day, the certainty and conviction I felt last night are murky, clouded by a jumbled mix of anxiety, longing, and sadness. We both said hurtful things; it wasn't the first time and likely won't be the last. All I really feel right now is the pain of the distance between us. I don't want to accept that a lifetime of friendship could be over, that the boy I grew up with has changed so much he's now a stranger.

At the door of his old bedroom, I press my ear to the wood and hear soft music. My heart kicks against my ribs as I knock.

"Wilder?"

When seconds pass with no response, I turn the knob and push the door open a crack. He's on the bed facing the window, his old gray comforter tangled around his jean-clad legs. From his deep, even breathing, he's fast asleep.

I slip into the room and close the door behind me. Approaching the bed, I step out of my sandals and crawl onto the mattress, then lie down and press myself to his warm back. I want to put my arms around him. Hold him. But that would be breaking the rules. I'm already bending them by touching him through his clothes.

I don't know how long I lie there, my cheek against his spine, but it's long enough for my tears to darken his soft gray T-shirt.

"Are you crying on me, Fairy?"

His gravelly words throw my heart into my stomach. It takes me several tries to find my voice. "You haven't called me that in years."

When I was five, a kid in my class called me a freak because of my heterochromia. I developed an immediate and overwhelming insecurity about my eyes. I begged my parents to buy me an eyepatch and when they wouldn't, I made one myself by gluing yarn to a piece of cardboard I'd cut from a cereal box. Then I refused to take it off my gray eye, even hiding it at night so they wouldn't find it and throw it away.

My mom told Rose what was going on, and Wilder overheard the phone call. When our families gathered that weekend, he pulled me aside. With all the solemn authority in his seven-year-old self, he told me that my pale gray iris didn't make me a freak. It made me a descendant of powerful fairies and meant I could see beyond the veil of the physical world to realities invisible to everyone else. Then he pulled off my homemade eyepatch and threw it away. I didn't make another one, and I never felt self-conscious about my eyes again. He called me Fairy until I was ten and told him to stop.

Wilder shifts on the bed, rolling over until we face each other. Three electrified inches separate us. Afraid to see his eyes, I stare at the base of his throat where his pulse flutters close to his skin.

"I'm sorry about last night," he whispers.

I close my eyes. "Me too. I don't..." I swallow back the urge to sob. "I don't want to lose you. I love making music with you—I do—but I can't ignore what I'm feeling anymore. I'm not happy."

"I know." His tone is low and agonized. "I've been such a dick to you. Getting away from me is the right choice."

"Why?" My voice aches like my heart. "Why do you say the things you do? Why can't you stop?"

My eyes fly open at a touch on my jaw. He stares at his fingers like he isn't sure they belong to him, but he doesn't move them. Long, dark lashes flicker as his gaze lifts to mine.

The world around us blurs; we're static figures in a shaken snow globe.

"I wish..." His throat bobs. "I wish I wasn't so afraid."

My brows draw together. "Of what?"

His thumb coasts across my cheek. Blood races to

the gentle pressure as if my very essence wants to catch and trap his touch.

"Everything," he whispers. "But mostly you."

My whole body turns hot and prickly. "What? Why?"

The barest of smiles curves his lips. "Silly Fairy who sees so much and so little at the same time."

His lips press to my forehead. Silky soft, dry, and warm. I freeze in shock, tingles radiating from the illicit contact and spreading down my limbs. My stomach swoops as his fingertips slide over my jaw. His hand forms a hot band around the side of my throat.

"I can't be what you want me to be," he murmurs as he draws away, "but not for the reason you think. Look at me, Fairy."

I lift my gaze. The brown speckles in his green eyes are black as pitch around giant pupils. His cheekbones are flushed, his brow furrowed like he's in pain. I've never seen this look on his face—abject hunger, spiraling torment.

"I'm poison." His gaze locks onto my mouth. "Sometimes I think you're the antidote, but at the end of the day, I won't risk infecting you. That's why I push you away. Not because I don't want you. As much as I need you, I have to save you from me."

Emotions punch me, one after the other: surprise,

elation, sadness, confusion, anger. "What the fuck? That's such bullshit."

His eyes flare. "Oh yeah? You think your pussy will banish all my demons?"

To my horror, my eyes begin to sting. "I've never asked you to have sex with me or be my boyfriend. The only thing I wanted was your respect."

I push backward, but he moves faster. One of his hands sears my bare thigh while the other whips up to reclaim my hair. He surges against me, bringing our bodies flush. I gasp at the unmistakable feel of his erection at the juncture of my thighs. That painful ache only he incites unfolds in my center, and a small, helpless sound escapes me.

"This happens every time you walk in a room," he grinds out. "Every time you open that pouty mouth or give me those glistening 'fuck me' eyes. You make me insane. Don't you get it? The problem is I *do* respect you. I respect your mind and talent more than anyone else on this planet does. You're *sacred* to me, Evangeline. But your body? That, I want to disrespect in the worst fucking ways."

Fear and uncertainty shiver through me, amplifying the sensation between my legs. I want him to kiss me. Take me. *Ruin me.*

I want to run as fast and far as I can.

His piercing stare tells me he knows exactly what I'm feeling. He always knows—he stole the book of my unspoken language years ago and memorized every word.

The fingers on my thigh clench and unclench, and he makes a sound in his throat that arrows between my legs. My hips twitch forward, primal need overruling reason. His nostrils flare, lips thinning, but he stays unmoving. A pillar of rigid heat and tensed muscle.

"You're wet for me, aren't you?" His voice purrs beneath my skin. "I bet you're always wet for me, just like I'm always hard for you."

Beyond reason, I nod, my gaze falling to his lips. Full and flushed, glistening from frustrated bites and swipes of his tongue. Two inches separate our mouths—two inches to freedom or catastrophe. I don't know which awaits us, and I'm starting not to care.

His frown deepens, his eyes narrowing to glittering slits. More fear pours through me, equaled only by my body's rising demand.

I say his name—a plea for him to stop this. Or finish it.

"You have no idea the depraved shit I want to do to you," he whispers harshly. "What if how I treat your body disgusts you? Would you get over it? Would we go back to partners while I use other girls as substitutes? Could you handle that? I don't think you could."

I can't breathe. Can't think. My greatest fantasy and worst nightmare are colliding, stripping me of denial. He's right—I couldn't handle that. And I was right last night—this is toxic.

But I don't move as he releases my hair. I don't stop him when he lifts my leg over his hip and nestles his hardness against my center. And when his hips swivel against mine, the friction makes me moan. He does it again and again. A tease and a threat I want him to make good on.

I want it all. I want him to fill me with his body like he fills me with his art.

"Open those fairy eyes," he demands.

My lashes part but immediately want to shutter again when I see his face. *Too much. He's too much.* Beautiful and savage. A provoked god of destruction.

His grip on my thigh tightens to the point of pain. "Did Eddie make you come when you fucked?"

"I..." Words fail me as his thrusts push me inexorably toward a sensory cliff's edge. Only this feeling is a thousand times more powerful than anything I've felt with my fingers.

"Answer me."

"We didn't have sex," I gasp out.

I must imagine it, but it feels like he grows even thicker, harder. He makes a noise between a gasp and a groan, and my legs begin to shake.

"Goddammit, Evangeline," he hisses.

He stills and releases my thigh. Before I feel the loss, his fingers dive between my legs from behind, yanking aside my cotton shorts and the gusset of my bikini bottoms, exposing me completely. I whimper as calloused fingertips graze my slit before confidently delving deeper. A finger pushes inside me, the invasion not deep but still shocking. My body tenses in resistance as he pulls it out and sinks it back in. His hand begins to move as well. Back and forth. Circling. Slowly at first, then faster. Discomfort shifts to a sparkling, consuming pleasure.

The sound of my wetness brings a mortified flush to my face. I duck my head against his chest.

"Fuck, fuck, fuck," he chants against my hair. "Tell me to stop."

He doesn't wait for an answer; I can't speak, anyway. His forearm flexes rhythmically against my ass, marrying the movements of his hand to the sinuous, purposeful drives of his hips. His jean-trapped cock grinds against my exposed clit, sending confusing signals of pain through the haze of euphoria. I clutch his shirt, small, animalistic sounds riding each of my panting breaths.

Another finger sinks inside me. It hurts, too. And feels better than anything I've ever felt before.

"Eyes on me," he demands.

My head weighs a thousand pounds as I lift it. His gaze flickers between my eyes, then drops to my lips.

"So beautiful," he whispers.

Prickling sensation eats my fingers and toes. Between my legs, the pain fades, replaced by languorous, spreading heat. I feel loose, unfolded, *possessed*, as my hips jerk erratically against his.

Wilder licks his lips. "Fuck yes. Chase it, Fairy."

My fingers dig into his chest. "Oh God—"

"I'm your god right now, and I want this virgin cunt spasming around my fingers and gushing all over my hand. Give it to me."

My mind recoils at his crass words, my head rearing back. His smile is slight, cruel, and knowing, his eyes hard on mine. I search his face frantically for anything familiar—any tenderness at all—but I can't find it, and it's too late to stop what my body has already claimed.

The orgasm sweeps through me. Devastating. Ecstatic. Humiliating. I smother my cries against his chest as I tremble and jerk, soaking his hand like he told me to.

I'm still pulsing, my senses floating, when he slips his fingers from my body and holds them between our faces. His skin glistens with my release. Eyes holding mine, he licks a line up his wet palm to the tip of one finger.

He groans. "You taste like sin."

Opening my jaw with his other hand, he shoves the same two fingers that were inside me against my tongue. Startled, I pull back. Not from the flavor—unexpected but not bad—but from the invasiveness. He pushes them in more, hitting the back of my tongue and making me gag.

This time when I shove him away, he doesn't resist. We stare at each other with a foot of space between us, both of us panting.

"Why?" My voice cracks.

His face remains marble, his eyes cold. "Go, Evangeline. Right now. Unless you want me to break you in half and make you choke on my cum."

Horrified, I scramble off the bed, yanking my bikini bottoms and shorts back into place. I snatch my sandals off the floor and back away.

Wilder watches me with narrowed, frigid eyes.

"What's wrong with you?" I whisper.

His brows lift mockingly. "According to a lot of women, absolutely nothing."

My fingers tighten on my shoes as my eyes burn with

unshed tears. "You know I'm not experienced. You were trying to shock me. You hurt me on purpose. Why would you do that?"

For a second, the mask over his eyes cracks. What I see makes my stomach bottom out—horror, self-loathing—before ice numbs everything. He sits up fast, feet thudding to the floor. I tense, ready to run, but he only grips the edge of the mattress, the tendons in his arms pronounced.

"You came to *my* room. Pressed your soft tits against *my* back. I got you off and you never once said no." His lip curls in a sneer. "Not everything you hoped it would be? Well, I'm sorry to disappoint, but I did warn you."

My mouth opens and closes. He rolls his eyes, then snatches his phone off the nightstand and swipes a few times. Ringing fills the room.

The line connects and a woman's voice croons, "Hey you. What's up?"

His eyes stay on my face as he says, "I need some relief. You free?"

"For you? Always."

"My place in twenty."

She giggles. "On my way."

He disconnects.

"I hate you," I tell him.

And this time, I mean it.

wilder

You stole seeds of me

And replaced them

With seeds of you

But you didn't know

We'll never grow

Because I'm poison

Evangeline wrenches open my bedroom door and flees at a run. Every muscle in my body tightens with the urge to go after her, but I curl forward instead and fist my hands in my hair.

"Eva? Whoa—what's wrong?"

She must ignore Rye, because seconds later his frame fills my open doorway. He scowls at me. "What did you do this time?"

The low laugh that comes out of me sounds batshit crazy. "Made sure she'll never come back to me."

His eyes widen. "On purpose?"

"You hurt me on purpose."

I didn't mean to. Fuck, I didn't mean to hurt her. I was barely hanging on to sanity, every shred of my self-control focused on not kissing her soft pink mouth. Not stripping off her clothes and feasting on every inch of her skin. Not freeing my dick and shoving inside her, stretching and claiming what no other man has.

I almost lost it a few times, overwhelmed by the way she looked at me, lust drunk and needy, and the texture and scent of her. Her blushing face, her supple thigh, her pussy... She was so wet. Drenched for me. So fucking soft. So hot and tight around my fingers.

My dick pulses angrily. I have no idea why I didn't blow my load in my pants, the fly of which is currently wet from her. Probably because I was so focused on every breath she took that—for the first time ever—I wasn't thinking about myself.

But I still fucked it up. I hurt her. Again.

Shame slithers around my shoulders, tightening around my neck.

"No," I say hoarsely, "not on purpose."

"What the hell, man?" Rye's voice is low and concerned. "I know whatever happened on tour made things more complicated for you guys, but why can't you apologize? Make it right?"

I shake my head, another unhinged laugh leaving me. "It's not that simple." Before he can say anything, I lift a hand and aim my glare. "Look, I get that you want to help, but leave it. Besides, you should be thanking me."

He frowns. "For what?"

I stand, grabbing my car keys. "Come on, dude. It's obvious you're in love with her." Ignoring the pound of trepidation in my chest, I force more poison out. "She's all yours now. Virginity intact. Maybe give her a few hours to recover from how hard she just came on my fingers, though."

The blood drains from Rye's face, making his freckles stand out even more. He takes a step into the room, his big hands clenched into fists.

I hope he comes at me. I won't even fight it.

I hope he breaks my fucking jaw.

"You're a piece of shit, Wild. I love Eva like a sister. She's my best friend in the whole world. I thought you were my friend, too. I thought you were *her* friend."

When I don't say anything, he shakes his head slowly. His anger drains away, replaced by pity. My skin crawls.

"You've always been a moody fuck, but the last year has been off the scale. Get some help, man. None of us want to see you crash and burn." He spins on his heel and stalks into the hallway, yelling back at me, "Burgers are ready, asshole."

Tossing my keys to the floor, I flop back onto the bed and press the heels of my hands into my eyes. A mistake I realize too late as Eva's delicious scent invades my nose. I hold my fingers to my face, breathing her in until I can't stand it anymore. Then I sit up and grab my phone, shooting a text to Christine to cancel.

Maybe I didn't mean to hurt Eva physically, but I definitely meant to shock and hurt her emotionally when I said that vulgar shit and called Christine right in front of her.

Rye's right.

I'm a piece of shit.

Muted footsteps in the hallway bring my head up. Twisted anticipation dies suddenly when Matt Sullivan appears. One look at his face tells me I'm about to get my ass handed to me. While I'm not worried that Eva ran downstairs and told her dad I fingered her, she *was* on the verge of tears when she left my room. Matt knows I'm the reason his daughter was crying.

I open my mouth.

"Don't bother, kid," he says, leaning against the doorjamb and crossing muscular, tattooed arms. "Shut up and listen. I came here to thank you."

My jaw drops. "What?"

A mirthless smile curves his lips. "Eva's been thinking about leaving the band since before you signed to Indigo. She stayed for you, to support your dream. You know something else? The music she makes alone sounds nothing like Night Theory. It's fucking good, though. Got this dark, electro-pop vibe."

She makes music without me?

"Anyway," Matt continues like he didn't just shatter a fundamental pillar of my reality. "I don't know what you did to make her finally cut the co-dependent cord between you guys, but regardless of your motives, it was the right thing to do. You feel me?"

I nod numbly.

"Also—and this is important, so open your punk-ass ears—I'm not happy Eva's hurting, but in the long run, it's a good thing. Because you and I both know you're not it." I'm confused until he adds, "She deserves more than you're capable of giving. On every. Fucking. Level. Wanna know how I know?"

My stomach churns at the implication he's aware that whatever Eva and I are, it's more than friends. Unable to hold his stare, I lower my head. Knowing it's futile, I still quip, "No, thanks."

"Tough shit," Matt says lightly. "I know because looking at you is like staring into the past. But unlike all the idiots on the outside, I'm not implying you're Julian 2.0."

I look up, stupidly hopeful.

His blue eyes spear me. "You're ten times worse. Stay the fuck away from my daughter, Wilder."

"Jesus Christ," I hiss, rubbing my face—again, a mistake, because all I smell is his daughter's pussy. At least my windows are all open, and my jeans are black, so he can't see the wet spot she made.

Matt knocks his knuckles against the doorframe. He turns to leave, then pauses. "Final piece of advice?"

"Sure, why not," I say bitterly.

"You're a helluva songwriter and musician. Maybe even better than your dad, though I'll deny it if you tell anyone I said that. But if you keep treating the people who love you like currency, you're gonna go bankrupt. And when that happens, all the fame in the world won't be worth a damn thing."

With a final nod, he disappears.

"Whatever," I mutter to myself. "That makes no fucking sense."

Except the longer I sit here thinking about the fact Evangeline makes her own music just fine without me, the more sense it makes.

I've been using her for years, since the first song we made together. Sucking away at the bond between us, treating her like a commodity to be consumed. All for my benefit. To make my dreams come true. Not hers— never hers. I don't even know what her dreams are, having always assumed they aligned with mine.

When was the last time I asked her anything about herself? Does she want to pursue a solo music career? Go to college? Why does she rent that crumbling house and never buy shit for herself when she has a giant trust fund?

A shaky feeling overtakes my body as I realize the one person I thought I knew better than anyone might actually be a stranger. What I thought was solid ground is crumbling under my feet.

Until yesterday, I had no idea she wanted to leave Night Theory. No idea she wasn't fully invested in our future as giants in the industry. Because our nine-year musical partnership was about me, not her. Not us.

She *does* deserve more than I can give her. Even if I don't know how to think of her as anything but mine. Even if I want to kill Eddie for kissing her, and the thought of some other man touching her body, of her wanting him to, makes me see red.

Maybe I don't know Evangeline like I thought I did, but she knows me in a way no one else does—not even my mom. I've already given her more of myself than anyone else; giving her the rest terrifies me. Maybe that means I'm a coward. Or maybe I'm simply obeying instinct, a cellular wisdom that transcends logic. It would explain why I've kept her at arm's length all these years. Why I haven't let myself know her. Really, really know her.

Because falling in love with Evangeline Sullivan will destroy me.

Sitting up, I look around at the poster-strewn walls that have heard hundreds of our songs and harmonies. Arguments, shouts of excitement, and belly-aching laughs. Tears sting my eyes, which finally drop to the nightstand and the black notebook my mom gave me.

My breath stills as a new emotion rises, faint but growing more defined every second.

Despite the betrayal still burning inside me at Evangeline's choice, despite feeling abandoned and fractured and bereft at the thought of her leaving the band—leaving *me*—I suddenly feel something else, too.

Something a lot like hope. A lot like freedom.

She doesn't need me.

Which means maybe I was wrong.

Maybe I don't need her, either.

NIGHT★THEORY
HOW
BABY THIS IS DESTINY
I'LL FOLLOW YOU INTO THE
I'LL COME FOR YOU YOU'LL BE
SET US FREE — YOU AND ME
DEAD OR ALIVE

PART TWO

verse

verse : lyrical or instrumental section of a song used
to advance the plot

evangeline

EVA 23 | WILDER 25

My front door opens, letting in a draft of cold, damp air before it closes again. Anna's voice filters to my ears along with Rye's deeper tones. I can't hear what they're whispering over the sounds of Slow Pulp from my Bluetooth speaker, but I have a pretty good idea.

"Hey, guys," I call over my shoulder. I catch a glimpse of Anna's wide eyes and Rye's grimace before I turn back to the counter and focus on chopping cucumbers for a salad.

They finally make it to the kitchen. Rye drops a kiss

on my head before heading to the fridge for a beer. Anna gives me a side hug, enveloping me in a cloud of perfume and stale marijuana smoke.

"Smells good in here," Rye says with forced cheer. "I love your lasagna almost as much as my mom's."

"Thanks. I made enough for you to take home and freeze."

"Hell yeah. You're a goddess."

"She is," Anna agrees. She grabs a cucumber slice off my cutting board and takes a bite, then grins at me. "An immortal goddess now."

"Anna," warns Rye.

She waves a dismissive hand in his direction, still grinning at me with manic, glazed eyes. "So, Eva? Have you listened to the song?"

I lower my knife before I stab her with it. "Yes, I've heard it."

Fifteen different people have sent it to me since it dropped online this morning, and that's not including family members. The only person to not contact me about it is Wilder himself. Probably because he knows as well as I do that the song doesn't mean anything. Maybe I inspired the lyrics, but I'm not naive enough to think they're about me specifically. That would be ridiculous.

Plus, his number is blocked in my phone.

Behind her, Rye mouths, "I'm sorry."

Still firmly in the bubble of my personal space, Anna bounces on her heels and screeches. The high-pitched sound makes me wince.

"And? Do you love it? You have to love it. It's unreal. So freaking good." She spins around, almost slapping me in the face with her hair-sprayed beach waves. "Where's your phone? Let's put it on."

I share another look with Rye. This time I let him see exactly how much I like his newest girlfriend, which is not at all.

"Anna, give it a rest," he says in a tired voice that tells me their four-month relationship is on its last legs.

She pretends she doesn't hear him—or she can't be bothered to read the room—because she grabs my phone off the counter.

"What's your passcode? Oh wait, I remember it." Her fingers fly over the screen, and I drown in regret for letting her borrow my phone last week to call hers when she couldn't find it in her purse.

The Slow Pulp song ends abruptly, and a second later, a dreamy, piano-driven intro begins. Moody and airy with a fuzzy bassline, it makes me think of salty ocean spray and moonlight.

Just like it's supposed to.

Sea glass and churning foam
Her eyes call me home
Now I'm trapped in her snare
But she isn't here
She's nowhere

Heterochromia
Heterochromia

Wilder's voice has changed in the last three years. I can tell he's worked on it with a professional. His range has expanded; his pitch is perfect. Now his baritone is so smooth it melts in my ears, with a raspy edge he uses to a spine-tingling effect on certain notes.

The track itself is arranged beautifully. The piano, the synth, the guitar and drums that build and culminate in the bridge, where they pound like a furious heartbeat.

There's a second chance
To be what you said you'd be
Come home to me
Come home to me

Another lovely transition leads to the last chorus and a fading outro. The final note of piano hangs delicately in the air until Anna shatters it with another screech. She throws herself dramatically against the kitchen table, rattling plates.

"I'm literally dead. Can you believe how beautiful that was? You're so lucky. I'd shit myself if someone as fuck-hot as Wilder Ashburn wrote a song about me."

Rye drops his head to his chest.

I pick up my knife and massacre more cucumbers.

♫

RYE AND I EAT ALONE.

We talk about our families, our jobs, and my show at a local venue tomorrow night. Rye is a natural chatterbox and carries us from one topic to the next with barely a pause. But the skin around his eyes is tight, his smile not its usual wattage.

A cord of tension hangs in the air, poised to choke us with all the topics we're avoiding. Like how after Anna made me listen to the song, Rye discreetly ordered her an Uber, then took her outside and dumped her.

And we definitely don't talk about the fact the song, "Waves," has racked up over a hundred thousand streams already, its instant popularity due to a two-month-long social media strategy. The kind that points to deep pockets, with professional behind the scenes videos of the four-man band, aesthetic track teases, and photoshoots with famous photographers.

After dinner, Rye does the dishes, then rejoins me at the table, where I'm slouched and picking at my cuticles.

"You okay?" he asks softly.

I nod and offer a smile that makes him grimace—which makes me laugh, albeit weakly. "I'm okay. Really. I'm happy for them. For him." Clearing my throat, I look away from the gentle understanding in his eyes. "You did good work on the track."

"Thanks, Eva. That means a lot coming from you. I'm still in shock that my name will be on the list of producers for the LP." He hesitates, his voice lowering. "It's good. Beyond good."

I nod a few times. "I look forward to hearing it."

"You don't have to wait. You can listen to the masters whenever you—"

"No," I say sharply, then blow out a breath as his face falls. "Sorry. I just mean I'll wait like everyone else. When's the release again?"

"Late April. Two more singles will land before then."

I whistle softly. "I take it the label is backing a full-scale release campaign? The whole nine yards?"

His smile is wry. "What is nepotism for five hundred."

I laugh.

Despite a nearly three-year delay in laying tracks for their sophomore album, Night Theory still has a recording contract with Indigo Records—the same company that signed Breaking Giants back in the day and has since become one of the most coveted pop and rock labels in the business.

"Good for them."

Rye grins. "You almost sound like you mean that."

"I do mean it." I pause, then concede, "It's bitter-sweet, I guess."

Mostly bitter.

As much as I don't regret leaving the band, and as much as I believe in Wilder's music and think his talent deserves the biggest platform possible, I still mourn the loss of what we shared. The loss of *him*. My childhood friend. My songwriting partner. The temperamental, driven, passionate person who made my world brighter. Sharper. More colorful. Who challenged me, inspired me, and ultimately betrayed everything I thought we were.

What we are now is... nothing.

I haven't seen Wilder in over six months, since our families' joint, end-of-summer barbecue last year. Our brief interaction followed a three-year pattern of avoiding and ignoring each other at gatherings.

The only difference last time was that Wilder brought a guest. A pretty brunette named Kendra, who ended up awkwardly introducing herself to me after Wilder walked past me with a muttered, "Hey."

According to my mom, Kendra is still around. Wilder's parents are happy for him. Everyone is happy for him.

Sensing my withdrawal, Rye scoots his chair back and stands.

"I'm gonna head out and let you get a good night's sleep. Excited about the show tomorrow?"

My smile is almost genuine. "Definitely."

After what happened with Wilder, I didn't write music for close to a year. I drifted for a while, living off my savings and the modest royalty payments from Night Theory's first album. Eventually, a tough love conversation with my dad snapped me out of my fugue. I found a part-time job at a music academy teaching piano and guitar to kids and enrolled at a local college.

I met Lily Aoki in my second semester during a music theory course. Our personalities are as different as night and day, but creatively we're a perfect match. We've been making music for a couple years, but in the last year we've gotten serious. Our talents are a marriage of mediums: I'm analog—notepads, keyboard, guitar— and she's digital, mixing and producing each song in ways I never imagined. We don't need anyone else with us onstage, either, because she does it all with her fancy laptop and DJ equipment.

We've performed a few dozen times at open mics around the city, but tomorrow night is our first legitimate show. We got a call last week from a booking agent at a small but respected venue in Fremont. He'd heard us at an open mic the weekend before and grabbed our flyer. When the original openers for tomorrow canceled, our flyer happened to be sitting at the top of the pile on his desk. He decided that despite our relatively unknown status, we were the right sound and worth the risk.

And the best part of it is he has absolutely no idea who I am—or rather, who my father is.

"It's going to be epic," Rye says, squeezing my shoulder before grabbing the container of leftovers.

I follow him to the front door, where I wrap my arms around his middle and take a deep breath of his comforting, mossy scent.

"Like hugging a tree trunk," I mumble into his flannel.

He chuckles and gives me a squeeze that forces the air from my lungs. "Like hugging a fairy—" We both freeze. "Fuck. Sorry, Ev."

"All good," I say brightly, stepping back and opening

the door for him. "I'm sorry about Anna. You really didn't have to... you know."

"Trust me, it was about to happen anyway." Winking, he adds, "You know I won't suffer alone for long."

I groan and shove him. "Get out of here."

Laughing manically, he saunters down the brick path to the curb. I wait until he's in his car before closing and locking my door. After cleaning the kitchen, I retreat to my bedroom, strip off my clothes, and pull on my heavy terry robe. Then I grab my phone and head for my hot tub.

The night is cold and clear. I don't bother turning on the string lights, the glow from the living room bright enough to buffer me from the dark. With a grunt, I pull up half of the cover and let it flop onto the other side. My robe hits the deck and two seconds later, I'm submerged in steaming, liquid bliss.

Dropping my head back, I watch the fog from my breath merge with the steam rising from the water. The urge to cry comes and goes like a tide, like the melody that trickles in and out of my mind.

There's a second chance to be what you said you'd be. Come home to me, come home to me.

When I realize I'm humming the words, I sit up and rub my face roughly. "Stop it," I admonish myself.

Ejecting the song from my thoughts, I focus on

what's important: the show tomorrow. I mentally run through the timeline of the day—everything from when I'll wake up to my usual voice-prep routine to what time we need to be at the venue and what I'm wearing—then review the song list Lily and I decided on.

Like she can hear me thinking, my nearby phone lights up with a text from her.

> Just got off work. Do you want
> company? We can make fake accounts
> and spam Night Theory's posts

A begrudging smile tugs my mouth to one side. She knows enough details about my complicated history with Wilder to loathe him on my behalf.

> Nah, I'm good. Thx tho.

> Here's an idea

> Unblock Wimpy's number and tell him
> the song sucks

My laugh is small but genuine.

> Not happening. I'm soaking now and
> going to sleep in a few. See you
> tomorrow. Get some sleep!

> Will do. Love you girl. Nite

I start to put my phone down, but a sudden impulse makes me swipe to my contacts and scroll to the bottom. To his name. I press it. Another swipe brings me to two little words.

Unblock Caller.

My thumb hovers, then descends. Before I can stop myself, I text him.

> Congrats, Wilder. It's a great song

It shows as delivered. I stare at the screen far too long before deciding I'm the biggest fool to ever live.

"Stupid," I whisper.

I step out of the hot tub, so angry with myself I don't even feel the cold. I towel off my legs and pull on my robe, then haul the cover back over the water and head inside. When the slider sticks a bit, I have the insane urge to smash my fist into the glass. Finally, it closes. I lock it and stalk toward the kitchen, where I chug a glass of water.

Wilder isn't going to text me back. I've given him the cold shoulder for years. He's given it right back. Whatever bond we had is gone. It's also close to eleven on a Friday night. He's probably partying with friends. With his super awesome girlfriend.

My phone rings in the pocket of my robe, startling a

yelp out of me. It takes three tries to pull it out, my fingers fumbling and numb.

Staring at the name on the screen, I read it over and over, seeing but not believing. Right before it goes to voicemail, I answer with a weak, "Hello?"

"You hate the song, don't you?"

His voice is warm and deep and dark. Both achingly familiar and shocking. An uncomfortable, spinning feeling consumes me—a blurring carousel of longing, resentment, and nostalgia.

"No." I clear my throat. "No, not at all. It's phenomenal."

"Liar," he whispers.

Against all common sense, my lips quirk. How many times have we spoken this script? Hundreds.

"Finished art is arrested progress," I tell him. "Time to let it go."

He says his line. "I don't know how."

And I finish it. "Write another song."

He's silent for one second. Two.

"Do you hate me, Fairy?"

My heart races. My face tingles. I drag my knuckles over my cheek, finding it hot to the touch.

"Yes."

"Good," he says, then hangs up.

wilder

Crossing the sidewalk, I yank open the passenger door of Rye's SUV and hop inside. When he just sits there, gripping the steering wheel so hard it looks like he's trying to shape it into a square, I slap the dash. He jolts and turns to me with panicked eyes.

"What's wrong with you?"

"She's going to kill me."

I scoff and finish buckling my seatbelt. "Come on. She won't even know I'm there."

"What about your parents? My parents? *Her parents?* Half the crowd is going to be people we're related to or friends of people we're related to. Plus, have you seen your Instagram account today? You have ninety thousand followers. Oh, and one of your videos went viral last night. God only knows why—you're eating a fucking burrito. But you seriously think no one will recognize you?"

I grimace at the potential truth of what he's saying. "I'll keep my hood up and stick to the back of the club."

"It's not a big club!"

Rye tugs at his earlobe, a lifelong tell that he's perilously close to a meltdown. They were epic when he was a toddler. I have no interest in seeing one from a two-hundred-and-twenty-pound former high school linebacker.

I make my voice calm and even—not difficult given the pill I took thirty minutes ago. "Like I already told you, I'm not trying to fuck up her night. I know she doesn't want me there. If I have to listen from the freaking bathroom, I will."

Rye nods a few times, relaxing marginally. Reaching into the backseat, he produces a beanie and tosses it in my lap. "Wear this. And don't look directly at her. I know it's been a while, but I doubt her Wilder-radar is broken."

Warmth spreads through me at the words, but I shake it off. Probably the Oxy kicking in, which I'm now regretting swallowing. I'll need to be careful to avoid my dad, who will take one look at my pinned pupils and lose his shit. But I wasn't thinking about seeing him—I was thinking about staying calm in a crowded room. Mostly, though, I was thinking about seeing Evangeline and dulling my reaction to her.

"Thanks for doing this," I murmur as I put on the beanie, pulling my sweatshirt hood over it.

Rye grunts and finally puts the car in gear. "I used to tell Eva all the time she needed to learn how to say no to you. I should take my own advice."

There's a pinch in my chest, but I ignore it and punch his bicep. It's like hitting a brick. "It's going to be fine, man. Trust me."

"I trust you as much as gas station sushi," he mutters.

I bark a laugh, then settle back for the short drive to Fremont.

I'm not unsympathetic toward Rye's dilemma. He's the center of Eva's and my Venn diagram, the only place we overlap these days. This is the first time he's felt the pressure of his position, the first time I've tested our bond against his loyalty to Eva.

Neither Rye nor I expected that sitting in the studio for months would spark a friendship completely separate from the drama of the past. His talents are incredible, and I would have been a fool to pass up having his input on the album over some beef that wasn't even with him. I'm doubly glad I didn't—not only is he as much of a perfectionist as I am when it comes to arranging music, I actually like the guy now.

Ten minutes later, Rye finds parking a block away from Side Stage, a black building covered in colorful, graffitied murals. It sits snugly against Tullamore Café, the beloved neighborhood landmark formerly owned by my mom and her cousin and now owned by my mom's longtime friend, Allison Montgomery, and her wife. About four years ago, they bought the lot next door and tore down the ancient fabric store. They renovated the café and built the attached venue.

Welcoming light pours out of the cafe's glass front, highlighting the short line in front of Side Stage's box office.

Rye turns off the car, then shoots me an unreadable look. "I don't even want to ask, but you didn't have anything to do with this, right?"

I frown in confusion. "With what?"

"Getting her the gig."

My brows jump. "Are you for real?"

"I know your parents are tight with the owners."

"So are her parents." When his suspicious expression doesn't change, I groan. "No, dumbass. I had nothing to do with it. You think I want Evangeline to hate me more than she already does?"

He sighs. "She doesn't hate you."

"She does," I say decisively.

He stares at me another moment, then shakes his head and exits the car. I follow, tugging the beanie down over my forehead.

Rye doesn't understand what happened between Evangeline and me. Hell, I barely understand it myself. All I know is that she hates me. She *needs* to hate me.

Three years of almost-silence, of seeing her from a distance at family functions, hearing her laugh, her voice, watching as the final vestiges of girlishness dissolved to reveal exactly how fucking gorgeous she's always been... all of it has proven one immutable fact.

I'm still an addict.

Believing she hates me makes it easier to abstain. It works for me. Or it worked until last night, when I made the impulsive mistake of calling her after realizing she'd unblocked my number.

When I heard her voice, when we played that old game, my craving was triggered.

Now I'm fiending for her.

"You all right?" asks Rye.

I realize I've stopped walking and am staring blankly at the ground.

"I, uh..." I glance to the side to see we've stopped in

front of Tullamore's front doors. "I'm gonna get something to drink."

Rye frowns and glances at his watch. "She goes on in five."

I nod. "I'll catch up in a minute."

"You mean creep inside, keep to the shadows, and pretend you don't know me?"

I roll my eyes. "Yes. I'll leave before the set ends and Uber home."

His frown deepens, but his love for Eva trumps his concern for my moody ass. "'Kay. See ya."

He strolls toward the box office.

I pivot and walk into the bustling café, making it five steps before my name, wrapped in surprise, is called from behind gleaming espresso machines.

Allison hustles around the counter, her familiar smile bringing one to my face.

"Hey, Auntie A," I say as she wraps her arms around my waist. She earned honorary aunt status when I was three and I've never considered calling her anything else.

"It's so good to see you, Wild," she says, grinning up at me. "It's been way too long. I don't remember you being this tall."

My smile turns smug. "Officially taller than my old man now, much to his annoyance."

She laughs. "I bet. Congrats on the single, by the way. Katie told me she heard it on the radio six times at work yesterday. Well deserved—it's incredible." Her smile softens, as does her voice as she leans closer. "Are you ready for what's coming your way?"

She looks meaningfully to the side, and I follow her gaze to a group of teenage girls at a nearby table who are staring at me and whispering. A quick glance around the café shows me they aren't the only ones.

I stomp my first instinct—which is to throw up in my mouth and run out the door—and instead give the table of girls a cocky grin. They turn bright red and dissolve into hysterical giggles.

When I look back at Allison, she squints at me like I've been body-snatched. "That was disturbing."

I agree with her. I'm disturbed every time I have to act like Wilder Ashburn, lead singer of Night Theory, instead of Wilder Ashburn, an introvert who'd rather stab himself than socialize.

From the corner of my eye, I see the girls stand, phones in hand.

Oh, fuck.

A steel band cranks tight around my chest. Soft ringing fills my ears.

I should have taken two pills.

"Come on," says Allison, grabbing my arm and

tugging me past tables, most of the occupants of which follow me with their eyes.

I'm naked beneath the piercing stares of strangers. My jaw aches with how hard my teeth are clenched. Every sound is too loud, every light too bright. I'm freezing and burning up, my stomach churning, sweat popping from my pores.

Allison squeezes my arm harder. "Hang on, almost there."

I keep my gaze pinned on her curly hair, peppered throughout with glistening silver strands. We enter a back hallway, passing a few people in Tullamore-branded shirts, who give me probing looks. Finally, she opens a door and pulls me into what looks like a staff lounge. Thankfully, it's empty and quiet.

"Sit," she says, pointing to a padded bench beside the door.

I drop onto the bench and hang my head. Slowly, my stomach settles and the ringing in my ears fades.

"Just like your dad," Allison murmurs.

I force myself to straighten. "I'm fine."

Her eyes narrow as she hands me a sealed water bottle. "Sure you are. Drink that, then I'll walk you next door through the staff entrance. You'll come out backstage."

I swallow half the bottle before shaking my head. "I have to go in the front."

The shrewd look in her eyes makes me feel like I'm five years old again and trying to convince her there's no mud in the mud pies I just made.

"Eva's onstage by now. As long as you don't make your presence known, she won't see you." She pauses, head tilting. "Have you heard her music?"

"A little," I admit. "A shitty recording."

Rye played the sample a few months ago for Eddie—who has no problem occasionally pumping him for information about Eva—and I happened to be in the same room. I've wanted to hear more since that first taste, the urge masochistic but undeniable.

"Then you're in for a treat." Allison glances at the clock on the wall. "All right, kiddo, let's go."

I haul myself to my feet and take an experimental inhale, relaxing when my lungs fill without pain. "Thanks for saving my ass back there, Auntie."

"Anytime." She scans my face. "Anxiety isn't something to be ashamed of, but it does need to be managed. Especially with the trajectory you're on."

Hearing her unspoken warnings and concerns—the same ones I get from my parents—I offer a disarming smile. I know better than to ask her to keep this from my mom, so I give her something else to tell her.

"Thanks, but this was a one-off. I don't usually venture out solo like this. And I have solid support from my bandmates."

"And Kendra, right?" she asks mildly.

My nod comes a second too late. I wince internally as Allison's gaze sharpens.

"Yep. She's great. Super supportive."

It's true. Sort of.

The door opens and a guy in a Tullamore shirt walks in, halting at the sight of me. His eyes widen and veer to Allison. "Oh, sorry—"

"It's fine," Allison says. "We were just leaving. Have a good break."

I give the man a nod, avoiding eye contact, and follow Allison out of the room. She leads me farther down the main hallway, around a corner, and through another door. This hallway is dimmed, the distinctive sound of live music apparent from the behind the door at the end. The popping bass makes the walls vibrate.

I can't hear her voice. But I feel it.

"Head up the stairs and turn left."

"Thanks," I say distractedly.

"Good luck, Wilder."

By the time I turn to ask her what she means, she's gone.

When I walk through the door, though, and Evangeline's voice wraps around me like thick silk, dancing with immaculate control atop a wicked beat, I begin to understand.

Then I see her and suddenly know exactly what Allison meant.

But it's too late for luck.

I'm fucked.

LOCAL MUSIC CORNER

At Side Stage last Friday, Eva Marie and Lily Aoki of Glow walked onstage with little fanfare. When they walked off thirty minutes later, they took my old, jaded heart with them.

Glow is a breath of fresh air. So fresh that for the first time in years, I'm scratching my head trying to apply genre conventions. Are they Electropop? Indie? New or Dark Wave? Post-punk? They're all of the above and so much more, and they deliver it with the kind of symbiosis and crowd responsiveness I rarely see live anymore. Just who are these young women?

Eva Marie is the daughter of Matt Sullivan of Breaking Giants, and you may also remember her as a former founding member of local Alt-Rock favorites, Night Theory. She met Tacoma native Lily Aoki two years ago in PacNorth's Interdisciplinary Music Arts program. The rest is history… or rather, the beginning of Glow.

Frontwoman and lead songwriter Eva brings a stunning trifecta of lyrical prowess, electrifying stage presence, and a voice so rich and versatile it'll make you believe in miracles. If that's not enough, she's also a multi-instrumentalist. Over the course of eight songs, she transitioned effortlessly between electric guitar and keyboard and even brought the club to a standstill with a violin solo. And she wasn't the only talent on stage making this old man gasp.

Lily Aoki is an alchemist of a DJ, her style reminiscent of early trip-hop greats and yet categorically her own. Her complex arrangements are disarmingly direct, with the unmistakable, shiver-inducing instincts of an orchestral conductor on a new music frontier. Paired with Eva Marie? It's a match made in music heaven.

I know what you're thinking. If Glow is so great, why haven't we heard of them? Well, despite support from famous faces in the crowd during their set, the duo has been climbing the ladder of success the hard way and not skipping any rungs. They've been on the open mic circuit for over a year, getting comfortable and earning their stripes.

In the opinion of this humble critic, we won't see them as an opening act much longer. Catching their set was the happiest accident in the last decade of my career.

Take note—Glow is here and they're about to light up the city.

ALEX ILOKA

evangeline

In the passenger seat of my car, Lily lowers her phone to her lap after reading the article for the five hundredth time since it landed online yesterday. I'm pretty sure she has it memorized at this point.

Her royal blue hair sways in my peripheral vision as she shakes her head in lingering disbelief. "*The* Alex Iloka. I can't get over it."

"It's pretty surreal," I agree, throwing a quick smile her way and an even quicker glance at the navigation screen on my dash. There are three more miles before I have to change lanes for a left-hand turn, but I put on my blinker anyway and merge over while no one is beside me.

I've freaked out over the article plenty myself, but right now navigating the dark, wet roads takes precedence. I'm hyper focused and ultra-defensive, my eyes swiveling between mirrors and the windshield, my palms damp on the wheel.

According to Rye, my aversion to driving at night is merely another trait in a long list proving I'm an old woman in a twenty-three-year-old's body. I tried explaining astigmatism once but got nowhere, probably because it was a flimsy excuse and he knew it. My astigmatism—if I even have one—is minor and nowhere close to the real reason, which is so embarrassing I've never told my best friend.

I'm afraid of the dark and have been since I was a little kid and got lost in the woods during a camping trip. Unfortunately, the phobia didn't fade as I grew up. It matured right along with me.

I almost wish darkness were still synonymous with monsters under the bed. It seems simpler, somehow. Now the threat is both bigger and more nebulous. The danger of the unknown and its hidden potential for shock and pain. Plus spiders.

Most days, I manage okay. The fear is easier to ignore when I'm with others, and when I'm onstage it doesn't bother me at all. I generally feel safe at home, too. As long as I take precautions, I'm even fine using my hot tub at night—although I still freak out occasionally and sprint soaking wet into my house.

But no matter where I am or who I'm with, I can't sleep without multiple nightlights. I won't check the mailbox at the end of my driveway if it's close to sunset. And I absolutely hate driving at night.

The only reason I'm behind the wheel right now is because I don't trust a stranger to drive us. That, and I volunteered to be the designated driver so Lily can unwind. Between her full-time job and classes, she deserves a night to let loose and celebrate.

Her sudden, giddy laugh makes my lips twitch. "You know what I can't get over? How we had no idea he was there. Just did our thing, totally oblivious."

"Same."

Especially since my first thought after reading the article was a cynical one—that someone had pulled strings on our behalf. Despite knowing Alex's reputation as strictly unbiased, I'd immediately called my dad and grilled him. He swore he had nothing to do with the critic's presence in the audience and even called the Ashburns to confirm they didn't overstep, either. I've since accepted that it was dumb luck. He'd been there to see the headliners, The Remnants, and happened to show up early.

"If we *had* known," I say dryly, "would we have made it onstage?"

"Definitely not. We would have been too busy

puking." Lily groans, palming her stomach. "Actually, even thinking about it in hindsight makes me want to hurl."

I smirk. "That's from the shots you did before we left. Told you they were a bad idea."

"I know," she whines. "I'm just really nervous."

"You're gorgeous and fierce as hell. Now eat the granola bar I hid in your purse."

She grabs it with a laugh. "Thanks, Mom."

I roll my eyes, then glance at the navigation screen. Seven more minutes until we arrive at the party The Remnants invited us to. Lily's nervous because she has a crush on their drummer, Tyler, after chatting with him last weekend and texting with him all week. I know she's anxious, too, about the party itself. It's not at a club, bar, or in someone's cramped apartment like we're used to, but in a private home in a nice neighborhood.

The Remnants and their ilk definitely aren't our usual social circle. To use Alex Iloka's metaphor, they're at least a dozen rungs ahead of us on the success ladder. While only a few years older than us, the men are full-time musicians with a label, four albums, and two international tours under their belts. Their sound is a little too niche for music charts or consistent radio play, but they have a rabid fanbase who think they're the second coming of Depeche Mode.

I'm nervous, too, but for different reasons. I haven't been to a party like this in three years and never without Wilder, Eddie, and Jax. It's a weird feeling. An almost vulnerable one. I won't have a clear purpose like I did before—Lily isn't Wilder. I won't need to babysit her so she doesn't do anything crazy or downright dangerous.

The thought should bring relief but instead leaves me unsettled, a feeling that intensifies as I turn onto a darker, residential street.

Lily finishes the granola bar and tucks the wrapper back in my purse. "Are you excited to see Michael again? That man looked at you with boners in his eyes after our set."

My stomach flutters at the mention of The Remnants' lead singer. "First off, ew. Second, I guess? Maybe? I don't know. He may not even talk to me."

"You're delusional. I think you should go for it. He's hot. Those dark eyes? The smile?" She fans herself.

I side-eye her. "You sure you're interested in Tyler and not Michael?"

She grins. "I can appreciate a good-looking guy, but you know I prefer the teddy-bear types. Perfect example: Rye Henderson. Now there's a bear I wouldn't mind pawing my underwear off."

I almost miss a stop sign, slamming on the brakes at

the last second. Thankfully, there are no other cars around us.

"Dude," I moan.

Lily giggles. "Sorry."

"I'll never understand your obsession with Rye," I grumble as I slowly accelerate.

"That's because he's basically your brother and incest is gross," she says flippantly, then peers out the passenger window. "Whoa, take a look at these houses."

Stately homes line the curbs, two- and three-story facades gleaming from the rain. Custom exteriors and manicured front yards glow beneath artfully placed lighting—and not the kind you buy from a hardware store and shove in a ground, either, like the ones all over my tiny front yard.

Lily's next laugh is shrill. "I had no idea we were headed to *rich*-rich territory. How close are we to the water?"

I swallow another surge of uneasiness. "A few blocks."

"I think I see the party," she murmurs, leaning forward in her seat. "Dang, that's a lot of people."

We're still a block from our destination, but the street ahead of us is lined with cars on both sides. To avoid having to circle around—or worse, attempt parallel parking in the dark in front of spectators—I pull against the nearest empty curb and park.

As I turn off the car, Lily says in a small voice, "I've changed my mind. Let's go back to your place. Hot tub and movies and bad tequila."

"Aw, honey."

My own nerves forgotten, I unbuckle my seatbelt and grab her cold hands. I'm one of the only people she allows to see beneath her tough exterior, and it doesn't happen often. On the rare occasion it does, there's only one way I know to help her—summoning the version of myself who grew up in a house like these, who walked the red carpet at the Grammys when I was eleven, and who isn't easily intimidated.

"We can leave, sure. Or we can walk in there like we belong, *which we do*, and give it twenty minutes. If no one impresses us, we'll bail. Just because we were invited doesn't mean we owe anyone our presence."

She cracks a smile. "I love it when you do the diva voice. I'm sorry, Ev. I know you don't even want to be here. You'd be in pajamas by now."

I nod. "Truth."

She laughs. "Fine, fine. If you can do it, so can I." With a sharp inhalation, she straightens and unbuckles her seatbelt. "You're right. We belong here. I'm an alchemist on a new-music frontier, and you're a power-house frontwoman. We're basically famous now."

After tucking my purse in the trunk, I lock the car, slip my keys and phone into my jacket pocket, and join Lily on the sidewalk. Worries forgotten, she links her arm with mine and propels us swiftly toward the split-level mansion.

We pass a few small groups loitering outside and approach the oversized front door. A massive deck facing the water sits a level above us to our right, packed with people talking, smoking, and laughing. Beat-heavy music punches into the damp air through open glass doors behind the crowd.

Inside is the same story—people, people every-where. Even with Lily's arm against me, I feel exposed. Off-kilter. A few smiles and nods are aimed our way, but I don't recognize anyone.

"This place is insane," Lily whispers, and I nod.

I hate to admit it, but I'm impressed. The style of the home is a classic for the area, but it's been fully remod-eled into a contemporary-modern masterpiece. I can't imagine the mortgage payment this close to the Sound. No doubt there are mountain views, too.

We walk up a short rise of stairs into the crowded living space that leads onto the deck. The first thing I see—besides more people—is the massive wall opposite us. My jaw drops as I take in the colorful, graffitied mural that spans the entire space from the baseboards to the high, beamed ceiling. Within the mostly abstract design are whorls of distorted musical notes and skewed instruments.

I instantly recognize the style of the artist who did the murals at Side Stage.

An artist I personally know.

"Whoa," Lily says with quiet awe. "That's a Riv original. Do you have any idea how much that probably cost?"

"A lot more than we can afford."

Unless they did it for free.

My stomach does a slow, downward roll, my skin prickling as I turn my head sharply to look around the room. I scan the crowded couches, deck, and nearby kitchen. When I don't see who I'm looking for, I release a slow breath.

I'm being paranoid. This isn't Wilder's house. It's simply a weird coincidence that his nineteen-year-old brother, River, graffitied an entire wall when I know for a fact he rarely takes commissions for private homes.

"Lily! You made it!"

The shout turns us toward the deck, where Tyler

breaks away from a group of guys. He weaves his way toward us, a huge smile on his face. As Lily's body relaxes against mine, I have a sudden suspicion I'll be leaving alone.

She confirms it with a whisper in my ear. "I'll text you when I get home?"

I smother a pang of disappointment and smile. "Sounds good."

"You're the best." She hugs me before hurrying to meet Tyler halfway. He waves at me; I lift a hand, then watch them until Lily gives me a thumbs-up behind her back, signaling that I'm officially dismissed.

I normally love her independence. I'm a lone wolf as well, so it works for us. But right now I wish I'd had the courage to be as honest with her in the car as she was with me. I could have told her I'm not as confident as I pretend to be. That it's been so long since I was a part of this scene, I'm not sure how to act.

With a mental sigh, I decide to give myself a tour of the house. Maybe I'll run into Michael or someone I know, or maybe I'll cut out early and head home to work on songs. Despite the prospect of driving alone in the dark, I'd actually prefer the latter.

Plan in place, I turn and take a step... right into a tall, broad-shouldered body. My face hits the middle of a hard chest, which rises on a swift inhale. I jerk back, but it's too late to prevent his midnight storm scent from invading my nose.

Steeling myself, I look up into narrowed, freckled green eyes.

"What are you doing here, Evangeline?"

evangeline

You used to be my lullaby

Your smile my favorite lie

I would have given you the sky

But all you wanted was goodbye

I yank my arm from Wilder's hold the second the door closes behind us. My skin hums from shoulder to wrist, like the contact sank through my leather jacket and top and is spreading like a toxin. I instinctively move away from him, deeper into the small room. A few seconds of disorientation later, my eyes finally partner with my brain to tell me where we are.

"Really? A bathroom?"

"It was the closest option."

His voice is calm. Unnervingly so. Despite that, the rich tone causes an immediate physical reaction. *Panic.* The walls of the arguably spacious bathroom seem to pulse closer, spiking my blood pressure. Not helping is the fact he's blocking the door, one shoulder resting on a brick wall painted as black as his heart.

I can't seem to make myself look at his face, so I focus instead on the fingers he's currently rubbing against his denim-clad thigh like they're tainted. The same fingers that were around my arm.

His hand stills, then he shoves up his long sleeves and crosses his arms over his chest. I stare at his muscled, veiny forearms, the golden skin now covered liberally with ink. My roaming gaze snags on a hyper-realistic lighthouse, the artistry as distinctive and familiar as that on the wall in the living room.

For a second, I forget the last three years—forget that he's a stranger. My mom's brother, Josh Marshall, is a world-renowned tattoo artist, and Wilder has been begging him to work on his skin since he was eighteen.

A smile quirks my lips. "My uncle finally agreed to tattoo you?"

He shifts against the wall. I risk a glance up to find his gaze fixed on the floor near my feet.

"Yes," he says shortly. "You didn't answer my question. What are you doing in my house?"

My smile dies, its echo reverberating in my chest. "I didn't know it was your house."

"Who invited you?"

"Michael Dresden."

He stiffens even more. "Stay away from him."

I suck in a breath, then release it slowly through my nose. There's a pinch in my chest, its source the same old wound: my inability to reconcile who he used to be with who he's become.

"Move. I'm leaving."

His eyes finally lift to mine. In the soft glow of the vanity's lights, their green is so dark I can't see the brown flecks. I'm grateful for the anger in my blood diluting the effect of him actually focusing on me, but I also can't stop my eyes from roaming, absorbing, *seeing* him in a way I haven't allowed myself to for so long.

His body is a man's now. Broad shoulders, narrow hips, long lines, and lean muscle. His face, too, has lost all vestiges of childhood. He's haughty and chiseled, almost ethereally beautiful.

I hate that he takes my breath away.

When one of his brows arches up, amusement flaring in his eyes, I wrench my gaze from his annoyingly perfect face.

"Whatever," I mutter. "You're pretty but your personality sucks."

He makes a small sound. Almost a laugh. Then he says, "Michael doesn't date. He fucks and ghosts."

Inwardly, I flinch. Outwardly, I scowl. "Don't pretend you care. Maybe I want to fuck and ghost *him*."

His lips curl, a challenge more than a smile. "Do you?"

I throw my hands up in exasperation. "What are we even doing right now? The first conversation we have in three years and we're already arguing? Clearly we need another three. Or better yet, ten."

"I don't want to argue with you."

He drags a hand through his hair—shorter than when I saw him last but still unruly—and makes a soft sound of frustration. When he looks at me again, my knees go weak.

It's *him*.

My friend.

"I saw the show last Friday." This time when his lips curve, it's a real smile. "Snuck in the back so you wouldn't see me."

Every muscle in my body locks.

"You were amazing, Evangeline. I'm in awe of you."

I stand in mute shock, my face burning and my mouth open. Wilder pushes off the wall. Two steps bring him to me. I have to crane my neck to maintain eye contact.

"What are you doing?" I whisper.

His gaze roams my face. "I don't know," he answers as softly. "I miss you. So fucking much. Do you really hate me?"

I swallow hard. My body burns; my scalp feels like mist. I have a sudden, visceral memory of the last time we were this close. In his childhood bed. His hand on my thigh. Between my legs.

Before I can do something stupid, I force the memory to play to its disastrous end.

"Yes."

I want to mean it, but I can hear my uncertainty and so can he. His teeth catch his lips, arresting a smile. Slowly, so slowly, he bends forward, caging me against the counter with his hands to either side of me. His head drops beside mine, warm breath cascading over my neck.

I stiffen, paralyzed between an urge to push him away and savor this dangerous moment. My toes and fingers tingle, and I can't stop myself from sucking in his scent.

"I wish that were true," he murmurs, my body vibrating with the low words. "God, I wish you hated me."

"I do," I choke out.

"Liar." His mouth grazes my skin above the collar of my jacket. Not a kiss. Worse, almost. He breathes me in, and with every breath, he sucks out more of my sanity.

You drank me dry so slow
I didn't notice as I lost my glow

The words shoot through my mind like comets, fiery tails dissolving my mental haze. I plant my palms on his chest to shove him back but freeze when I feel him shaking. The world shifts and presents itself from a new angle, one in which he isn't intentionally provoking me but collapsing against me.

"Please." His voice cracks. "Don't push me away. Just for a minute, let me come home."

My heart pumps painfully against my ribs. There's something in his voice I've never heard before. Sharp barbs and fathomless shadows. Coupled with the trembling of his body, it scares the shit out of me.

My arms automatically wind around him, anchoring tightly and pulling us flush. With a choked groan, he wraps his arms around me in return. His heart thunders against my ear. Every quake in his frame spikes my worry further.

The fact that this is our first hug registers only dimly

as I rub his back and massage the tight muscles of his shoulders. Slowly, his trembling abates.

"Fuck, that feels good," he whispers.

"Wilder," I say against his chest, "what's going on?"

His hold relaxes a fraction. "Nothing."

I try to lean back but he doesn't release me. "Please talk to me. Tell me you're okay."

He sighs, a hand shifting to cradle the back of my head. "I'm okay. A cockroach, remember? Ugly and indestructible."

I fight the urge to smile. "Grudge much? I was eight when I called you that. Right after you told me I was a toothpick with a cotton ball for a head."

This time when he shakes, it's with laughter. His fingers dive into my hair, spreading across my scalp. When he begins to lightly massage me, my knees melt. His other arm tightens, holding me up.

"Does that feel good?" he whispers.

It feels really fucking good. So does his big, hard body, still curled around me like a heated, muscly blanket. I haven't been held in close to a year and never by someone built like Wilder.

Never by *Wilder*.

All the things I should be feeling—alarm being the foremost—are nowhere to be found. I feel fuzzy and warm. Oddly safe. A tapestry of colorful patchwork memories surrounds me. Lying in the shade of the sycamore in his parents' backyard, scribbling in our journals and playing guitar. Arguing about whether *place* rhymed with *decay*. Comparing calluses on our hands.

Our first sold out show as Night Theory, the screams of the crowd in our ears as we looked at each other and realized we'd done it. Built something special, something *magical*, together.

My voice wavers with emotion. "I'm really confused by what's happening right now. We're hugging. Is this an alternate dimension?"

I can't see his smile, but I feel it.

"Never hugging you is now on the list of my biggest mistakes."

A warm hand encompasses the back of my neck. I shiver as he nuzzles his face into my neck and drags in a deep breath. "You smell the same," he whispers, a gravelly note in his voice that makes my stomach drop.

The arm around my back flexes, canting our hips together, and the world tilts again. My body wakes up apocalypse-style—boiling seas and giant plumes of fire.

That is *not* his belt buckle growing harder and bigger against my stomach.

"Wilder," I squeak.

This time when his lips find my neck, there's no

mistaking his intent. A small, involuntary moan escapes me as he presses a soft, open-mouthed kiss beneath my ear. His hands float down my spine and seize my hips. He lifts me onto the counter, immediately pressing forward between my legs. My fingers dig into his waist as his tongue touches my pulse. I moan again because logic has clearly left the room and *it's been so damn long* and *holy shit I forgot how enormous his dick is.*

The last time his hands were on me, I wasn't ready for it. My heart was too invested; we were both hurting. I was a virgin and his experience was daunting. He shocked me on purpose to push me away.

I may not be that much more experienced now, but I'm three years older. No longer a virgin. I'm not afraid anymore. My body screams for what he can give me and my head suddenly doesn't care about the consequences.

"Fuck, I want you so bad." He nips at my earlobe as one hand dives between our bodies. His thumb circles, manipulating the seam of my jeans against my clit. "Tell me to stop."

"No." I gasp. "Don't st—"

My voice chokes off as a fist pounds on the bathroom door.

His head whips up and he snarls, "Go away!"

"Wild?" asks a concerned female voice. "It's me. Are you sick? I'm coming in."

The doorknob rattles. Wilder leaps backward so fast he collides with the brick wall. Our eyes meet for one second—a second that stretches for years—before he jerks into action, grabbing the door before it can swing open all the way. I glimpse Kendra's pretty, worried face before he slips out and closes the door behind him.

Over the pounding of my heartbeat, I hear the rumble of his voice.

"I'm fine... She followed me in... Yeah, just some girl..."

My eyes close.

Just some girl.

wilder

The hands that were on Evangeline's luscious body are now on Kendra's shoulders, steering her away from the bathroom. Halfway down the hallway, she digs her heels in and spins to face me. Brown eyes full of a familiar blend of cunning and curiosity narrow.

"The bathroom? Really?"

My eyelids twitch as she echoes the same words Evangeline used but with an entirely different meaning. I glance back to see the door still closed. All I want is to go back inside. Be inside *her*. I want it so badly I can barely breathe.

I force my focus back to Kendra. "It's not what you think."

She glances below my waist, then lifts a sculpted

eyebrow. "You know I don't care. Why all the secrecy?" She takes a sultry step toward me, pressing herself to my chest. "We usually share."

"Not this one." The rough words slip out. Kendra's eyes instantly shimmer with suspicion.

"Why not?"

Her gaze veers past my shoulder, narrowing on something. *Someone.* My spine stiffens, prickling under the scrutiny of mismatched eyes. When the sensation fades, I glance back to see Evangeline walking away from us, back toward the party. Hips swinging. Blond hair waterfalling over a cropped leather jacket.

She's probably going to find Michael Dresden.

Fuck that guy.

"No. Not her."

My head swivels back to Kendra. Despite the Botox keeping her forehead smooth, it's easy to see she's furious. I'm not surprised. She doesn't know much about Evangeline's and my history, but she possesses the same instincts as all women. She recognizes a great white shark in our waters.

I want to laugh in her face. Laugh at our fucked-up excuse for a relationship. We barely tolerate each other unless we're high, and we both sleep with other people. Sometimes together, sometimes separately.

Rye hates her and thinks she's using me. I know she is. But I'm using her, too.

"She'll never accept your life, your needs," continues Kendra, misinterpreting my silence. Her voice is smooth now. Cajoling. "I know you don't want to lose what we have."

She lifts a hand to my face, cool fingertips on my jaw. Evangeline's fingers were warm.

Irritation flares inside me. Pulling Kendra's hand from my face, I frown. "You think I can't find someone else? There are at least ten people in my living room right now who would happily set me up."

Her lips compress, nostrils flaring. Just as fast, her expression clears and a soft smile forms. The same smile that sucked me in when we met. When I thought she was a nice, normal girl. Someone I could tolerate and have a good time with. Introduce to my parents so they'd get off my back and stop thinking I was hung up on Evangeline.

By the time I found out Kendra's smile was as fake as mine most days, I lacked the motivation to cut her loose —due in large part to the pills she sells to me.

"Wild." My name is wrapped in syrupy superiority. "Think about what you're saying. You can't trust any of these people. You think they want you to succeed?" She shakes her head, eyes pitying. "You and I both know they'd love nothing more than to bring you down. You don't want to risk that, do you?"

Unfortunately, she has a point. Outside of Rye and the guys in the band, the list of people I trust starts and ends with my family. But even that trust only goes so far. None of my friends or family know about the rigid control I maintain day in and day out. How I self-medicate in order to show up as the frontman my band needs. They don't know that once every few months, I cut myself off and spend a week in the misery of withdrawals.

They all think my weird, periodic ritual of locking myself in my room for days is a part of my songwriting process. It's not entirely a lie—I wrote the bulk of our next album while my skin felt like it was melting off my bones. But it's not the whole truth. I do it so I won't become a true addict, upping my doses over and over until I can't function without the drugs.

There's only one person who actually knows my secret and that's the woman in front of me... who just *oh so subtly* threatened to sell me out if I dump her.

I wish I could hate her, but thanks to a night last year when she poured out all the details of her twisted childhood to me, I have a damned soft spot for her. I understand why she is the way she is, and if she doesn't quite understand why I am the way I am, then she accepts it. Accepts me.

Would Evangeline accept me as I am? The narrow line I walk? The method I use to manage my demons? *Definitely not.* And the kicker? If she did, I'd lose respect for her. She'd cease to be the woman I've put above all others in my mind and heart.

My muse. My Fairy.

Kendra slips her arms around me. I don't pull away, but I don't embrace her, either.

"I'm sorry, Wild. I had a knee-jerk reaction, and that's not fair to you." She exhales noisily against my chest. "You know what? If you need to sleep with her once to get her out of your system, then go for it. I trust you. You won't break what we have."

My heart stutters, adrenaline shooting through my veins. "You don't mean that."

Kendra gazes up at me. Her face is impossible to read, but the look in her eyes is sly. "I do. In fact, the more I think about it, the more I think it will be a good thing."

I frown. "That's an abrupt shift. Me sleeping with Evangeline will be a *good* thing? Why?"

She draws away from me and shrugs. "I've heard rumors about her."

My eyebrows shoot up. "From who?"

She inspects her manicure. "An old friend of mine dated her for a while last year. You don't know him."

I swipe a hand over my face, exhausted with this conversation. "Enough with the manipulation tactics. Spit it out."

She gives me a satisfied smirk. "He said she's a bad lay. Boring. He wasn't her first, but he said it was like fucking a virgin."

For a few seconds I just stare at her, stunned by her audacity and an overwhelming need to rip this random guy's head off.

Then I replay what happened in the bathroom. The way Evangeline arched against me, rubbing herself against my hand. Her breathy moans and clutching fingers, panting breaths and flushed cheeks. How her body fit against mine like a puzzle piece I've been searching for my entire life.

I think about how she came apart on my fingers three years ago even though she fought it. How she initially fought her reaction to me tonight, too. How she gave me the fucking green light, and if it weren't for Kendra's interruption, I'd be balls deep inside her right now.

Sex with Evangeline will be explosive. Call it masculine instinct or learned experience, or maybe I'm finally realizing how bored *I've* been. Kendra knows all the tricks—so do the women she brings into bed with us—but something has been missing for a while. Authenticity. True abandon. I'm sick of performative sex with women who are more concerned with moaning at appropriate times than actually enjoying themselves.

There's never been anything artificial about Evangeline's response to me or mine to her. Not mentally, emotionally, or physically. Time apart didn't dilute our alchemy. I'm starting to wonder if anything ever will.

"Wild? What are you thinking?"

My eyes narrow on Kendra. "Talking shit about another woman's sexual history is low."

She flushes, decent enough to be embarrassed. "I only repeated what he said."

"Uh-huh." I pause, eyeing her like she's a scorpion about to strike. "Do you really mean it?"

She doesn't bother pretending confusion, though her nod lacks confidence. "Sure. *Once.* And don't bring her here."

I can't completely smother my reaction. Excitement. Anticipation. Relief. Kendra sees it all. She doesn't say anything. Neither do I. But in our silence is an acknowledgment that on some deep level we know this is a mistake. It's in the pinched skin around her eyes. The layer of disquiet that sits atop my elation like oil.

But I can't stop myself.

"Tonight?" Kendra asks softly.

I nod shortly. I can't wait anymore. I've waited so long already.

She looks past me toward the party. Toward the dozens of people, most of them superficial friends and hangers-on, who show up whenever I want. When she turns back to me, she wears a bright, false smile.

"In that case, I think I'll have some fun, too."

She wants a reaction. My jealousy. Possessiveness. Sometimes I pretend I feel them for her sake because while I don't love her, I'm not a complete dick. But I can't pretend tonight. I can't feel anything but my need.

Bending forward, I brush a chaste kiss on her cheek. "Be safe," I tell her.

"You too," she whispers.

She walks away, her head held high, off to find an unsuspecting man or couple to keep her entertained. I wait thirty seconds, then follow, weaving through the throngs of people in search of a white-blond head. When I don't see Evangeline in the living room or on the deck, I swallow a surge of trepidation. Has she left? Did she leave *alone*?

When I see Michael Dresden chatting up a brunette on a couch, I breathe a sigh of relief and pull out my phone to text her. My fingers hover over the screen.

What the fuck am I supposed to say? *My girlfriend says I can fuck you, so are you down?*

I rub my forehead.

"Wild! Did you see Eva?"

I turn to find Eddie and Jax approaching me from the deck, matching grins on their faces. The brothers look so similar they're often mistaken for twins—or they were until Eddie adopted his signature neon-green mullet last year.

"I did," I say, my fingers curling around my phone.

"It was so good to see her, right?" asks Jax. "She said she's already getting calls from venues after that writeup from Illoka."

Eddie nods rapidly. "She's killing it. We have to catch her next show."

I like Eddie and Jax. They're great musicians, low-drama roommates, and all-around decent guys. I've even forgiven Eddie for kissing Evangeline before me.

But right now I want to strangle them both.

"I'm actually looking for her. Any idea where she is?"

Jax's expression falls. "Sorry, man. She just left. Said she was tired."

Eddie laughs. "She still hates parties."

A knot of tension inside me releases.

I slip my phone in my pocket, then clap my hands to

their shoulders. "Can you hold shit down here? Kick these fuckers out before dawn?"

Eddie blinks in confusion, but he's thankfully too buzzed to put two and two together. Jax, on the other hand, raises a knowing eyebrow.

"Sure," he says dryly.

Eddie lifts his beer in a salute, turning away from us to shout, "The Thompson brothers are in charge, assholes!"

There's a chorus of laughter and cheers. Jax rolls his eyes. Someone cranks the music higher, and under Eddie's encouragement, the entire living room turns into an impromptu dance floor.

I nod at Jax, then slip away in the chaos.

evangeline

Within twenty minutes of arriving home, I'm curled on my couch in pajamas, a cup of steaming tea on the coffee table, my Kindle in my hands. Everything is exactly as it should be. I'm relaxed. Alone. My peace restored.

No one will ever know that when I got home, I ran around like a crazy person turning on every light, opening every closet and door, until there were no more shadows.

What happened tonight—*what almost happened*—has gone the way of all my other memories of Wilder. Locked in a box, chained closed, and thrown into the Mariana Trench of my mind.

I refuse to go back to the dark place I was in after I

left the band, when dwelling on the loss of him and everything we'd shared felt like slow suffocation.

Never again.

I'm so engrossed in my book, my ears dismiss the first knock as a part of the music playing on my nearby speaker. It isn't until the song ends that I register the sound of a fist pounding on my front door.

Then his voice. "Evangeline!"

I rocket to my feet. My stomach doesn't come with me, clinging to the couch cushions, most of the blood in my head racing to join it. For ten frenzied seconds, my body is a statue while my mind erupts like Vesuvius.

He's here.

Why is he here?

Oh God, he's here.

Another song starts. Wilder's voice pushes into my ears over the intro. "Open the door, Fairy!"

The nickname is what propels me into motion—what breaks chains and locks and releases what I've been trying to forget. I stalk to the front door, unlock the deadbolt, and yank it open. Wilder's head whips up, relief etched on his features.

I look around pointedly. "Sorry, no Fairy here. Just *some girl.*"

He catches his lower lip in his teeth, wincing. "I panicked. Can I come in?"

It's ridiculously hard to ignore the puppy eyes he's giving me, but I manage to scoff. "Absolutely not. What happened in the bathroom was a mistake. Momentary insanity. Go back to your girlfriend. Or, wait—did she dump you? Good for her!"

His lips twist as he smothers a smile. "Kendra and I have an open relationship. She knows I'm here."

I blink a few times, hoping the words will become less presumptuous. Nope. They don't.

"You think I'm going to sleep with you?" My voice rises with every syllable. "You're out of your mind. I don't even like you!"

He steps closer, hands lifting to grab the top of the doorframe. Ducking his head, he pins me with a heated stare. "You may not like me anymore, Evangeline, but you still want me. You told me not to stop."

I used to love that he was one of the few people who called me by my full name. Now it feels aberrant. An unwanted intimacy.

Wilder's gaze travels down my body, lingering on my braless breasts. I cross my arms over my white T-shirt.

"It's cold out," I snap.

Leaning toward me even further, he murmurs darkly, "Don't lie to me." He licks his lips, a quick flick of his tongue that echoes as a pulse between my thighs. "We've been dancing around this for years. There's no pact anymore. Let's get it out of our systems. Tomorrow we can go back to strangers."

"Get fucked," I snarl.

His brows twitch up. "Trying to, actually."

With a growl, I swing the door closed. His boot catches the wood, then he's pushing into my house. He slams the door behind him, locks it, and faces me. My heart gallops, my darting gaze capturing him in ecstatic bursts like furious notes on a piano. Flushed cheekbones. Heaving chest. Twitching fingers. Eyes full of naked longing.

He's a siren song of chaos and desire, so beautiful my conviction disperses like sea foam. I'm swept away.

"Evangeline," he whispers.

We reach for each other at the same time. It happens fast but feels like slow motion. I'm waiting forever—*I've waited forever*—for his hands on my waist. They clench and lift me, slamming our chests together. My legs wind around his hips, my arms locking around his neck. Planting one hand on my ass, he sinks the other into my hair. With a sharp tug, he angles my head and brings my mouth to his. So close I can feel the condensation of his breath.

"Kiss me, Fairy."

It's a plea. A prayer.

I can't resist.

His lips are exactly how I remember them from our brief kiss when I was sixteen. Silky soft and warm, firm and full. They part slightly but he doesn't kiss me back. Doubt surges, but when I start to pull away, the hand in my hair tightens to hold me still.

"No," he whispers.

His thumb finds my chin and presses down, opening me to him. He breathes into my mouth. Hot, heavy, slow. Sucking me in, filling me up. Shivers wrack my body. My fingers and toes vibrate.

His groan expands my lungs, and then he's kissing me like I've never been kissed before. Like he's pouring the entirety of our lives into my mouth. Our tongues tangle like our verses used to: seamlessly, effortlessly.

I had no idea a kiss could feel like this. Like arriving somewhere I've never been but where I've always belonged.

I don't notice we're moving until we're falling onto my bed, until the weight of him reminds me I have a body instead of only lips and tongue. I gasp when he breaks the kiss, instantly bereft without his lips on mine.

He rises above me and tugs my shirt up my chest. Hot, rough hands slide over my bare stomach to encompass my breasts. He squeezes them gently, his expression rapt in the too-bright room.

"I've thought about touching these for so long. Fucking them. Giving you a pretty pearl necklace."

A choked moan leaves me as he circles my nipples with his thumbs. Lightly at first, then with more pressure until my breasts ache and my nipples are flushed and tingling. With a satisfied hum, he lowers his head. When his mouth covers one peak at the same time he pinches the other, I gasp his name.

"You like that, huh?" He punctuates the low words with flicks of his tongue and finger. His teeth scrape over hypersensitive flesh—I whimper. My hips lift, searching for him, but he shifts out of reach.

"I know you can be louder," he says, dark amusement in his voice. "Let me hear you sing."

He devotes himself to making me lose it, suckling my breasts, blowing onto wet skin, biting and massaging and *feasting* until I'm giving him what he wants. Making sounds I've never made before. Feeling sensations I've never felt, like my breasts have a direct line to my clit.

Suddenly there's pressure right where I need it, a heavy hand rubbing roughly. Fireworks explode in my head and I explode with them. He swallows my cries, kissing me with feverish intensity until I melt, boneless and twitching in the aftermath.

I open my eyes to find Wilder smiling down at me. His real smile. A little lopsided, one dimple deeper than the other. I haven't seen the expression in so long, my heart tugs in my chest, aching and overfull. I touch his face, my fingertips dancing over his cheekbone where a single, small mole rests.

His smile falls. "Don't," he whispers. "This doesn't end like one of your romance books. I'm no hero."

Another tug in my chest, this one a scythe slicing through old, stale hopes. The *maybes* and *could have beens.* Silly wishes of a girl for her perfect love story, her perfect prince.

The pain fades fast, though, more nostalgia than anything else. I grieved that girl and her foolish dreams three years ago. I grieved the idea of *him.* Right now I'm not interested in a pretty, boring prince.

I want the villain.

I swallow, finding my voice. "Trust me, I know. You're an asshole, and I'm ghosting you tomorrow."

His lips twitch even as darkness flickers in his eyes. Tension ripples down his body. To break the unbearable moment, I arch into him. His gaze lowers to where I'm rubbing myself shamelessly against his erection.

"What are you waiting for? An invitation?" I angle my hands between us, coasting my palm over his cock before grabbing his belt buckle. "Fuck me like you hate me, Wilder."

"Jesus Christ," he hisses.

The next seconds are a blur as we tear off our clothes. His hands and mouth are everywhere. My stomach. Neck. My ankles, knees. Thighs. He shoves a foil packet between my teeth, his hand transferring to my throat and staying there as he slides down my body. One of my legs is yanked up, my knee shoved outward and held to the mattress. I spit out the condom foil, which slides off my chest.

He bites my inner thigh, then covers me with his mouth.

I gasp, arching. "Yes."

He eats me out like it's his calling. No hesitation, no tender exploration or reading my cues. He takes my pleasure like he owns it, and before I know it, I'm bucking against his mouth and crying out his name through another orgasm.

I'm still twitching with aftershocks as the hand on my throat releases, calloused fingertips floating over my chest and stomach and lifting goosebumps. He rises from between my legs like a fallen angel, all chaotic hair and straining muscles and inked skin. The lower half of his face glistens with my release, speckled green eyes catlike with smugness.

He licks his lips. "You still taste like sin."

I'm useless, panting and drugged by back-to-back

orgasms, and can only watch as he straddles my hips. His hard cock juts out over my stomach, and of course it's as pretty as the rest of him. He strokes himself slowly, his grip loose over the long, thick shaft and a broad, flared head that shines wetly at the tip. Something else shines, too—silver balls that disappear and reappear as his hand passes over them.

My eyes widen.

"Apadravya piercing," he says with a smirk. "Consider those orgasms appetizers to the main course. I'm about to blow your mind."

I squirm, an uncomfortable emptiness taking up residence between my legs. His other hand plays with my breasts lazily, but I can't focus on his touch because I'm fixated on his cock. I wish his hand were my mouth. I want to roll my tongue over the silver balls and taste them. Taste *him*.

But when I try to rise, to reach for him, his hand plants on my chest. "That's not on the menu."

"You don't want a blowjob? Who are you?"

He doesn't answer. Doesn't look at me as he begins to tease my nipples again until my breaths turn to pants and I'm making small, needy sounds. His too-perceptive eyes lift to mine.

Shaking his head, he *tsks* softly. "How many men

have tried and failed to read your music? How many have left you unsatisfied?"

The words rattle me, but they anger me, too. If he thinks I'm the same girl he shocked in his childhood bedroom, he's about to find out that I abandoned her on the floor where we used to write songs.

Stretching my arms over my head, I fake a yawn. "Sorry to break it to you, but you're not special. I'm one of those lucky girls who gets off easily." I nod at his hand, still working over his shaft. "Are you going to do something with that or just wave it in my face?"

For two absolutely perfect seconds, he stares at me in shock. Then he laughs. It's not a nice sound, though, but a sinister chuckle.

"You're such a fucking liar."

I glare at him, but he only smiles slightly and reaches for the condom. He tears it open and rolls it on with brisk efficiency.

Don't think about how many women have watched him do this. Don't think about it...

Too late.

I grimace, my eyes closing.

Hands grab my face. My eyes snap open as he covers me with his body, blanketing me with heat. The tip of his nose touches mine, his eyes so close I can count the freckles like stars in an alien sky. I grab his forearms for stability because it suddenly feels like I'm plummeting down from space.

"No," he whispers, pressing a soft kiss to my mouth. "You stay right here. It's just us. You and me. Like it's supposed to be."

My body goes rigid. "You can't have it both ways. And you're not a hero, remember? So stop acting like one. Either fuck me or get the fuck out."

An emotion crosses his face too swiftly for me to name, but it bounces in my chest like I'm an empty chamber. Heavy and hard.

His jaw clenches. "You want me to treat you like them? Fuck you like I don't give a shit about you?"

No.

"Yes."

He bares his teeth. "Fine."

I yelp in surprise as he flips me onto my stomach. My hips are wrenched into the air. His knees bump mine apart. My hair is gathered, spiraled into a chord, and yanked until my spine bows. He shoves two fingers inside me and pumps hard.

"Fucking dripping."

He says it like it's a curse, like he's angry my body likes his aggressive handling. I'm a little confused myself, but there's no time to think about it because the head of his cock drags over my center. Up and down, up and down.

"If it's too much, tap my thigh," he growls.

"Wh—"

The rest of my question is lost—*I'm lost*—as he slams inside me with one brutal thrust.

CHAPTER TWELVE

evangeline

I spent years describing love

using too many words

specifically verbs

before finally realizing

you weren't really listening

only nodding along

Every time I shift in my chair, phantom fullness pulses between my legs. Two days after Wilder broke my vagina, I still feel him. Every time I wipe. Sneeze. Bend over. Muscles that have no business interfering with my life are sore and cramping. Yesterday I was convinced I was starting my period. But no—just another consequence of the most intense, depraved, earthshaking sex of my life.

"Not hungry, Eva?" asks my dad, his eyes lifting from my untouched waffle and narrowing with concern.

I summon a smile. "Not really. Filled up on fruit."

"I'll take that," Hunter says, snatching my plate. At eighteen and still growing, he's perpetually starving. He's already finished off two servings of waffles, bacon, and scrambled eggs.

Mom shakes her head with a fond smile while my uncle Josh chuckles. "I remember that age well."

The conversation veers in a safe direction—namely, away from me—as they reminisce about keeping my uncle Patrick fed when he was a teenager. I devote myself to my cup of coffee, pretending to listen while trying not to think about how sore I am and ignoring my dad's periodic, searching glances.

He's always been the worrier in the family, especially when it comes to me. His overprotectiveness used to piss me off when I was a teenager. Now I'm grateful for it. *Mostly.* Right now it's knives sawing on my already frayed nerves.

Unfortunately, Sunday brunch at my parents' requires an excuse to skip. A worthy one in the realm of sudden hospitalization or amnesia. My mom is militant about the tradition. In the early years, it was chaos with both sets of grandparents and four aunts and uncles every weekend. Now most of my parents' siblings have families of their own. Uncle Josh and his wife don't have kids, and since she works most weekends as a trauma nurse, he still comes more often than not. My grandparents are usually fixtures as well, but they travel a lot during the colder months. This month all four of them are on a cruise to Panama.

"Eva."

My mom's gentle voice jolts me. I look up, blinking in surprise when I see that Hunter's gone and Dad and Uncle Josh are clearing the table.

"Sorry. Spaced out."

My dad opens his mouth, that familiar frown of concern on his face, but my mom gives him a *look*. He closes his mouth fast. He and my uncle trade a humored glance and head for the kitchen with plates.

Mom rounds the table and smiles down at me. "Come on. I have something for you."

Whereas my dad is all about frontal assault, Sophie Sullivan is the master of sneak attacks. With her gentle spirit and angelic beauty, she's a Trojan Horse of life lessons I'm never ready for.

Sighing, I push back from the table and follow her down the hall. She veers into her art studio, a bright, colorful space that's one of my favorite places on the planet.

Growing up, I spent countless hours curled in the armchair by the window, watching her draw. Sometimes I fell asleep, but mostly I read books, listened to music, and later, played guitar. Most of our difficult conversations have also happened in this room. The Sex talk. The Red Flags and Safety talk. The Why-Your-Best-Friend-Isn't-Your-Best-Friend-If-She-Kisses-Your-Boyfriend talk.

Leaning against the doorjamb, I cross my arms and school my expression.

"What's up?" My voice is unconcerned, masking my unhinged inner dialogue.

You're fine. Everything's fine. You did not have life-altering, semi-hate sex with Wilder. And he definitely didn't shred your G-spot with his pierced dick.

A vivid flashback hits me—the tender, fierce expression on his face when he ripped off the condom and came all over my chest, then rubbed his cum into my breasts.

My whole body flushes. Between my legs, a painful pulse makes me wince.

Thankfully, Mom has her back to me as she rummages through a small closet. I take slow, deep breaths until I feel calm again.

"Ah, here it is! I found this in the attic last week and thought you might like to have it."

She turns around, offering me a small black box, the kind you buy in a craft store for keeping mementos. It's covered in band stickers.

My face goes numb. "I don't want that."

There's nothing remotely normal about my voice this time.

"Oh, honey." She sets the box down on a drafting table. "Come sit."

With no reasonable excuse not to, I drag myself to the armchair and collapse into it. Mom pulls over her rolling stool and settles in front of me. Grabbing my hands in hers, she leans forward until we're eye to eye.

"It's the new song, isn't it? I'm sure it brought up a lot of complex feelings."

"Um, yeah."

She leans back an inch, her brows lifting.

I screw my eyes shut. "Don't look at me like that."

"You just lied to my face." There's amusement in her voice. "You haven't done that since you were four and tried to convince me the cat covered *himself* in pink marker."

Slipping my hands from hers, I rub my face. "I'm sorry. I... I didn't really lie. The song did throw me for a loop." *And started this mess.*

When she doesn't say anything, I make the mistake of looking at her calm, compassionate face. My defenses crumble.

Cheeks burning, I whisper, "He came over Friday night."

Her eyes widen and flicker to the left side of my neck. Specifically to the spot where I piled concealer over a hickey. My skin crawls. I'm hoping it's a prelude to spontaneous combustion.

"Oh," she whispers, then sits back, blinking fast. "*Oh.*"

I groan, dropping my head back to stare at the ceiling. "It was a mistake, Mom. It was—" I choke, my eyes stinging. *Perfect. Mind-blowing.* "I hate him so much."

There's a long pause. "You don't hate him, sweetie."

"It's just us. You and me. Like it's supposed to be."

As his words whisper through my mind, I finally allow myself to feel them. My gut clenches, my heart pounding in thick misery. Tears push against my closed eyelids, forcing their way through my lashes.

"You're right," I concede, angrily swiping wetness from my cheeks. "What I hate is that he changed. I wish I knew what happened my senior year. One day he was the Wilder I'd always known, and the next day he was different. Like he had a... a poison inside him that spread so slowly I didn't notice until it was everywhere. I think that's the worst part—the guilt. I feel like he needed me to help him, but I didn't even know something was wrong until it was too late. I lost him before I knew he was slipping away."

My mom makes a soft, sad sound. She grabs my hands again, squeezing hard.

"Listen to me very carefully, Eva. You're not responsible for anyone else's mental health. The road Wilder is on is his to walk. We all worry about him, Rose and Julian especially. But they know there's nothing they can do but provide support, set boundaries, and be there for him if he decides he's ready for a change."

My lungs atrophy, turning my voice brittle. "What are you saying?"

She sighs, her head briefly bowing. When it lifts, determination and sorrow shine in her eyes. "What changed back then was Wilder started having debilitating panic attacks. He refused to see a therapist or consider medication. Rose thinks he started using drugs to manage his anxiety and that over the years his using has progressed."

Shock erupts from me in a breathless laugh. "What? No. I mean, sure, he smoked a lot of weed back then." *We both did.* "And I'm sure he drinks and stuff now, but he's always been super careful because of his family history..." I trail off at the unchanging expression on her face. My spine stiffens further. "He's not an addict, Mom. He wasn't loaded on Friday. I would have known."

"Maybe not," she says softly, but I can tell she thinks I'm being naive.

Maybe I am.

Was he on drugs?

The idea nauseates me.

I jerk to my feet, forcing her to push back the stool. "I have to go."

"Eva, please—"

"No! He's not a fucking addict!"

Buzzing silence follows. I've never yelled at her like that. Shaking my head in dismay, I whisper, "I'm sorry."

"It's okay, honey. It's okay."

She reaches for me, but I back away.

"I can't do this right now."

Movement in the doorway makes me flinch. My gaze flies to my dad. His expression is neutral, but his voice emerges hard. "Julian says it's opiates. Probably pills. He's careful around his family, but he's not fooling his parents. He's always high these days." He pauses. "Stay away from him, Eva."

"I haven't seen him since the barbecue last year," I blurt.

My dad's eyes narrow. "You think after years of watching him toy with you that I didn't recognize the look on your face the second you walked in this morning?" His gaze drops to my neck. "Please tell me that's not from him."

Mortified, I slap a hand over the spot.

His shoulders bunch, then relax. He shakes his head slowly, blue eyes filled with such disappointment that shame spreads like ink through my chest. My chin wobbles. He's *never* looked at me this way.

My mom takes a few steps toward him. "Let's take a breather," she says softly.

He stays laser focused on me. "Deep down, I knew it was only a matter of time before he came after you, but I really, really hoped you'd be smarter than this."

"Matthew," hisses my mom.

He ignores her again. "I know you guys were close growing up. You had a bond anyone could see. Hell—Julian, Rose, your mom, and I used to joke that the two of you were a done deal. *Soulmates.*" His lips twist over the word. "We were wrong. What Wilder feels for you isn't love. Maybe it could have been, but the second he decided to take the coward's way out, he became incapable of the feeling. If you let yourself believe the bullshit he's telling you, he'll drag you down with him. He's an addict. He's *using* you. Did he tell you he was single now? He's not. His girlfriend moved in with him two months ago."

"Enough!" snaps my mom. "Take a walk, Matt."

He looks at her, but it's like he doesn't even see her. His jaw ticks, then he spins on his heel and disappears into the hallway. I stare after him, silent tears spilling over my cheeks.

My mom wraps her arms around me; I barely feel the embrace. "He shouldn't have said all that. It was coming from a place of pain that has nothing to do with you."

"His dad?" I ask weakly.

She nods against my shoulder. "And Julian. There was a rough period in the early days before he got sober. It almost broke up the band. But it's not an excuse. He went too far." She leans back, framing my face in her hands and smoothing away my tears. "Expect him to be groveling tomorrow."

Preternatural calm descends on my shoulders, numbing and welcome. My tears slow and stop.

"You agree with him, though. Don't you?"

Her gaze flickers away from mine, her hands falling. "I won't lie and say I don't have some of the same fears." She looks like she wants to say more, but instead presses her palm to my chest over my heart. "Be careful with this, okay?"

I manage a small smile. "Don't worry. I have no intention of seeing Wilder again, at least not on purpose." I pause. "He told me he was in an open relationship. Do you know if that's true?"

She frowns. "I don't, sorry. Do you want me to ask Rose? I can be discreet."

I shake my head, regretting letting the question slip out. "No, that's okay."

I know exactly who to ask.

♫

ONCE AT HOME, I make myself tea and take it onto my back porch. The sky is a pale, crystal blue, the air cold enough that I have a blanket wrapped around my shoulders and my tea has doubled its steam.

Despite the still-bare branches of the maple above me, green stalks are pushing through the soil along my fence. In a few weeks, white and yellow daffodils will bloom. I've always loved this time of year—the first yawn of spring—but for the first time, I can't connect to the symbolic beauty of new beginnings. All I see is barrenness.

Dropping into a chair, I take a few sips of chamomile.

Then I make the call.

Rye answers on the second ring. "Yo! Good timing. Just got in the car to head home from Casey's. I can't wait for you to meet this girl, Eva. She's super cool. No crazy vibes at all."

"Is this a different Casey from the one you dated before Anna?"

There's a telling silence, then a deep groan. "Shit. Oh, fuck me. Her name is Kelsey. I totally called her Casey this morning. No wonder she gave me that weird look."

I try not to laugh, but it's impossible.

"What am I going to do?" he whines.

"I'd start with an apology. Was it a first date?"

He makes an affirmative sound. "I was going to be a gentleman and drop her off at home, but then she dragged me in—"

"Got it," I say quickly. "If it was a first date, she might accept an apology. No promises, though. Getting her name wrong after spending the night gives major fuckboy energy."

He laughs, unoffended. "Anyway, what's up? How was the party on Friday?"

I lean back to stare at the bare branches above me. "It was at Wilder's house. Is that why you suddenly had last-minute plans?"

"Uh, maybe?"

I sigh. "You don't have to pretend you're not friends with him, Rye. I don't care about that. I'm calling because I have a question. After you answer it, we're going back to never talking about him. Cool?"

"Cool." He clears his throat. "I'm sorry, Eva. We were in the studio for months—"

"It's fine," I interject. "My question is about Wilder and his girlfriend. Do they have an open relationship?"

This time the pause is so long that if it wasn't for the background hum coming from moving tires, I'd think he'd hung up.

When his answer comes, his voice is uncharacteristically serious. "They both sleep with other people. But I wouldn't even call it a relationship. It's super fucked up. They don't even like each other. Why are you asking? What happened?"

I open my mouth, but before I can speak, he explodes.

"Oh, *shit*! He seduced you, didn't he? That motherfucker. Were you drunk? Do I need to beat his ass? I knew I should have gone with—"

"Rye, chill!"

He falls silent, but his breathing is harsh through the line.

"I wasn't drunk, okay? I went home early and he

showed up at my house. We slept together. It was consensual. He left. The end."

Memory seizes me.

Wilder buttons his jeans and buckles his belt, bare chest and arms flexing with the movements. I know I have to get up to lock my door behind him, but I need another minute. I'm not sure my legs can hold me yet.

"You really have no idea," he murmurs, heavy-lidded gaze dancing down my body.

I sit up, dragging the sheet with me. "About what?"

Avoiding my eyes, he grabs his shirt and pulls it on, then slips his feet into unlaced boots. His socks are tucked into a pocket.

Finally, he looks at me. "Be stronger than me. Block my number. Don't open the door if I knock."

I swallow so hard I hear it. "Obviously."

His smile is tender. Sad in a way I don't understand. "I mean it. Someday you're going to realize the way it is between us isn't the norm. But when that happens—when you're tempted—remember that I'm not worth it."

Before my shock can transition to anger, he stalks to the bed and grabs my throat, then presses his lips to mine in a short, hard kiss.

"Goodbye, Fairy."

Then he's gone, striding from the bedroom. He doesn't look back.

"Eva?" asks Rye in a tone that tells me he's been talking but I haven't heard a word he's said.

"Sorry. I'm here."

"Are you sure you're okay?"

I force confidence into my voice. "Yep."

He hesitates. "Are you guys talking now? Is this going to happen again?"

A sudden gust of wind throws my hair across my face and whistles through high branches. I shiver, then grab my tea and stand.

"No. It was a one-time thing."

Rye says nothing.

He doesn't have to.

I'm not sure I believe me, either.

CHAPTER THIRTEEN

wilder

You gave me what I asked for

Then took it with you out the front door

Now I'm broken open

Everything unspoken

pouring out of me

So I spin... spin

On this carousel of sin... sin

A game I'll never win... win

Without you

Six long weeks have passed since Evangeline's gasps and moans became my favorite soundtrack. I've replayed our night together so many times the vinyl is worn out. Muffled and muddy, the melody distorted.

Sometimes I'm not sure it really happened.

The only time it feels real is when I'm asleep. In my dreams, I experience it all again. The silky slopes of her hips under my hands. Her arching neck. Sweat-slick spine against my chest, her hair in my mouth, in my fist. The graceful, serpentine waves of her moving body as she matched me note for note. Bright, lust-drunk eyes and her voice sobbing my name.

Evangeline is a perfect song, but she's stuck in my head like a bad one.

Kendra is *not* happy.

I've successfully avoided having sex with her, but I'm running out of excuses. Thus far, she hasn't confronted me. As much as I need her, she needs me, too. The threat goes both ways. She's not willing to risk losing all the perks of being my girlfriend, so she's pretending everything's fine while I pretend I'm not revolted by the idea of touching anyone but Evangeline. And that, of course, is off the table.

Evangeline did what I told her to and blocked my number. I may not be a good person, but I'm not enough of an asshole to push her or show up at her house uninvited again. Even if I fantasize about knocking down her door a hundred times a day.

I'm in a constant state of hunger, but the only sustenance that will sate me is one I can't have.

The band is my saving grace. Our second single released and the response was even more insane than the first. Whatever anonymity we enjoyed before is gone, at least with the under-forty crowd in the city we call home. I wasn't a fan of social outings before, but now I can't even hit up my favorite record store or local coffee shop without being forced into conversation with strangers.

Not that I have much free time.

Between multiple daily rehearsals, the guys and I have been running ourselves ragged. Every day there's somewhere we have to be or something we have to do. Interviews. Photoshoots. Music videos. Our social media accounts have ballooned so much we've hired an agency to handle them. A team of people now generates our content, one of whom is currently recording us while we watch a basketball game in our basement.

Our keyboardist, Zander, shoves his glasses up his nose, his eyes darting from the TV to Eddie. "Are we supposed to be talking?" he hisses.

"Just act natural," chirps the woman behind a tripod holding her phone.

The first two replacements for Evangeline only lasted months before being fired. Zander has been with us for over a year. He's normal. Kind of quiet. So far, he seems to be handling all the attention pretty well, but he's definitely more freaked out than the rest of us. We, at least, remember our first tour. Although that brief flare of fame was nothing compared to what's happening now.

"This is so weird," Zander mutters.

Next to me, Jax chuckles. "If you think this is weird, wait until we hit the road."

Eddie throws a piece of popcorn at him from the other end of the L-shaped couch. "Stop scaring the newbie."

Ignoring his brother, Jax leans toward me and lowers his voice. "How are you holding up?"

"I'm fine."

His eyes fall to my hands. I curl my fingers, subduing their spastic drumming.

I'm on day ten free of pills. Normally by now, I'd have taken a quarter of a pill, my usual starter dose for reentry into my life. But after I cut the tablet, I couldn't bring myself to swallow it.

This detox was more brutal than any I've gone through before. The withdrawals more painful, the cravings so intense I almost broke a dozen times. It scared the shit out of me. My skin still feels raw, like I'm recovering from a sunburn. My head is a mess, my thoughts a fireworks show—blinding, loud, chaotic. At least my stomach settled today and I can swallow without gagging.

"Dude," Jax whispers. "You've gotta stop."

Five days ago—my worst day—Jax heard a crash in my room. When I didn't answer the door, he busted in and found me on the floor, moaning, sweating, and shaking. My mumblings about having the flu went down like a lead balloon.

I ended up telling him the truth minus where I get my pills. He yelled a lot. I puked on his shoes. It was a fucking mess.

"I told you," I whisper back, "it's under control."

Jax frowns. "When the tour starts—"

"Did you guys see this?" Eddie interrupts as he jumps to his feet. He veers around the coffee table and shoves his phone in our faces. "Glow is headlining tonight at the Cathedral!"

Jax whistles. "Damn, go Eva. Main stage?"

"Side stage," I murmur, having already seen the post on the band's Instagram. Cathedral's main stage has a capacity of six hundred, but the attached hall for lesser known acts is nothing to sneeze at with a cap of three hundred.

Eddie bounces on the balls of his feet. "We have to go!"

"Sounds good to me," says Jax with a shrug.

Zander stands fast, his relief obvious. "I'm down."

Eddie and Zander head for the stairs, Eddie rambling about how awesome Evangeline is and how he's going to text everyone he knows to come to the show in case ticket sales are lackluster. They're not. I checked fifteen minutes ago and the show is nearly sold out.

I wonder if Eddie would be as supportive of Evangeline if he knew I fucked her into a coma last month.

Sighing heavily, I press the heels of my hands to my aching eyes.

"Can we have the room?" Jax asks the woman whose name I can't remember.

She smiles brightly and removes her phone from the tripod. "Sure thing. Are you going to the show, Wilder?"

I start to shake my head but pause. If everyone leaves, I'll be here alone with nothing to distract me from the craving beating in my blood. I have no idea where Kendra is—she stays away during my detox—but she's the last person I can talk to about this, anyway. The last person who would tell me *not* to take a pill... or three. Much more likely, she'd crush them up and snort a line, then offer me the straw.

"Yes," Jax answers with a quick glance at me. "He's coming."

I cock an eyebrow in his direction but don't object. Do I want to see Evangeline? More than I want my next breath. But that doesn't mean seeing her is a good idea, especially not in my current state. My impulse control is hanging by a thread. If I see her fingers on a guitar, hear her sing, I'm probably going to do something stupid like weasel my way backstage and use my effect on her to get under her clothes.

Blood flows south at the thought, and I suddenly can't remember why that's a bad idea.

The social media woman claps her hands in excitement, shattering my daydream about Evangeline's tits in my mouth.

"Awesome! I've been wanting to see Glow, so this is perfect!" Leaving the tripod, she runs up the basement stairs.

Jax sighs. "Mae is a lot."

"That's her name?"

He snorts, then grabs the remote to turn off the TV. Sensing that I'm about to get lectured, I sigh and face him.

"Look, Jax, I'm sorry I worried you—"

"Let's do a dry-thirty. You and me. No booze, no drugs for a month. Gym, vitamins, the whole nine."

I stare at him, floored, as the words cycle through me and incite an uncomfortable blend of fear and yearning.

The last time I was sober for that long was after Evangeline left the band. I don't even remember why I did it, though it probably had something to do with the shame of all the fucked-up shit I did on tour and what happened after. I'm sure some part of me also thought if I could show her I was changing, she'd come back.

She blocked my number instead, and I got blackout drunk the night I realized it.

"It'll be good," Jax continues. "We'll reset our systems before the tour."

Without thinking, I say, "I don't know if I can go that long," then immediately wish I could take the words back. They make it sound like I'm admitting...

I can't even finish the thought.

Jax grabs my shoulder, his expression determined. "It's going to suck for me, too. I don't think I've gone more than a few days without weed for—shit, probably two years. Point is, we'll be miserable together. But then we'll be jacked from all the gym time and so healthy our piss smells like lettuce."

A reluctant smile pulls at my lips.

"Is that a yes?" he asks, grinning.

Yearning briefly eclipses fear, and my chin jerks down.

He squeezes my shoulder, then stands. "Come on. We have time to clear out our stashes and tell Eddie and Zander to lock their shit up."

Just as fast, fear rises again, this time a monster with fangs dripping venom. Panic curls through me, accelerating my pulse. I stand, locking my knees when they wobble. The urge to take a pill hits me so hard my vision tunnels.

"Jax." My voice is strangled.

He turns at the base of the stairs, his expression swiftly shifting from questioning to concerned.

I open my mouth, close it, and finally force out the words that don't want to come. "I need your help getting rid of the pills. Like you're going to have to do it because I don't... I don't think I can."

His expression softens in understanding. "You got it."

I swallow the lump in my throat, pushing back against the pressure inside me. "One more thing. The Oxy... Kendra gets it for me."

He stares at me for several seconds, processing, then blows out a heavy breath. "A lot of shit about your relationship suddenly makes sense." He pauses. "Do you love her?"

I shake my head.

He nods decisively. "Kick her to the curb tonight,

then crash at your parents' for a few days. Eddie and I will move her shit out and get the locks changed. Okay?"

A frenetic energy sizzles through me. Not fear or panic. Something far more dangerous.

Hope.

I nod. "Okay."

♫

As DESPERATE AS I am to see Evangeline, I know she isn't the answer to my problems. She can't change the way my brain works, can't protect me from the feeling I've had since I was a kid that I was different from my peers.

For as long as I can remember, I've thought of it as the Shadow.

There are three manifestations. Sometimes it's subdued or muted, usually when I'm hyper-focused on music. For minutes or hours, I'm able to forget about it.

Other times, the Shadow overtakes me like a fog, becoming a veil between me and the world. It's a haze that numbs me. Separates me. Those are the times I withdraw because I'm afraid that when people look at me, they'll see it. My *wrongness*. They'll recognize I'm not like them and everything I've worked for will vanish.

The third manifestation is the worst. When the Shadow isn't distracted or numbing me, it hovers around me as a constant threat. When triggered, it snaps closed like a medieval Iron Maiden, piercing me with dozens of sharp spikes. I'm hypersensitive. Raw, exposed nerves and emotions. The world and all its madness and loudness invade me, overwhelm me. I lose perception of time. Lose control of my breath and senses.

I panic.

When I was six, I drew a picture of the Shadow. A crayon kid surrounded by a cloud of swirling black and purple with needles sinking into the small body and making it bleed. My mom found the drawing and showed my dad. They put me in therapy. I don't remember the therapist's name, but her voice was soft and I liked her smile. We played with sand trays and drew pictures more than we talked.

I stopped going after a year. My parents and the therapist seemed excited about me not coming back. It was a celebration to them, but I was sad. I'd liked the one hour a week I spent in her office full of toys and no expectations.

More than that, though, I liked that my parents were happy. So when the Shadow next appeared, I didn't say anything. Didn't draw any pictures. I kept my weird thoughts to myself and started watching how other kids acted. Classmates at school, Rye and Evangeline on the weekends. I learned to mimic them, how they interacted with each other and adults. I was still a quiet kid, but I learned to smile more. Say the right things.

Pretend there was no Shadow.

When the topic came up again, I was eleven. My parents were worried because one of my teachers expressed concern that I didn't have friends at school. But by then I'd become adept at faking normalcy. I convinced them I was fine by making friends I didn't really want. A lot of friends. I joined after-school activities: drama, musical theater, and even soccer for a couple of years. I went to birthday parties and hangouts. Spent my free time at home entertaining my younger siblings, playing guitar with my dad, and learning piano from my mom.

I distracted myself, which distracted the Shadow. During the day, at least. Almost every night, I'd wake up gasping and shaking beneath an enormous pressure on my chest. When the numbness invariably came, it was a relief because for however long it lasted, I could sleep.

Then Evangeline and I wrote a song.

It was the first time in my life the Shadow actually disappeared. Almost like it had been waiting for that moment. Waiting for her and our music.

For years afterward, I went through each week knowing that relief was coming in the form of Evangeline every weekend. Being around her, making music with her... she made me feel both normal and extraordinary.

I overheard my mom once referring to Evangeline as an old soul. I didn't understand it then, but I do now. She was a calm kid. Slow to anger. Perceptive and compassionate beyond her years. She always smiled with her eyes. She always knew what she wanted. Said what she thought. She was brave. Real. Those traits only grew as we did.

Unlike me, her insides have always matched her outsides. She's never been a fraud pretending to be someone she wasn't.

With her influence, I stayed in control of the Shadow until I was almost twenty. And when I lost it, it was also because of her. Because my mom showed me a picture of her at her senior prom. A grinning boy had his arm around her waist. She was smiling up at him. I asked who he was, and my mom told me he was Evangeline's new boyfriend.

That night, the jaws of the Shadow snapped closed with more force than ever before. It wasn't my first panic attack, but it was by far the worst. There were moments when I thought I'd die from it, alone and unable to call out.

The next day, shaky and weak from the worst night of my life, I texted a friend who I knew stole Xanax from his mom. I'd tried them before. They didn't make the Shadow disappear, but they dimmed its effects.

He offered me Vicodin instead.

Relief.

I KNOW Evangeline can't fix me.

But she's still my favorite high.

evangeline

Both Lily and I are breathing hard and dripping sweat when we collapse onto a worn leather couch in the small dressing room attached to Cathedral's side stage. We sit in giddy silence, listening to the cheers and whistles slowly tapering off outside the walls.

The last six weeks have been a whirlwind. In addition to coursework and our jobs, we've played shows around the city every weekend. Each one bigger than the last.

Thanks to Rye pulling some strings to get us studio time and his skills as a producer, we also recorded fifteen songs: all the crowd favorites and a few newer ones we've barely debuted. As of yesterday, we have eight thousand monthly listeners on Spotify, and CDs and merch Rye's been peddling for us at shows are dwindling fast.

"Did you see the first rows?" asks Lily in a dreamy voice. "They knew the words of almost every song. Every beat drop. Fucking nuts. What is this life?"

A smile stretches my aching cheeks as I roll my head toward her. There are tears in her eyes.

"It's really happening, isn't it?" she whispers.

"I told you it would."

She laughs, sniffing. "You did. I believe you now."

There's a knock on the door.

Lily sits up and wipes her face, then stands and quickly checks her reflection in the mirror. I don't move except to reach over to the mini fridge and grab a bottle of water. I have a feeling I know who's outside—and it's not Rye like she thinks. I saw a familiar man offstage with Cathedral's general manager, and I'm fairly certain Lily's about to have her mind blown.

I'm content to watch. She deserves this moment, one I experienced at eighteen.

She swings the door open, her smile huge. When she sees the man waiting outside, her jaw drops and her complexion pales noticeably. I grin behind my water bottle.

"H-hello," she squeaks. "How can we help you?"

"Ms. Aoki," comes a warm, masculine voice. "My

name is Cory Donovan. I'm here on behalf of Indigo Records. Do you and Eva have a minute to chat?"

Lily blinks at him a few more times before her brain restarts. "Yes, absolutely." She shifts back into the room, throwing me an *I'm-freaking-the-fuck-out* look before sitting on the arm of the couch beside me.

The sandy-haired vice president of Indigo Records walks into the room. His eyes find me and he grins. "It's about damned time."

I push to my feet, smiling as I shake the hand of my father's longtime friend.

"Good to see you, Cory. I take it you got the demo?"

From the corner of my eye, I see Lily's head whip toward me. I didn't tell her I gave my dad a USB last week to pass on to Cory. Maybe because I wasn't a hundred percent sure this moment would come, but more likely because I'm still reasoning through why I finally felt okay using my family connections.

Now that the moment is upon us, I have no regrets. It doesn't feel like we skipped any rungs on the ladder; we're already being courted by two small labels. Both have solid reputations, but they can't launch us like Indigo can. And for Lily—for myself—I want the best of the best behind us.

Indigo would never screw us over, and not only because of who my father is. They're a well-oiled machine. While their roster isn't enormous, their acts routinely go platinum, sell out tours, and bring home industry awards.

Cory chuckles. "I sure did. You were already on my mind after that Illoka article, but when I listened to your demo..." He shakes his head, his gaze turning speculative. "Any chance you'll tell me why you haven't reached out before? You've clearly been ready for the next step for a while."

I glance at Lily, who watches me with ecstatic hope in her eyes, then shrug at Cory. "We were earning our stripes the old-fashioned way."

His smile grows. "Well, it shows. I heard you were booked to headline at McClane Concert Hall next month?"

Lily and I exchange a grin. "We were."

McClane beats Cathedral's main stage in size and capacity, and their booking process is strictly *Don't Call Us, We'll Call You.* When that call came two days ago, Lily and I barely kept it together for the duration, then lost our fucking minds.

Cory grabs a nearby chair for himself and gestures for me to sit back down. Unbuttoning his suit jacket, he settles and props elbows on his knees. "All right, ladies. Let's get down to business. I've been informed there are other offers on the table. What's it going to take?"

From the hallway, a low, familiar voice says, "Don't fuck around, Cory. They get the same contract Night Theory has or better."

A wave of shock ripples down my body, followed by a surge of crackling heat as Wilder steps into view. He leans against the doorjamb, arms crossed over his chest, his gaze steady on Cory.

Six weeks of forcibly compartmentalizing our night together peel away one by one. My eyes drink in the dark hair held to his cheek by the side of his sweatshirt's hood. Full lips currently compressed. Sharp, unshaven jaw. Lowered brows. Eyes like shadowed emeralds against black lashes, the golden skin beneath them smudged by stress or sleeplessness.

I want to touch him so badly I can't breathe.

Lily's hand clamps hard on my shoulder. I suck air into my oxygen-starved lungs.

"I should have known you'd be lurking around here, Ashburn," Cory says with a boisterous laugh. He stands and shakes Wilder's hand. "You don't have to worry. You know I'll do right by Eva."

Wilder nods. "Good." His eyes flash to me for an instant. "Great show tonight."

He slips back into the hallway.

I'm on my feet before I process moving. "I'll, uh, be right back."

Ignoring the surprise from Cory and panic from Lily, I race into the hallway right as Wilder turns a corner.

"Wait!"

He jerks to a stop but doesn't turn as I catch up to him. I stare at his back, every part of mé buzzing. My skin, blood, and bones.

Words slip past the knotted mess of my thoughts. "I thought I felt you."

He shifts, giving me his profile. "Felt me?" he asks softly.

My stomach spirals downward. "In the audience. You know, the infamous Wilder-Eva radar?"

His head bows, then lifts as he turns to face me. Soft, sad eyes fix on mine. "I shouldn't have come back here."

Feeling like a passenger in my own body, I take a step toward him. "Why did you?"

His chest expands on a swift inhale. "The guys are here, too. They're helping Rye pack your gear. I saw Cory walk back and wanted to make sure—" He shakes his head, glancing over his shoulder. "I should—"

"Wilder." I take another step toward him, frowning as he stiffens.

My mind is quite static now.

This isn't the man who pounded on my door and gave me the best sex of my life. But I remember this version of him, one I haven't seen in years.

Uncertain, vibrating, awkward.

I grab his hand, wrapping my warm fingers around his cold ones. "Hey. It's me."

"That's the problem," he murmurs, his fingers spasming in mine. "I want to be wherever you are. I don't know how to let go. Tell me to leave you alone."

My lips part and the truth ejects. "I can't."

His eyes find mine. For endless seconds, we stare at each other.

Then he says, "Fuck it," and yanks me forward.

Our mouths collide and I open for him instantly, a starving flower finally feeling the sun. The low, rough noise he makes tells me he feels this, too. How our mingled taste fills up parts of us that are otherwise empty.

I forget where I am.

Who I am.

Until Lily says loudly, "Ahem!"

I break the kiss with a gasp.

Behind us, Cory says, "Great to meet you, Lily. I'll see you and Eva Monday afternoon," then a bit louder, with clear amusement, "Have fun, kids!"

Mortified, I jerk backward but barely move, belatedly realizing Wilder's arms are locked tight around me.

"Let go," I hiss.

His hold only tightens, pulling me against the bulge

in his pants. He stares down at me, cheeks flushed, lips glistening, eyes feral and hopeful and bewitching.

"I broke up with Kendra," he whispers fervently. "I haven't touched anyone since you. I'm yours if you want me. Only yours. Say yes, Fairy. Say yes to us."

The world drains away. We're alone in space. Just us. Like it's supposed to be.

I nod, and his smile is a sunrise.

evangeline

After a final, searing kiss and a promise to meet me at my house in an hour, Wilder retreats to the stage to help load our gear into Rye's SUV. Lily drags me back to the dressing room, closes and locks the door, then spins on me.

"What the ever-loving fuck? What did he say to you? You look like he knocked your brain out."

I swallow, my tongue moving over my teeth, tasting him. Mint and storms. "He dumped his girlfriend," I tell her, lingering shock in my voice. "He said he wants to be with me."

She blinks fast, then frowns. "That's a complete one-eighty from what he told you last month, what he's been telling you since you guys were teenagers. What changed?"

"No clue. I guess sleeping together made him reevaluate? It was... super intense."

"No shit. You limped for three days." She pauses, her voice lowering. "What happens if he wigs out again? This is the same dude who knew you had feelings for him but still paraded groupies into his bed right in front of you. Who gave you just enough attention to keep you tethered to him and starving for more." She shakes her head. "We've talked about this, Ev. Tortured bad boys with magic dicks are only acceptable in fiction."

I wince. "I know. But I couldn't say no, Lil. I've wondered for so long, wanted him for so long. I've never felt anything like what I feel when I'm with him."

She drags me to the couch and pulls me down, threading our fingers together. Her eyes brim with worry.

"I know we're not the type of women who share every little feeling with each other, but you're still my best friend in the whole world. If I could grow a wiener, I'd put a ring on your finger right now and fuck Wilder out of your system."

I laugh weakly. "Thanks."

She grins, but it fades fast. "This is coming from my love for you and your giant, beautiful heart: this is a bad idea. You've told me a thousand different times how toxic your friendship—or whatever you'd call it—was toward the end. Think of what happened when you left the band. All the shit he's said to you over the years."

You're my muse.

I'm poison.

Nothing will ever compare to us.

I need you.

We're musical destiny.

This isn't a love story.

I hear her words and remember his. I even remember my father's warning. *He's an addict. He's using you.* But nothing penetrates the golden haze of Wilder's declaration. I can't feel doubt or fear.

All I feel is a lifetime of us.

His haughty, little-prince voice telling me to stop following him around and me never listening. Wearing him down until he played with Rye and me—but mostly me. Endless games of hide-and-seek and him begrudgingly pushing me on the swings in my backyard. Piggyback rides and popsicle-stick crafts and sneaking into the kitchen before dinner to swipe frosting off cupcakes. Backyard barbecues and pool days and camping trips. Sharing a blanket under the stars as one of our dads played guitar. Singing together, our small voices harmonizing in a way that made our parents trade surprised looks over our heads.

Sunlight shifting around sycamore leaves. His

frowning face as he scribbled in one of our journals. Falling asleep on his bedroom floor while he puzzled through melodies on his guitar. Rare, throaty laughter. Freckled, mood-ring eyes. The expression on his face whenever I sang, like I was the only person who mattered in the world.

Stage lights and cheers and that perfect, glowing space of our creation. Our eyes and hands and voices and lyrics. The connection between us burning like a star, infinite explosions drowning out all background noise. Everything beyond us reduced to colorless ash.

His flexing hips and supple, ink-littered skin. His tongue licking sweat from between my breasts. Eyes holding mine as he drove me toward oblivion and then commanded me to jump like it was the most natural thing in the world. Like he was and will always be the architect and master of my body's secret codes.

"Shit," whispers Lily.

Her face comes back into focus, as does her apprehensive expression. I quickly press my hand to her bouncing knee.

"Whatever happens with Wilder, my number one focus right now is our future. If he wants to be a part of my life, that's up to him. But I'm not going to sacrifice everything we've worked toward for him. I can promise you that."

As I say the words, I hear the truth in them. So does Lily. Her shoulders relax, but she still asks, "And if he pulverizes your heart again?"

I force a smile. "What's that Grace Cunningham quote you were obsessed with last year after that asshole dumped you?"

"'Love is good for music, but heartbreak is good for art.'" She makes a face. "To clarify, I liked that quote before I knew Wilder's grandmother said it."

I laugh. "Fair enough."

A knock on the door is followed by Rye's voice. "All loaded up and ready to go!"

Lily smirks and calls back, "The gear or your dick, Henderson?"

"Date me and find out, Aoki!"

I roll my eyes and stand to gather my things from around the dressing room. Lily lets Rye inside, and they trade flirtatious comments as she does the same.

In the last month and a half—with Rye acting as our roadie, merch-man, and producer—I've grown used to their glaring chemistry. And ever since Lily ended her fling with Tyler from The Remnants, their banter has taken on an increasingly sexual charge.

My best friends' private parts are on a collision course, but I've come to terms with it. In fact, I have a feeling when they finally give in, they'll discover they're actually perfect for each other.

Ten minutes later, I give Lily a hug goodbye and she hops into Rye's passenger seat. He lingers beside my car with me, flipping his keys around his fingers.

"Thanks for taking her home, Rye. Don't knock her up, okay?"

He almost drops the keys. "What? I wouldn't. I mean —Lily's not like that. Or I'm not like that. With her. *Fuck.* Shutting up now."

Laughing, I open my car door and drop into the seat. Rye bends down to make eye contact, his solemn face wiping the smile from mine.

I swallow hard. "You don't have to say it—I know. I can't tell you this isn't a huge mistake. But I have to find out. I hope you understand."

He nods. "I do understand. I think it's true for both of you. It's time to find out." He looks like he wants to say more, but instead smacks the hood of my car and grins. "You good to drive, grandma? It's pretty dark out there."

I roll my eyes. "Goodnight."

He winks. "Night, Eva."

He jogs toward his car and Lily. I start my car and drive home. To Wilder. To *us.*

I don't notice the darkness.

CHAPTER SIXTEEN

Bells were ringing

At the end of time

The sky was on fire

But you were mine

Sitting against Evangeline's front door, I wage a mental war on the doubts and fears assailing me. Do I regret what I said to her? Not even a little bit. I want her—want *us*—more than anything. More than the drugs my body and brain still crave. More than success or recognition or acclaim. I'd burn everything down for her. Give up everything I think I want and need.

And therein lies my greatest fear: the complete lack of control I have over my feelings for her. I don't know how to stop needing her. Craving her. Suffering when we're apart.

At eleven years old, she stole pieces of my soul. The best pieces. I'm not whole without them, without her, and I never will be.

Three years ago, I thought I could learn to live and thrive and make music without her. And I tried. God, I fucking tried. But it wasn't until I gave up and started writing down all my memories of her that my music came back.

Every damn song on the new album is about her in one way or another. Even with a chasm between us, she shaped every note and word.

Now, sitting here in the shadows on her small porch, my skin twitchy from nerves and the aftershocks of withdrawals, I finally admit to myself a truth I've known all along.

I love her.

I've loved her all my life and have been in love with her since I was seventeen.

The epiphany ricochets, punching me with the same truth upside down. There's something wrong with my love. Wrong with me.

My love has hurt her.

Will it be different this time? Or will I hurt her again?

My phone lights up with a text, pulling me from my bleak thoughts. It's Kendra again. I don't read it. I'm sure it's more of the same—anger, denial, threats. She's called me eight times and sent a dozen messages in response to the text I sent her on the way to the show.

I'll have to deal with her at some point. Do the right thing and have a face-to-face conversation. I owe her that much. I should probably be worried about her threats, too, but the freedom I feel right now drowns out potential consequences. If anything comes of it... that's what lawyers and PR teams are for.

Headlights momentarily blind me as a car pulls into the narrow, weed-choked driveway beside her bungalow. My pulse jumps. I stand fast, gritting my teeth at a punishing wave of dizziness, then quickly turn off my phone and tuck it in my back pocket.

As Evangeline exits the car and walks toward me, my various physical discomforts fade. *Background noise.* My eyes suck in her angles and curves, her colors and textures. Neon pink fishnet tights and calf-high boots. An electric blue halter dress that would be sleazy on anyone else but on her looks edgy and cute. The crown of braids on her head a wispy mess after the high-energy show.

She steps up to me, chin lifted and lips lightly pursed. I can't read the look in her mismatched eyes.

My heartbeats are bruising.

I clear my throat, bracing myself. "Regrets already?"

She hesitates. "No. I just didn't expect you so soon." She glances down at herself. "I was hoping to shower before you got here."

Tension drains from me so swiftly I almost sag against the front door. "I could use a shower, too."

"Is that so?" She fights a smile, her gaze flitting down my body. My cock jerks in my pants, and I have to bite my tongue to keep from groaning.

She adds, "I need to eat, too."

I nod quickly. "Shower, food. What else? How do you wind down after a show these days?"

She shrugs. "A book. Tea. Sometimes a movie or a soak in the hot tub. I usually eat and pass out, though."

I grin. "Same as always, then."

Her soft laugh is silk on my raw skin. "Pretty much. Right this second, though, all I want is for you to move so I can open my front door."

I smirk and make space for her, stooping to grab my backpack.

"Think you're spending the night, huh?" she asks cheekily.

I shrug, feigning indifference when there's nothing I

want more. "I don't have to, but I'm staying away from the house for a few days. Kendra's moving out."

Her eyes narrow. "Wait—when did you break up with her?"

I wince. "Uh... today."

To my surprise, she laughs and rises to her toes to give me a soft kiss. "You can stay."

This must be what winning the lottery feels like. My heart can't decide if it wants to stop or race.

As soon as she turns toward the door, I step into her. My chest against her shoulders, my erection above the swell of her ass. Keys rattle as she misses the lock.

"I'm gross, Wilder. No touching until I shower."

"Not happening."

Lowering my face to her hair, still damp from sweat, I suck in her scent. Then I bend further, my mouth finding the soft, warm skin beneath her ear. I gather her essence in my nose, on my tongue. Salt and musk and the natural fragrance of her skin that comforts me as much as it drives me wild.

"You smell and taste like heaven. Someday I'm going to eat you out the second you step offstage."

She chokes. "That's nasty."

Sliding my free hand around her hip and under her dress, I cup her between the legs. Heat bathes my palm. She shivers, her thighs clenching.

"You want me nasty," I whisper against her ear. "Don't you?"

Her breathing speeds up. "Maybe."

"Open the door," I say hoarsely. "I'll give you a sixty-second head start. Shower or bed—your choice. But when a minute is up, my mouth is devouring this pussy."

She squeaks and finally gets the door unlocked, then runs across the house to her bedroom, flipping on lights as she goes. I lock the door behind me, smiling to myself when I hear the shower turn on. I knew it would. Despite her body's response to my suggestion, she's not mentally ready for my filthy appetite.

I don't even know if *I'm* ready for it. The shit I want to do and say to her... it shocks even me. No woman has ever incited such unhinged sexual need in me. With Evangeline, all my self-control is stripped away. For better or worse, I'm fully myself with her.

When I make it to the bathroom doorway and see her already in the shower, suds and water dripping over her head and down her gorgeous body, I jerk to a stop and squeeze the head of my dick so I don't fucking erupt.

I'd almost forgotten how much Oxy dulls physical sensation. I didn't *feel* high the first time we had sex, but the drugs were still in my system. If she's hoping for a marathon like last time, she's going to be disappointed.

I'll make it up to her.

Sparkling eyes rise to my face. "Problem?"

I exhale a laugh. "Nope. It's just been six weeks."

Those eyes widen. "You haven't even... you know?"

"Rubbed one out imagining your cunt spasming around me?"

She rolls her eyes even as her cheeks flush scarlet at my crude words. "Obviously."

"Oh, I definitely have." Keeping a firm hold on myself, I allow my gaze to wander down her body. My eyes linger on her pink nipples and the trimmed, fair hair between her legs. Breath shudders out of me as I drag my gaze back up. "Memory doesn't compare to the real thing, though."

She smiles tentatively. "Aren't you coming in?"

I shake my head. "Changed my mind."

Taking two steps into the bathroom, I lower to my knees on a thick bathmat. The flash of disappointment in her eyes shifts to curiosity.

"What are you doing?"

I point at my mouth. "Waiting to be fed."

Her blush spreads down her chest as her eyes roam over my face. "You're serious."

"Deadly. Finish up and get out here before I starve."

I've never seen anyone wash so fast; she's out of the shower less than a minute later. To my surprise, she doesn't bother reaching for a towel before walking right up to me. Her wet hands sink into my hair, guiding my face upward. She bends down until her lips hover over mine, hair dripping all over my face.

"Time to eat, Wilder."

I blink in surprise. Then I laugh in sheer joy.

She's perfect.

So fucking perfect.

My eyes on hers, I back her up until her ass hits the counter. I lick a line up her stomach, making her spasm before yanking one long leg over my shoulder and spreading her open for me.

"Goddamn," I whisper as I drag my index finger lightly around her silky, rose-colored center. "So pretty."

I blow on her and she jerks.

"Quit teasing."

Looking up, I take in her heaving breasts and quivering stomach. Her parted lips and dilated eyes. Water droplets slide down her body. Drip onto the floor and me. She shivers, goosebumps blooming all over.

"Cold?"

She nods.

I spread her with my fingers and press a kiss to her clit. Her legs shake. "Lean into it. Feel that chill as you feel this." I lick her heavy and deep. Her breathy moan makes me feel like a starving god whose chains have broken.

I devour my feast.

It doesn't take long for her to fall apart. She cries out softly, pulsing against my mouth.

"More," I demand.

I push two fingers inside her. She flutters around me, tight and scalding. I give her no quarter, sucking and flicking her clit with my tongue as I curl my fingers and pulse them. My other hand dives around her thigh and up. I hook my pinky inside her and apply counter tension to my still-moving fingers, then press my index finger to her asshole and massage the tense surface.

She jerks. "Wilder!"

My mouth is too full to respond, but I lift my eyes to her startled face. It takes a few seconds, but with a trembling breath, she nods.

Fuck yes.

She's so wet, it takes barely any pressure for my finger to sink into her ass. Her beautiful voice fills the steamy room as I work. Gasps and cries and pleas. My balls tighten in warning but I hardly notice.

She whimpers my name as she unravels, her pussy and ass clamping hard on my fingers. It's too much sensory perfection—I groan against her as my cock jumps and I nut in my pants like a preteen.

evangeline

Wilder sits back on his heels and wipes his face on his sleeve. His cheekbones are flushed, a grin teasing his lips as he peers up at me.

"I think I'll take a shower, after all."

I'm so wrecked from that second orgasm, it takes a few beats for me to register the wet spot near the fly of his jeans. I bite my lips but it's no use—a giggle slips free.

He climbs to his feet, his grin lighting up his eyes. Warm hands slip around my back, tugging me against his front. His nose nuzzles mine.

"Go ahead and laugh. We both know you'd be just as big of a mess if I hadn't licked it all up."

My already flushed skin burns. He chuckles and gives me a brief, wicked kiss, then moves to the shower and turns it back on. His shoes come off. Then his socks and shirt. A belt buckle clanks. Jeans and boxer briefs hit the floor. I ogle his perfect ass and muscled back as he steps into the tub and pulls the glass door closed.

His head tilts back. Water cascades over his face, misting above his open mouth, running down his chest and rippling abs to his half-hard cock.

"If you're going to stare, you might as well do it from in here."

My eyes flash up to his playful smile.

Am I dreaming?

I almost say it out loud. Maybe Wilder senses the words because he says, "This is really happening, Evangeline. You and me. Come on."

He opens the shower door. Steam billows out, stirring air and making me shiver.

My feet carry me toward him.

Like they always do.

THE REMAINS of a pizza sit on my kitchen table, half-eaten. We each managed a slice and a half before gravity forced a collision of our mouths.

We're on the couch now. I rock in his lap, the position both torturous and exquisite, his cock so deep inside me it passes the line of intimacy into possession.

Making the moment even more intense is the fact he won't let me break eye contact. His hands frame my face, fingers in my hair, gentle pressure holding me still or adjusting my head when I try to look away. Between consuming kisses, his freckled eyes stay on mine, penetrating me as deeply as his body.

I've never felt so safe and threatened at the same time. He's familiar and new. A fantasy I'm not completely convinced has become real. Our history melts around us, viscous and powerful as it reshapes everything I know about my own heart.

There are no clothes between us. No condom, either. He didn't bring any and Lily stole the last of mine a few weeks ago. When Wilder and I surfaced from lust long enough to realize what was missing, it was already too late. At least for me. He tried to stop me from sliding down his length, but my rational brain was offline. The second my body took an inch of him, his brain likewise ejected reason.

I shift from grinding to lifting slowly and dropping back down. Every time his piercing hits a spot inside me, scorching heat flashes through my entire body.

"Holy fuck," he groans, neck arching and eyes closing. "Slow down, baby, or I'm not going to last."

My heart thuds at the endearment. I don't slow down. The sight of him beneath me, all flushed skin and clenched muscles, his abs flexing as he struggles not to take control, makes me feel like a goddess.

"Does it feel good?" I ask breathlessly.

"Better than anything."

His hands sink further into my drying hair. Calluses snag on strands, igniting pinpricks of sensation that make me pant harder. He pulls my head back, bowing my spine, and his tongue laves my nipples.

I whimper and move even faster.

"You're so wet. Hot. Soft." He yanks my face back down, his tongue diving between my lips. "I'm so fucking glad you're the first person I've felt without a rubber. Worth. The. Wait." He punctures the words with bites on my lips.

"Same," I whisper. "This first is yours."

His cock throbs inside me, turning to steel. A hiss whistles through his clenched teeth. "I'm super close." He tries to lift me off him, but I sit fast and clamp my knees on his hips.

His eyes widen with panic. "Evangeline—"

"I'm on the pill. Fill me up, Wilder."

His eyes darken, features tightening. Releasing my hair, one arm snakes around my back. He presses his other thumb to my clit.

"You're coming with me," is all the warning I have before he takes over from below, rolling his hips into mine with deep, devastating precision. Those flashes of heat from his piercing build and compound until they become an inferno that swallows me whole.

"I'm—" The rest of my words are a stuttering cry.

He groans. "Oh, fuck yes." His hips lose their rhythm, jerking hard against me as his body goes taut. The sound he makes—the feel of him pulsing inside me—heightens my orgasm to catastrophic levels. The feeling is so intense reality slips away.

"Hey," he whispers, "it's okay. I've got you."

My senses return and provide context for his low, tender tone. I'm cradled in his arms and sobbing into his neck.

Shit.

I sit up fast and wipe my face, sucking back the next sob before it can release. "Sorry. I, uh... Need to pee."

Avoiding his searching eyes, I shift my legs to climb off him.

"Not so fast." His arms flex and I fall back against his chest. "Tell me what's going through your head."

This is a dream.

A huge mistake.

You'll hurt me.

Turn on me.

Leave me broken again.

"Nothing," I mumble.

A quick twitch of his hips makes me gasp. He's still inside me, hard enough that his thrust triggers an aftershock. I screw my eyes shut, fighting the instant rise of desire.

"Let me see those fairy eyes."

The words trigger a three-year-old memory. A frisson of old hurt follows, tumbling fast into anger. When I look at him, his eyes widen, shoulders stiffening.

"What's wrong?"

"We need to talk," I say with forced calm. "But I can't have this conversation with your dick in me. And I actually do need to pee. I don't want a UTI."

He studies my face another moment, then closes his eyes. When they open, they're full of resignation. "I'll get dressed and make us tea."

He lets me go. I scramble off him, wincing as he slips out of me, and escape to my bathroom. After peeing, I use a washcloth to clean my wet thighs, then splash cold water on my face and study the woman in the mirror. I barely recognize her beneath a glowing complexion, swollen lips, love-marked skin, and tangled hair.

"What are you doing?" I whisper to her.

Her eyes hold no answers, only naive hopes. *She*

wants nothing more than to fall back into the fantasy, the pretend world where Wilder has never hurt me, where his offer backstage at Cathedral came with no strings, no history, no fears.

The woman in the mirror has been in control the last few hours, but the real me is back in the driver's seat. Ironically, I have that brain-melting orgasm to thank. It broke my delusional bubble, reminding me of the many tears I've spilled over him.

I reach for my robe, then decide I need more than terrycloth between us for this conversation. A minute later, I'm armored in leggings, a sports bra, and a sweatshirt I stole from Rye that covers me to mid-thigh.

I find Wilder in the kitchen, sweatpants riding low on his hips. To my relief, he also pulled on a T-shirt. When he hears the creak of my footsteps on old floorboards, he glances over his shoulder.

His jaw clenches, nostrils flaring. "Please tell me that's Rye's sweatshirt."

I love his jealousy.

I hate that I love it.

"It is."

He blows out a breath, turning back to the counter. "Go have a seat. I'll bring your tea. Two spoonfuls of honey still?"

"Yes," I say weakly, then retreat to the living room.

My steps slow and stop when I see the couch, specifically the lack of cushion where we'd been sitting. The cushion itself sits near the slider, stripped of its casing. I'm still staring at the empty space when Wilder comes up behind me.

"I put the cover in the washer. The cushion should be fine."

There's something in his voice that brings my head around. Amusement mingled with... *pride*? I squint at him, growing more confused by the second. We couldn't have made that big of a mess. Could we have?

"Thanks," I say uncertainly.

He hands me a mug. I wrap my hands around the warm ceramic as he takes a sip of his tea to hide a smile.

"What are you not telling me?"

Twinkling eyes snap to mine. "Have you ever squirted before?"

I almost drop my tea. "*What*?"

He grins. "I didn't notice until I stood up, probably because that was the most intense orgasm of my life." His smile turns smug. "Apparently it was good for you, too."

Closing my eyes, I will the heat crawling up my neck to recede. It doesn't work. Warmth eclipses my entire face. How did I not notice? My thighs had been excessively wet, but I'd thought it was sweat.

"That's definitely never happened before."

"Hey." His thumb stokes my jaw and my eyes pop open. "It was a first for me, too, and I'm not even remotely weirded out. There's nothing your body could ever do that would make me not want to worship it." He pauses, then smiles slightly. "Remember that night on tour when you did too many tequila shots and spent an hour puking in the hotel parking lot and I held your hair back for you?"

I grimace. "Yes. Why?"

His smile widens. "I still wanted to fuck you."

A startled laugh escapes me. "Ew."

He chuckles and heads for the other end of the couch, then flops onto one of the two remaining cushions. I follow slowly, my thoughts bouncing between gratitude for how fast he normalized what happened and trepidation for the conversation we need to have.

A few steps from the couch, I realize that sitting next to him will be too much of a distraction. And if he touches me, I'll forget everything I need to say. So I veer to an adjacent armchair and sit, tucking my feet under me.

Wilder sips his tea and watches me with a cocked eyebrow. "What's on your mind?" he asks, a note of wryness in his tone.

I swallow the sudden lump in my throat. "I'm not sure how to start."

He puts his mug on the coffee table, sinking back into the couch and crossing his arms over his chest. While the position is defensive, his expression remains easy to read. Resigned. A little wary.

"I bet I can guess at least one thought banging around in that beautiful head." When I don't say anything, he continues, "Since you're close with your parents and hate keeping anything from them, you told them we hooked up last month and your dad flipped out. He probably reminded you what a piece of shit I am. And now that the orgasm endorphins are wearing off, you're remembering I'm a piece of shit, too."

I stare at him, my vocal cords paralyzed. I shouldn't be surprised by how well he can read me, but I am.

Wilder's smile is a sardonic twist of lips. "We may not know all the boring little details about each other's lives these days, but don't forget I've known you since before you could walk." The smile dies. "I know I've hurt you. I wish I could undo the past, but I can't."

I find my voice. "I don't think you're a piece of shit. I think you've made mistakes. We both have."

Dark eyebrows lift. "But?"

My stomach clenches with unease as words rush to

the tip of my tongue. Words that might send him out the door—words that still need to be said.

"If this is going to work, if you really want a..." My throat closes.

"Relationship with you," he supplies, eyes steady on mine. "Yes, I want it. I've been obsessed with you for years, but I was a fucking coward. I'm not saying I deserve your forgiveness or even that I want you to forget what a shithead I was. But I hope you'll give me a chance to be the man I know some part of you believes I can be."

My chest tightens; my eyes sting. Fear and hope seesaw.

"What is it?" he asks softly. "I'm a big boy. Just say it."

The words finally pour out of me. "You were pretty close—about my dad's reaction. But he also said you're an addict. And my mom said your parents suspect you've been using opiates since you started having panic attacks at nineteen. Is it true?"

His body stills, expression going eerily blank. My heart pounds like a drum. Tea sloshes in my mug as a tremor moves through my body. It's warm in the house, but I'm suddenly freezing.

"Were you high two months ago, Wilder? When we had sex the first time? Are you... are you on drugs right now?"

A bit of life, of *hurt*, returns to his face. "You really can't tell if I'm high?"

I study his clear eyes. "I don't think you are," I begin hesitantly, "but honestly? I don't trust my own ability to tell. I also know my dad wouldn't have said that without reason. And your parents..." I shake my head helplessly.

He makes a rough noise, his gaze falling to his lap. "No wonder you're freaked out." He sighs heavily. "It's my fault. I don't return their calls enough and ignore most invites to the house. It makes sense that they'd think I'm fucked up. I've been so focused on the band for the last two years, I didn't realize they were so worried."

His gaze lifts to me. "It's not an excuse, but I don't have the kind of relationship with my parents that you have with yours. You know it's always been hard for me to open up to people. Even them. You're the only—" He cuts himself off with a grimace. "To answer your question: no, I wasn't high when we hooked up last month. I'm not high right now. Have I used drugs? Obviously you know the answer to that. But I'm not a fucking junkie."

The beginnings of relief tingle in my body. "And the panic attacks?"

His eyelashes flicker; discomfort radiates from the tense line of his shoulders. "I get them. Have since I was little. They became intense in my late teens. I don't have them too often anymore, but I still get anxious. Usually in social situations or around strangers. The only place I'm truly comfortable is onstage." He pauses. "And with you."

More hope rises in me, carried on a wave of sympathy and affection. He's being honest. Opening up to me. It feels precious, like a new beginning.

My voice softens. "Do the guys know?"

He shrugs a shoulder. "They know I have limits on how long I can handle fan meets and press stuff. They're used to my weirdness by now."

"I don't think it's weird to have boundaries to protect your peace."

His lips quirk. "You're giving me too much credit. Most days, I'm winging it and hoping for the best."

Flashes of memory pass through my mind, years and years' worth, building a picture of Wilder I never fully saw until this moment. How he always stayed on the edges of gatherings, outside the raucous mingling of our families. Disappearing often to sit alone with head-phones on. His dislike of casual touch. Shadows under haunted eyes. How he did shots right when we stepped offstage before we were swarmed. His lyrics, which have always shown a mind that experiences the world differ-ently than me—than most.

My heart fractures at the thought of his long, silent struggle.

I shake my head slowly. "I wish I'd known. I wish you'd told me. I could have supported you better. Maybe what happened three years ago—"

"No," he interjects gently. "Nothing that went down is on you. You were right to cut me out of your life."

I almost contradict him but pause and acknowledge that who he was—the things he did and said—still hurt. Not like they once did, but regardless, even if I understand him better now, how he treated me back then wasn't my fault.

Wilder leans forward, resting his elbows on his knees. His head hangs down for a few moments. When he looks up, the raw, glassy-eyed expression on his face steals the air from my chest.

"Can I be real with you?"

"Of course."

He holds up his hands; the strong, graceful fingers visibly tremble. "My heart is going a mile a minute right now. I'm fighting the urge to bolt. It's not you—I don't *want* to feel like this. But talking about this, letting you finally see how fucked up my head was, still is..." His voice drops to a whisper. "Please, please don't regret me."

My mug meets the coffee table and then I'm

climbing into his lap and wrapping my arms around him. A shuddering breath leaves him before his arms squeeze me in return. His head drops to my shoulder, warm breath showering my collarbone.

My heart is a furnace inside me, its fiery glare dissolving the stains of our past.

There is only now and a future so bright it stings.

"Never," I swear.

evangeline

I wake in the morning to sparkling sunlight. The bed is empty, the space where Wilder slept cold. Before the thought that he left fully forms, I smell freshly brewed coffee and hear a soft melody being plucked on my acoustic guitar. A familiar melody: "Waves." It sounds different, though—lighter and more hopeful.

He's here. He stayed.

After our talk, we were both so wiped we stumbled to bed and passed out. I remember little of the following hours, save for the pervasive warmth of his body wrapped around mine and a feeling of deep contentment.

The need to see him infuses my limbs with energy. Scrambling out of bed, I dart into the bathroom to pee and brush my teeth, then yank on yesterday's leggings and force myself to walk at a reasonable pace into the living room.

Wilder looks up from the guitar in his lap, his fingers flattening against the strings. My stomach flutters as his gaze caresses me, a small smile deepening one dimple.

"You're so beautiful."

The sincerity in his voice makes my face warm. A deliriously happy smile spreads across my face.

"Good morning to you, too."

Rising to his feet, he sets my guitar back on its stand. "Come here."

Despite willingly obeying the command, he meets me halfway. Warm palms cup my face.

"Good morning," he whispers before giving me a kiss so sweet and tender that I sigh. "I ordered bagels. Do you still like bagels?"

I don't normally eat breakfast right when I wake up, but I'm so touched by the gesture that I nod eagerly. He releases me to stride into the kitchen, asking over his shoulder, "Everything with cream cheese?"

"Sounds good. Thanks."

I follow and pour myself a cup of coffee, watching him askance as I do. He cuts a bagel and pops it in the toaster, then braces his hands on the counter and stares at the glowing grates like his focus will speed time. His fingers tap rhythmically on the tile, making the tendons on his tattooed forearms pulse. A wavy chunk of dark hair obscures one eye.

The longer I watch him—the longer he stares at the toaster, ignoring my focus—the more surreal this all becomes. Despite last night's emotional closeness and the euphoria of mere seconds ago, I'm once again engulfed by the disquieting feeling of not really knowing him.

Can you know someone's soul—their deepest, truest self—without knowing anything about their actual life? He thinks so. He believes he knows me. But do I know *him*?

I thought I knew him once. I thought the bond we shared was unbreakable, and it wasn't.

Who are you, Wilder?

Unable to stomach the silence or my spinning thoughts any longer, I clear my throat. "Did you sleep okay?"

His gaze snaps from the toaster to me. The stark relief in his eyes tells me this is as surreal for him as it is for me, which in turn calms my erratic pulse.

His lips curve. "I finally know why you always talked about missing your mattress. Best night's sleep I've had in weeks."

I laugh. "I'm glad."

His smile fades from his face but stays in his eyes. When he continues staring at me, I shift on my feet.

"What?"

He shakes his head. "Nothing."

The toaster pops, burnt bagel slices leaping. We both jump, then share a short, awkward laugh. With a little plastic knife, Wilder slathers cream cheese on each side. I bite my tongue when he uses far more than I normally like, then snort at the thought.

He gives me a questioning look.

"Sorry, I just—" I wave aimlessly, struggling to keep nervous laughter at bay. "You're making me a bagel. It's weird, right? This is weird."

His lips quirk before he gives in to a wry smile. "Yeah. But I like it. I like this. Us."

"Me too."

His smile heats, making my toes curl. "Come eat." He brings the plate to the table and pulls out two chairs. I sit and look at the bagel—more cream cheese than bread—and take a gulp of coffee.

"Will you eat half?" I ask as he settles next to me.

There must be something in my voice because Wilder glances at the bagel and grimaces. "Hold on." He jumps up, grabs the knife, and starts scraping off the pillowy excess. Some plops onto the table. The remaining bagel is black with a thin white glaze.

His shoulders tense. "Shit. I'm sorry. I can make another one."

Before he can move away, I grab his hand. He freezes, the fingers beneath mine vibrating. My ribs contract, pinching my heart.

Growing up, he might have shown me more of himself than he did others, but he never showed me *this*. The man beneath the mask. I wonder if he was ashamed of this part of himself. Or maybe he was afraid I wouldn't accept him, that it would change us, and that fear became a self-fulfilling prophecy.

Oh, Wilder...

"Please sit," I say softly.

He drops into the chair with none of his usual grace, gaze flickering but avoiding my face.

"The bagel was a really sweet thought, but I'm more of a coffee-only person first thing in the morning."

His eyes find mine, glittering with what I now recognize as anxiety. The desire to help him—to fix this for him—overwhelms me. Questions rise: is this an all-day, every-day battle, or is this a side effect of our conversation last night? Does he really believe therapy can't help? Are there supplements that would benefit him? Is he eating right?

Then my mom's voice jumps into my mind. *"You're not responsible for anyone else's mental health."*

The reminder halts the questions but doesn't alleviate the spiky, weighted feeling inside me. The same one I lived with constantly from that fateful summer when he changed until I left the band. An intuition that no matter how hard I try to reach for him, he'll always orbit just outside my reach.

One day, I tell myself, *you've had less than one day with him.*

"I'm sorry," he mumbles. "I'm already fucking this up."

The tangled threads of my thoughts unwind. He's *trying,* and that means more to me than he'll ever know.

"The only thing you fucked up is the bagel and my vagina last night."

His eyes widen, a startled, raspy laugh tickling my ears. When his shoulders and expression relax, warm satisfaction spreads through me.

He grabs a strand of my hair, curling it around his fingers. "Can I ask you something, Fairy?"

"Of course."

He gives the strand a gentle tug, the sensation echoing between my legs. Only the serious expression on his face keeps me from squirming.

"Will you tell me about yourself? About your life the last three years? Everything I know is second-hand from Rye or my parents."

The warmth inside me intensifies. "What do you want to know?"

"Everything. You're working, right? At a music academy?"

"Yep. Weekday afternoons. I teach guitar and piano to kids."

He grins. "I bet they love you."

I laugh and shake my head. "I'm actually one of the tougher teachers. Most new students don't last more than a few months, but I do have a few who've been with me for a couple of years. Amalie and Jordan are pianists and already composing, and Micah is my guitar prodigy. You should hear him shred. It'll blow your mind."

"I'd love to hear him." The look Wilder gives me makes my heart stutter. He tugs my hair again. "And you're in school, too?"

"Yes. Mostly online." I take a hurried gulp of cooling coffee, then voice a thought I haven't even told Lily. "I'm not sure I'll keep going after this semester, though. We have the meeting with Indigo on Monday and if we sign—"

"*When* you sign."

"When we sign," I amend with a smile, "so much will change. I guess it all depends on the contract, the size of the advance, timeline for an album, how fast they want us on tour..." I trail off.

"The advance is going to be a lot." His voice is soft and careful. "Based on the fact Donovan himself showed up last night and salivated all over you two, I'm guessing mid six-figures."

My jaw drops. "What? No way. We're unknowns."

"You're not, though," he says with another tug on my hair. "Before you think I'm talking about who you're related to, let me put it to you this way—no matter how close Donovan and your dad are, he's a businessman first. He wouldn't sign you at all if he didn't think you'd make him truckloads of money."

"Yeah," I say vacantly. "Logically, I know that."

I don't realize I'm chewing on my thumbnail until he gently pulls my hand from my face.

"Come back, baby."

My eyes jerk to his. He holds my gaze in a way only he can, with a magic that makes the world stop. "You can't change who your parents are or that some people will automatically attribute your success to nepotism. It's a shadow we can't escape. You have to learn to ignore the negative noise."

"Is that what you do? Ignore it?"

He smirks. "My music speaks for itself. Anyone who says I don't deserve what I've earned is just jealous."

My laugh blends with a groan. "Still an egomaniac, I see."

He chuckles, then sobers. "I know it's going to be hard for you to hear this, but you and Lily aren't run-of-the-mill talent. You're the Holy Grail—young and attractive, with a unique and commercially viable sound. I'm confident in Night Theory's staying power in the industry, but in a hundred years we'll be forgotten. Glow, on the other hand, has the potential for immortality. Your sound might very well shape a new generation of artists."

At my horrified expression, Wilder laughs and kisses my forehead. "So cute. I can't wait to remind you of this moment twenty years from now when I'm putting up yet *another* shelf for your awards."

Before I can even begin to process either of his predictions—my success, our longevity—he continues, "Back to what to expect after Monday. You're right to think your life will change fast. The pressure will be on immediately and it'll be intense as fuck. The landscape has changed even in the last few years, too. There's so much more to do now. Social media is probably the most demanding and time-consuming, at least when you're starting out. Then there's a million small networking events, random shows, last-minute festival slots they maybe give you twenty-four hours' notice for... and in the midst of it, recording an album, writing the next one, rehearsals, tour planning—" He stops suddenly, misinterpreting my blank expression. "Sorry. You already know all this."

"I don't, actually." My skin prickles as I drain my mug, then slip off my chair to refill it. With my back to him, the next words are easier. "After leaving the band, I sort of disconnected from everything music and industry-related. I didn't write songs for a year. Barely touched a guitar outside of giving lessons. For a while, I even thought I'd never go down this road again. Then I met Lily and it just... happened. My passion came back. I'm excited again. But I'm also freaked out because it feels overwhelming in a way it didn't before."

When he doesn't say anything, I turn to find him staring at his lap with an expression I can't read. Sensing my attention, he looks up.

"I'm glad you found Lily," he says softly.

I study him, reading the tension around his eyes, and make myself address the elephant that has stomped into the room. "Are you? Glad that I'm making music with someone else?"

His chest rises sharply. "Yes. It would have been a tragedy if you gave up music." He smiles, but a veil of sadness lingers in his eyes. "I guess everything happens for a reason."

"Maybe," I say mutedly. "It's scary, though."

"What is?"

A lump rises in my throat. I swallow it and avoid his eyes. "Doing it without you."

His chair scrapes over the floor as he rises and comes to me. My mug is pulled gently from my hand and set on the counter. His arms enfold me, warm and solid. *Midnight rainstorms.* I lean against him, clinging shamelessly.

"You won't have to do it without me," he says into my hair. "I'm right here, and I'm not going anywhere. I'm sorry if I overwhelmed you. Next time tell me to shut up."

I shake my head but don't speak, afraid if I open my mouth all my fears will spill out. About the future. About *him*. About the darkness I can't see but worry hovers outside the light of this moment.

Wilder lifts my face in his hands. Sunlight streaks through a nearby window, turning his eyes into my favorite kaleidoscope of green, gold, and brown.

"I couldn't write, either," he murmurs. "That's why the album took so long. Eventually I stopped fighting myself and wrote for you again. You may not have been next to me, but you were inside me. Every note, every word. You're still my muse, Fairy."

Lightning streaks down my centerline. My breath hitches.

His eyes darken. "I'm going to kiss you now," he

rumbles, "and I'm not going to stop until we need another shower."

I kiss him first.

CHAPTER NINETEEN

I wanted to give you all my

Glass-house truths

But I loved you too much

To shatter on you

Three hours later, the temporary catharsis of worshipping Evangeline's body has worn off. I'm anxious and twitchy again, this time due to the front door looming in front of me.

My parents' front door.

While I would have preferred staying naked in bed with Evangeline all day, she had lunch plans with Lily. Inviting myself would have exposed what a needy bastard I am, so I kept my mouth shut and my insecurities to myself. Instead, I gave her a goodbye kiss that left her flushed and told her I had somewhere I needed to be, too, and would text her later. Playing it cool when I felt anything but.

Unfortunately for me, my first plan of heading home for the distraction of a grueling workout was quashed after a call to Jax. Kendra and three of her friends descended like a pack of hyenas this morning and are causing a ruckus as they pack her stuff. Jax and Zander are supervising so they don't fuck anything up, but he did me a solid and sent Eddie to meet me a few blocks away with my car.

At least I have wheels now. And, after a deep dive into my text threads, a place to be. Not that I actually want to be here. The alternative, though, is sitting in Evangeline's house, crawling out of my skin as I wait for her to come home.

My pulse ping-pongs around my throat as I finally ring the doorbell. A handful of seconds later, the door swings open.

"Hey, Mom."

She stares at me in shock. Right when I'm on the verge of expiring from how fucking uncomfortable I feel, she snaps out of it. Launching at me, she slams against my chest and squeezes the air from my lungs.

"Can't breathe," I huff, patting the curls on her head.

Her arms tighten even more. "Hug me back or I'll cry," she mumbles into my shirt.

The smile that was forming on my face dies as I realize she's probably not joking. I haven't seen her since Christmas and not for lack of trying on her part. I think the last time I answered her call was two or three weeks ago. All I gave her was five minutes before making an excuse to get off the phone. I didn't even answer her text that invited me over today.

If her hug wasn't restricting my oxygen, toxic guilt would surely suffocate me. My arms weigh a thousand pounds as I lift them around her, and the sound she makes nails my heart to my spine.

Fuck. She's crying.

Movement in the doorway brings my head up. My gaze connects with River's. A small, humorless smile on his face, he drawls, "The prodigal son returns." Lifting his wrist, he checks the time on an invisible watch. "Thirty seconds to make Mom cry. A new record."

My molars grind, but I keep my mouth shut. I deserve worse. I haven't just shut out my parents for the last two years but my siblings, too.

"Give him a break, Riv," Mom says, sniffing as she finally releases me. She grabs my hand. "Come on. Katherine will be so happy to see you. Can you believe she's turning seventy-five? I can't. I have more gray hair than she does."

River steps to the side as she tugs me into the house. His eyes, the same golden-brown as our dad's, follow me with a mixture of skepticism and resignation.

I'm braced for my mom to drag me to the living room at the back of the house where I can hear the rest of the family, but halfway there she veers into the empty kitchen. River pauses outside, then shakes his head and continues down the hall.

Releasing my hand, she moves around the island to grab two glasses from a cabinet, then opens the refrigerator to pull out a pitcher of iced tea. In spite of the almost frenetic energy buzzing in her movements, watching her is soothing. Like listening to an old, familiar song.

It suddenly hits me how much I've missed her, the emotion so visceral my stomach clenches hard.

"Have a seat," she says gently, glancing my way as she pours our drinks.

I drop onto a stool at the island. She sits beside me and slides a glass my way. Cradling it, I swipe my thumbs across the cool surface. The prickling under my skin slowly fades. Calm descends deeper with every inhale of my mom's perfume and the intangible aura of my childhood home. Citrus, herbs, and safety.

My sisters' voices carry down the hallway, along with Katherine's raspy laugh and my father's lower tones. Nostalgia and comfort filter through me.

My mom clears her throat lightly. "How's Eva?"

My head whips gracelessly in her direction. Her eyes shine with mirth. "You're tagged in a bunch of photos from her show last night, including a few of you walking backstage. Speculation online is you broke up with your girlfriend and are pursuing her." She waggles her eyebrows, her smile teasing.

Despite her effort at levity, my head bows in embarrassment. My own mother scours the internet for news on my life. Fucking pathetic.

Steeling myself, I meet her gaze. "The last couple of years..." My tongue tangles. Eventually I mutter, "I've been a self-centered ass."

"You're forgiven," she says, blinking away a glassy sheen from her eyes. "Is it true, though? You broke up with Kendra?"

I confirm with a nod. Though she tries to hide it, her relief is obvious.

"That's too bad."

I laugh shortly. "Nice try. I know you never liked her."

She winces. "True. I have no idea what it was—she was a nice girl—but something about her rubbed me the wrong way." Her eyes narrow. "Maybe because once she came into the picture, my firstborn son stopped answering my calls."

It's my turn to wince. Thankfully, she continues before I have to decide how to respond.

"So... Eva?"

I shift in my seat. "It's new. Like last night, new."

She lays a hand on my forearm, squeezing lightly. "It's not new, though, is it? The two of you have always been..." she trails off, and another voice finishes.

"*Fated* might be the word you're looking for."

Our heads swivel to the smiling woman standing in the kitchen doorway. Katherine is technically my great-aunt—the twin of my maternal grandmother—but she raised my mom after her parents' deaths and is the only grandparent I've ever known. And my mom's right: despite signs of time on her face, she doesn't look anywhere near seventy-five. Long, dark hair spirals to her waist. As usual, her lips are curled as though holding back secrets. Her clothes have always been eccentric, and today she's wearing a floor-length, crushed velvet dress that could easily pass for a Halloween witch's costume.

Dad believes she's psychic. Mom refuses to admit it, but her denial is more habit than conviction. As for myself, I've witnessed enough of Katherine's eerily accurate predictions over the years that I'm a believer. I don't know if she has actual psychic powers or if she's simply a thousand times more observant than the average person, but either way, there's something undeniably supernatural about her.

Katherine meets me halfway for a hug, and it's only then I'm confronted with the passage of time. Her body is more frail than I remember, her incense and rosewater musk pronounced. I feel like if I squeeze too hard, she'll disperse into smoke.

Releasing her, I kiss her soft cheek. "Hi, Granny. Happy birthday."

She lays a cool, soft palm on my cheek. From the way her eyes pierce mine, sparkling dark and eerily calm, I know what she's going to say before she says it. My fingers and toes tingle in fearful anticipation.

"I have a message for you, my boy."

I barely hear my mom's groan over the ringing in my ears. I've been waiting six years for those words. For an answer to the question I asked the first time I felt like I was losing everything.

Losing Evangeline.

"Can't you read your cards or talk to your spirits or something?"

At my irreverent demand, humor crinkles the skin

around her eyes. "I'm sorry, Wilder. I don't have a message."

I stop pacing and face her. "What if she falls in love with this douchebag? Am I supposed to watch it happen? You said—"

"I remember what I said," she interjects softly, something like regret briefly eclipsing her expression before it smooths.

"No message?" I ask in a final, desperate plea.

She shakes her head, then sighs. "How about a word of advice from an old lady with two eyes and a lifetime of experience?"

"Please," I whisper.

"A flower needs water, sunlight, and space to grow."

The memory tumbles into others from the following years. They all clash before merging into a glaring epiphany. Back then, I'd decided she meant I shouldn't pursue anything romantic with Eva. That conviction worked for me, complementing my fears. But hindsight is clear—Katherine was warning me not to suffocate her. Which I ended up doing anyway by putting her in a box built of my selfish needs.

Cold radiates down my spine.

Is that what I'm still doing?

My heart races, my muscles tensing. All I see are

Katherine's ageless eyes. I'm suddenly not sure I want her message.

Pounding footsteps and squeals in the hallway drag my attention from Katherine. She steps aside right as Olive and Ivy careen around the corner. They gape at me for two seconds before darting forward and almost knocking me over with their double-strength hug. Their voices fill the room, words overlapping and creating a familiar, beautiful chaos in my ears.

"I can't believe you're here!"

"Freaking finally."

"Your hair is so short!"

"And you have a thousand more tattoos."

"Ohh, he has to listen to our new song."

"No way, Liv! It's not done."

"Fine, fine. Selfies!"

Over their heads, I meet my dad's amused gaze. He mouths, "Welcome home."

wilder

After helping River clean the kitchen and put away leftovers, I step onto the back patio and take a deep, cleansing breath.

The sun sits low in the sky, its golden light filtered by giant pines. A dog barks somewhere in the neighborhood, the sound muted and echoey. Closing my eyes, I focus on the familiar susurration of evergreen leaves and bare branches. The wind is cool, damp, and earthy in my nose.

I can't remember the last time I felt this mentally exhausted, but it's not the frazzled fatigue I'm used to. I feel calm. Almost peaceful.

"Beautiful evening, isn't it?" asks Katherine.

I open my eyes and turn, finding her on a bench

angled toward the sunset. Her eyes are closed, that familiar, enigmatic smile on her lips.

"It is," I agree, making my way to her. She pats the bench and I settle beside her.

I'm still wary of whatever she has to tell me, but my initial apprehension has faded. Evangeline texted an hour ago to ask if I wanted to hang out and watch a movie tonight. I said yes, obviously, though all I plan to watch is her face when she comes.

No matter what Katherine says, it won't change the fact Evangeline is finally mine. That she's waiting for me right now. I can almost taste her. Smell her. My skin aches for the pinch of her nails, my ears for her strangled moans.

"I'm glad you and River were able to reconnect."

Shifting in my seat, I glance at Katherine. Her eyes are still closed. It's probably my imagination, but her smile looks different. Knowing. My neck heats. *No way she knows what I was thinking about. Right?*

I cough over my embarrassment. "Me too."

River was smarmy and passive-aggressive toward me most of the afternoon, but at some point between hauling plates to the kitchen and loading the dishwasher, the friction smoothed. We had a long, animosity-free conversation about graffiti, tattoos, and music.

"He's going to need you," Katherine murmurs.

I stiffen, thoughts of Eva vanishing. "What does that mean? Is he okay?"

Her eyes find mine. "Right now, yes, but there will come a time when he isn't. You're not as dissimilar as you think you are. He has his own shadows."

My chest burns. I suck in air, the reflex alone alerting me that I was holding my breath. A tremendous weight descends on my shoulders, like giant hands pressing me down. Making me smaller. Reminding me how powerless I am.

"Don't worry," Katherine continues, her gaze shifting to the tree line. "When the time comes, you'll be ready."

The vague reassurance doesn't help, the spectral hands on my shoulders moving to my lungs and squeezing, *squeezing*. I can't hear the wind in the trees anymore. I can't hear anything but my heart pounding on my eardrums.

A soft hand covers the fingers clamped on my knee. "We need to talk about Evangeline."

Shaking my head like the movement will dislodge the demon using my chest as a stress ball—it doesn't—I force my eyes to Katherine. My mouth opens to say, *Stop. No. Don't tell me,* but nothing emerges save for a harsh exhale.

I shouldn't have come outside.

Katherine's face sags slightly, her eyes losing focus. Tiny fires ignite all over my body as she begins to speak.

"Force and effort. One destroys harmony, one maintains it. What you cannot hold gently will be destroyed. To become who you're meant to be, let go of who you think you are."

She sucks in a breath, her eyes closing. Beneath fragile lids, her gaze darts back and forth. Whatever she sees brings a lattice of wrinkles to her forehead and makes her fingers twitch around mine.

"Ah, I understand now," she murmurs. Her eyes open and look at me—no, look *through* me. Every hair on my body stands up. "If you're both afraid of the dark, there will never be light. One cannot exist without the other. There must be balance. Be brave again. Dive into the dark and find the light inside you. For yourself and for her."

An old memory rises and pops like a bubble, splashing me with sights and sounds from a multi-family camping trip when I was seven. Thin, cool air. A crackling fire. Itchy mosquito bites and sunburns. The sun falling fast over jagged mountain peaks. Adults panicking because no one could find Evangeline. An hour's long search with flashlights.

My legs carrying me in a direction opposite everyone else. Crunching pine needles. Scratching brambles. My shaking hand on a cold metal tube, the glowing orb bouncing with my steps, my too-fast breaths.

A small body curled in a depression at the mossy base of a tree. Pale hair like a beacon.

"Fairy," I whisper now, as I did then.

"She cannot survive in your dark," Katherine murmurs.

Goosebumps roll up and down my body like sound waves on a loop. "Am I going to lose her?"

Not again. Not again.

Her mind back from whatever strange place it went, Katherine pats my hand. Wrinkles deepen around her eyes as she smiles softly. *Sadly.*

"She's a woman, Wilder. Not an object to find, keep, or lose."

"I know that."

"You don't. Not yet. But you will."

wilder

By the time I let myself into Evangeline's with the key she gave me, it's past midnight. I almost didn't come, and it took hours of driving aimlessly for me to get here.

The house is quiet and dark—or as dark as she can stand it, with nightlights plugged into multiple outlets in every room. At the threshold of her bedroom, the sight of her sleeping face almost takes my knees out. I grab ahold of the doorframe to steady myself.

She's curled on her side, a nightlight glowing on a flushed cheek, pale hair rioting across the pillow and around her shoulders. She looks ageless. Both young and ancient. Her thick, dark blond eyelashes flicker with dreams; from her furrowed brow, unpleasant ones. Probably about me.

She cannot survive in your dark.

Katherine's words whisper through me for the thousandth time since I left my parents' house hours ago.

The need to protect Evangeline from harm bucks against another need, just as potent and driven by selfishness. I *want* her. It consumes me. Owns me.

How can I protect her from me when I can't even protect myself?

"Wilder?" She rubs her face sleepily and sits up. The comforter slips down her torso, giving me a glimpse of her breasts outlined by a silky camisole before she shivers and yanks it back over her shoulders. "Are you okay? I was worried. You weren't answering your phone."

She's too sleepy to be as annoyed as she should be. Her gray eye shines silver in the light from the bathroom, her darker one shadowed. That single, otherworldly gaze spears me like nothing else can. I'm a naked, quivering fool beneath it.

I'll never be worthy of her. She's a goddess of truth and goodness, and I'm a formless, slithering shadow.

Find the light inside you.

How am I supposed to find my light when all I see is hers?

I have no idea what expression I wear, but when Evangeline reaches a hand toward me, the ache in my chest increases a hundredfold. The pressure of regret and longing and fear presses down so fast and hard I gasp.

Then she says, "Come to bed," and desire ignites like a flash fire inside me. My fingers curl with the impulse to take, consume, *feed*. Warp her and mark her. Brand her with my body so deeply she'll never want another. Only me. Only us.

"Are you sure?" My voice is a dangerous rasp, the crackling death of my good intentions. Her eyes flare, pupils expanding, chest lifting on a swift inhale.

"Yes." Her consent is both a demand and a plea.

My feet carry me across the room. I shed my clothes as I go, already hard for her, leaking in anticipation. She lifts the covers and I slip beneath, my hands finding purchase on soft skin. I yank her against me. She's music and light and warmth. Infinite sunrises in my black world.

I press my face to her neck and breathe. Just breathe.

Her fingers weave into my hair, short nails grazing gently over my scalp, sending tingles down my spine. She's soothing me even though my grip is punishing enough to leave bruises, a thought that makes me even harder—makes me hate myself even more.

I'm afraid to move my hands. Afraid of not being

able to stop myself from hurting her. *Using her.* I'd rather die.

I've never felt this out of control.

"It's okay," she murmurs. Like she can hear my thoughts. Like she *knows* me.

A full-body tremor rattles my bones and tightens my skin. I open my mouth against her neck, the tip of my tongue finding her racing pulse. A new urge rises and eclipses all others.

I want to taste her pulse and swallow it.

Swallow *her.*

Evangeline squeaks as I suddenly lift her, rolling onto my back and dropping her knees to either side of my head. My hold keeps her upright as I press my nose to the soaked cotton between her legs, then gently bite the swollen folds beneath.

She gasps. "Oh God."

I bite harder, making her jerk. Her head drops forward, our gazes clashing. "That's not my name."

Her pupils blow out, black swallowing gray and green. She licks her lips. "Wilder." So soft, barely audible, then louder and ragged with need. "*Wilder.*"

"That's my girl."

Releasing one of her thighs, I drag her camisole up and grunt at the sight of her breasts rising and falling as she pants. Pebbled nipples framed by spun-gold hair.

Gorgeous, heart-shaped face and half-lidded eyes hazy with lust.

Mine.

Flattening my tongue, I lick the fabric between me and what I crave. She whimpers and rocks forward in search of friction, but I don't give her what she wants. The next sound she makes is an angry one, causing my dick to jerk and my lips to curve.

"You want to suffocate me with this perfect cunt so badly, don't you?"

Her lips part on a silent gasp. My tongue finds her clit, flicking it through the cotton. This time her gasp has tone, a pure note of desperation. Her body pulses against my hold, thighs flexing beneath my hands.

"I need to hear it, baby," I murmur into her heat, my eyes never leaving hers. "Tell me what you want and I'll give it to you. I'll never say no."

The look in her eyes darkens until all I see is the pieces of me inside her reflecting the pieces of her inside me. Two jagged halves locking together seamlessly.

She licks her lips. "I want to be your perfect little slut."

Shock and a dagger-like stab of arousal vacuums the air from my lungs. My arms weaken, depositing her on my chest, while every other muscle group in my body stiffens with the same resistance I felt the first time we slept together. When she asked me to fuck her like I hated her. Like she didn't mean anything to me.

Denial tangles in my throat with an equal truth: I want what she's offering with every depraved inch of me.

Her fingers dip into my hair and tug gently until I look up. I'm flayed open by her gaze, which I'm terrified sees too much. *Everything.* All my sick desires, my compulsion to break her apart so I can steal more pieces of her soul for myself. Tarnish her perfection with my shadows. Imprint myself into her every cell so she can never be rid of me.

She's offering me exactly what I crave, and it feels both unbelievably right and unbearably wrong.

"Eva, I—" Her palm presses gently against my lips, quieting my weak protest.

"Before you say no, listen." She moves her fingertips to my jaw, painting a line of heat up to my ear. Her gaze flickers away from mine, her cheeks turning deep rose. "You were right when you said no one has been able to read my music. I've never been able to climax with anyone but you." Her eyes return to me, flashing with determination. "I feel safe exploring this with you. I know you respect me, Wilder. I'm asking you to safely, consensually *disrespect* me. I want this. I've wanted it for years, since that day in your bedroom. And I know you want it, too."

Blood surges to my cock, making it pulse in time with my heart. Her words have the opposite effect on my thoughts, which shift from whitewater rapids to a placid lake. My skin stops feeling like it's stretched too tight. The burning in my spine dissipates.

She feels safe. She wants this. *Me.*

"You mean that?" I ask unnecessarily. If there's one thing I trust in this world, it's that Evangeline says exactly what she means.

Confirming it, she rolls her eyes. "Obviously."

I swallow once, twice, my fingers tensing on her waist. "Then yes, of course I'll explore this with you. But if I say or do something you don't like, you'll tell me immediately. Promise me."

Triumph shines in her eyes as she nods. "I promise."

The last of my doubts float away.

"In that case..." Lifting her back to her knees so she hovers above my face, I yank her underwear to the side. She's wet as fuck, as aroused as I am, and the knowledge turns my next words guttural. "Grab the headboard and sit on my face."

She doesn't hesitate and neither do I. The second her weight comes down, I'm lost in her flavor and scent. The music of her moans, gasps, and cries. When she stiffens, her hips jerking, pussy fluttering on my tongue, I throw her to the mattress and follow her down.

Her chest heaves against mine, her eyes wide. "I wasn't done." She sounds so irked, I fall in love with her again. Deeper. Even harder.

I wrap a hand around her throat, squeezing lightly. Angling her face up, I drag my teeth over her chin, then kiss her hard and deep, forcing her to taste her release. She writhes beneath me, legs tightening around my waist.

"More," she whines.

I find her ear and bite the lobe, whispering, "You're a greedy little slut, aren't you?" And when she moans breathlessly and grabs my cock with both hands, I briefly wonder if I died on my drive here and accidentally wound up in heaven.

My vision blurs as she feeds the first inch of me into her hot, tight body. Every instinct demands I thrust all the way in, but the erotic euphoria of her wiggling as she tries to impale herself is too fucking perfect to miss.

"That's right, baby, stuff yourself full. Take every inch you can. God, I love stretching this pussy. I love how soaked you are. How you drip all over my cock."

My rough words make her even wetter. More desperate. When I'm seventy percent inside her and she can't get me any deeper because of the hovering position of my hips, she growls in frustration. It's the cutest sound I've ever heard.

"Wilder, I swear—"

I give her throat a gentle squeeze. "Shut your mouth unless my tongue is in it."

I don't give her time to think about what I said, punching my hips forward with every ounce of my pent-up hunger. She cries my name, her spine bowing and her eyes closing. I fuck her hard and fast, the slap of our bodies as rhythmic as a metronome.

"Look at me," I snarl. Her lashes flutter, parting on hazy, victorious eyes. "This is what you wanted, huh? Me off the leash? Fucking your cunt like it's mine?"

She nods.

"Good. You *are* mine. Do you understand? My dirty, needy girl. My little toy. No one else's. This pussy only comes on *my* cock, *my* mouth, *my* fingers."

"Y-yes," she pants. "Only yours."

"Right answer. I think you deserve a reward."

Scooping a hand beneath her ass, I hold her against me as I shift to a tight, rolling grind that stimulates both her clit and G-spot. She starts to shake and gasp.

"Such a perfect toy," I whisper, inhaling puffs of air from her parted lips, "telling me what I want to hear, stretching for me and clenching me so tightly. I can't wait to find out how many inches I can fit down your throat. See your pretty tears as you gag for me. I bet you want my cum dripping from every hole in your body, don't you?"

The hot gush and constriction around my cock tells me the answer even before her eyes roll back in her head. "I'm—oh—"

Another orgasm crashes through her, her body clamping down and throbbing hard. I watch her face, enthralled, my own release taking a back seat. Knowing she's never experienced this with anyone but me feels better than a stadium full of screaming fans, better than any high.

As she relaxes, I kiss her languidly. "Say 'thank you, Wilder.'"

"Thank you, Wilder." She smiles up at me, soft and open, all her defensive walls abolished. She's never been more beautiful. "Was I good?"

My breath stalls in my lungs. My heart turns to fiery goo. I'm one thousand percent here for all her kinks, but something about her wanting praise does me in. My cock agrees, jumping with renewed vigor, begging for friction.

I press my forehead to hers. "So good, baby. So, so good. But it's my turn now. You're going to take everything I give you, aren't you?"

She moans. "Give me everything. I want it all."

Holy fuck.

I yank her legs from my waist, bending them so her knees are pressed to her armpits, then drop my weight. My hands seize fistfuls of her hair, close to the scalp so I don't actually hurt her as I pull her into me with every thrust. Slow at first, then faster and harder as I chase my release.

I'm already close to the edge, acute physical pleasure compounded by the visual perfection beneath me: her gorgeous face slack with ecstasy, her eyes a doorway to the secret world that exists solely for us.

My tongue finds the succor and sanctuary of her mouth. On my next and final thrust—as my orgasm explodes like a nuclear blast in my body and she clutches me to her, holding me with all her strength—I understand how foolish I was to think I could steal more pieces of her.

Evangeline Sullivan is a law unto herself: impossible to subvert, immune to external force.

She'll never need me like I need her.

As more fragments of my soul break free, flying into her keeping, I decide it doesn't matter. She can have them. Every last piece of me.

I'd rather be lost in her than found anywhere else.

CHAPTER TWENTY-TWO

evangeline

How fast does a heart beat

When it can't tell time?

And how long must I wait

For you to be mine?

"Ms. Sullivan? Did you hear me?"

I jerk on my stool, blinking at my student, Micah. He's frowning so hard his eyebrows are almost touching. Annoyance shines in his big brown eyes.

"Yes," I say on reflex, then sigh and shake my head. "No. I'm sorry, Micah. What did you say?"

He squints at me like I've been possessed by a stranger. Fair point as this is the first time I've ever been less than fully immersed in a lesson with him in the two years we've been working together.

"I asked if you were okay," he says, each word enunciated with the singular condescension of a twelve-year-old. I almost smile, until he adds, "You don't look so good. Mom's gonna be pissed if you get me sick."

"I'm not sick," I assure him. "I just…" I trail off, my gaze bouncing around the familiar, cluttered room. Over assorted instruments, amps and mics, bookshelves of sheet music, bundled cords and the ancient whiteboard.

A soft pain spreads through my chest. When I look back at Micah, I see he feels it, too. And he knows.

"You're leaving?" he asks in a cracked whisper, all traces of bravado gone.

I nod and clear my tight throat. "I am."

His thoughts play clearly across his face—panicked reasoning, then relief—so I'm not surprised when he asks, "Where are you going? My mom will totally drive me. Or if you're, like, moving to another state, we can do online lessons, right?"

My smile hurts, not because it's forced but because it feels like the rest of me: happiness eddying against the cliff of unavoidable loss.

"Actually, I signed a recording contract with Indigo Records yesterday. After next week, I'll be taking a hiatus from teaching."

His jaw drops. "Indigo Records? Holy shit! That's amazing."

I laugh even as I wag a finger at him. "No cussing. And thank you." I glance at the clock over the door. "We have twenty minutes left, so let's use them. We can talk more about it when your mom gets here."

Unsurprisingly, my words fly in one ear and out the other. "This is so freaking cool. I'll know someone famous. Will you hook me up when I'm older? Introduce me to people? I can't wait to tell my friends at school. They're gonna flip."

Biting back a smile, I say as sternly as I can, "Let's focus, Micah," but a sudden knock on the door undermines my effort. Micah grins at me as I sigh and call out, "Come in."

The owners' daughter, Molly, pokes her head inside. A student at the nearby University of Washington, she works the front desk occasionally. Her cheeks are flushed, eyes shining with a manic light as they veer from Micah to me.

"You have a visitor," she stage-whispers.

I frown. "I'm in the middle of a lesson. They can wait or leave a message."

She expels a breathy giggle and glances at Micah again. "Actually, he said he's here specifically to sit in on your lesson. And I *really* think Micah would like him to."

Understanding hits, knocking my stomach down an elevator shaft.

Wilder.

I haven't seen him since Sunday morning. He was still sleeping when I left for brunch at my parents' and was gone when I got home. He later texted to tell me he would be rehearsing late. We've exchanged sporadic texts for the last two days, a fact I've shoved in a mental box along with the nagging fear that something changed Saturday night. That what we shared—which made me feel closer to him than ever before—had the opposite effect on him.

Even if I'd *wanted* to confront him about the sudden distance between us, there's been no time to do so. Yesterday was a whirlwind. Lily and I spent the morning with my dad and his lawyer, prepping for the meeting at Indigo. After the meeting—which went exactly like Wilder said it would—we met my family, Rye, and Lily's dad for a celebratory dinner that lasted several hours. By the time I got home, all I had the energy to do was shower and pass out.

Wilder did call me this morning, but I was listening to an online lecture for one of my classes. And even though I had time before work, I didn't call him back. I'm not entirely sure why.

Now that he's physically here, suppressed emotions

roar through me. Uncertainty. Anxiousness. Yearning. I want to see him almost as much as I want to hide in the nearby supply closet.

"So? Can I show him back?" asks Molly.

I look at Micah, his confused but curious face making the decision for me. I nod at Molly and she disappears.

"What's going on, Ms. Sullivan? Who's here?"

Instead of answering, I reach over and switch on the amp his guitar is plugged into. A soft, crackling hum fills the air as the door opens again.

Wilder walks inside with his battered guitar case, looking like dirty sex from the toes of his boots to his inked arms, faded Misfits T-shirt, and jeans that fit so well they should be outlawed for the sanity of humankind.

I can't control the wave of heat that spreads from my chest, pooling and pounding in my head and between my legs.

He flashes me a look so carnal I have to fight not to squirm on my stool. Thankfully he glances away just as fast, approaching Micah with an easy grin.

"Hey, man," he says to the boy whose face has gone slack with shock. "I was wondering if I could join you for a bit?"

evangeline

After saying goodbye to Micah's tearful mom—doubly overwhelmed by news of my leaving and a rock star's surprise appearance in her son's lesson—I head back to the room where I left Wilder.

Outside the door, I pause to listen to him playing. He unplugged his guitar so the sound isn't as rich, but there's no question of his innate talent. Or the song, which is one of ours.

"I see your shadow on the glass, Fairy."

I press a hand against my tumbling stomach. *Get your shit together.* Steeling myself, I walk inside. The latch clicks behind me, the tiny sound making me flinch.

Wilder's fingers flatten over the chords, his smile falling, brow furrowing. "Hey, what's wr—"

"Thank you," I blurt. "I can't tell you how much that meant to Micah. And me. How did you even know when —" I pause when I realize the answer is obvious. "Rye."

He nods, still frowning. "I want to say 'you're welcome,' but from the look on your face, I'm not sure you actually meant that." He lays his guitar in its case and stands. "I, uh—I wanted to see you. I'm sorry if I crossed a boundary I shouldn't have."

"Why haven't you come over the last two nights?" The words burst out of me without permission, expelling from the tender place inside me I've been studiously avoiding.

He looks startled, then relieved, then ravenous as he takes a step toward me. I suck in a breath and he stops, scanning my face.

"The truth?" he asks.

"Always."

"I was going to come back over after rehearsal Sunday, but when I was getting ready to leave, the guys laid into me. They said I was giving off needy, codependent vibes. So I've spent the last two and a half days freaking out about it while missing you and trying not to call you a thousand times or show up at your house."

I blink in surprise, then laugh as the underlying emotional strain of the last days drains away.

Wilder takes another step toward me, his shoulders

losing some of their coiled tension. "Tell me why you're laughing?"

I shrug, my grin slowly fading. "Next time, can you talk to me about what you're feeling? I've been low-key wondering if I scared you off Saturday night."

Long legs eat the space between us until we're chest to chest, his hands cradling my head as I stare up at him.

"Nothing would *ever* scare me away from you." The low, fervent words hum in my marrow. "Saturday night was perfect. *You're* perfect." He sighs. "The guys did have a point, though. I'm needy as fuck when it comes to you. I could barely sleep the last two nights without you, so we might as well check the box next to codependent as well. Shit, if you wanted to put a collar on me and drag me around by a leash, I'd let you."

"Okay," I whisper.

His brows rise, lips twitching. "Okay, what? Okay you like the idea of a collar on me, or okay you forgive me for not knowing what the fuck I'm doing when it comes to you?"

"The second one." I tilt my head. "Maybe the first one, too."

He drops his forehead to mine. "I don't deserve you."

Lifting onto my toes, I kiss him softly. "I don't know what I'm doing either. Case in point, instead of asking you what the hell was going on—"

"You got all up in your head about it, then shoved everything in a little box at the back of your brain."

My mouth drops. "What?"

He kisses my forehead. "You're my favorite song. I know every note. Plus, you're a Taurus. Overthinking and compartmentalizing are your thing."

My scowl of annoyance makes him laugh. Releasing me, he walks back to his guitar and closes the case. Over his shoulder, he asks lightly, "How was Sunday brunch?"

The shift in topic startles me. Then I understand what he's getting at—*he knows me*—and I cover my cheeks to hide their quick flush.

"I, uh..."

Wilder chuckles as he stands, case in hand, and approaches me. He sets the case beside us, then tugs my fingers away from my face.

"I promise I'm not trying to make you feel bad. I know why you haven't told your parents about us—for the same reason that when I told my parents, I asked them not to mention it to yours."

Sadness tinged with guilt swiftly eclipses the surprise that he told his parents about us. Brunch on Sunday was exhausting, and not just because of Wilder's welcome interruption of my sleep the night before.

I hate lying to my parents, even if it's lying by omission. I hate even more that it's becoming easier by the day. But I can't handle the alternative, which is telling them Wilder and I are officially together. The look on my dad's face weeks ago is a thorn in my memory. I never want to be on the receiving end of that expression again.

"They don't hate you or anything," I say quickly. "It's... complicated."

"I get it. It's going to take time to prove to them that I'm not a fuckup anymore. But we have time. Right?"

My mouth goes dry at the careful words, the suggestion of a deeper question beneath them.

"What are you asking me?"

He takes one more step, and I tilt my face up to maintain eye contact.

"Will you be my girlfriend, Evangeline?"

My pulse trips over itself. "Aren't I already?"

His eyes simmer. "Answer the question."

"Yes," I say breathlessly. "I'd love to be your girlfriend."

His smile expands, deepening dimples and filling my head with sparkling fog. "Good. What are you doing tonight?"

You, I think, and his eyes flash like he heard the thought.

"Why? You want to take me on a date?" The skin around his eyes tightens, his smile freezing. Realizing my mistake, I add quickly, "Not in public or anything. I don't expect that. Especially since, you know, my parents... and people with cameras, and crowds, all that stuff." I laugh, the sound a tad shrill. "Do you even read the comments on your socials? They're wild. I'd be worried someone might knock me out and kidnap you—"

His index finger presses to my mouth, silencing me. I gasp and he takes advantage, dragging his finger along the inside of my lower lip. My breaths turn choppy. His eyes flicker up long enough for me to see his wide pupils, then lower back to my lips.

"Such a pretty, pretty mouth," he whispers, sinking his finger past my teeth. "Suck."

All rational thought suspended, I close my mouth and suck, shifting forward at the same time so his finger sinks deeper. He grunts, hips twitching. The hardness behind his zipper grazes my belly. My mouth waters. I grab his belt buckle, ready to drop to my knees and finally, *finally* taste him, but his other hand seizes mine.

A whine of protest warbles in my throat. Wilder sucks in a breath, his finger curling against my tongue. "Fuck, baby. You want me in your mouth? Stretching your jaw and throat like I stretch that pussy?"

My clit throbs at the gruff words. I press my thighs

together against a sudden sharp pang and nod. His eyes close briefly and he rocks into me.

"Dammit," he hisses, shaking his head. Lust and conflict sit clearly on his face. "I can't believe I'm saying this, but you're not giving me a blowjob right now. Remember where we are?"

A modicum of sense returns. I hear muted piano keys being struck in a nearby room, the bright, metallic sound of a snare, muffled voices of teachers and students. My eyes widen in horror, my libido shutting off like a faucet.

Wilder smirks as he slips his finger from my mouth, popping my lower lip against my teeth before lowering his hand and tucking it in his pocket. All the while, he watches me with that impish, cat-like precision.

"You're welcome," he murmurs silkily.

I rub my palm over my burning forehead. "Thank you. I don't know what I was thinking."

He bites his lip, a smile shining in his eyes. "I'm at least seventy percent to blame. You're incredibly hard to resist."

"So are you," I whisper.

His expression softens. "The reason I asked what you were doing tonight is the guys and I were wondering if you wanted to come over for dinner. Kind of a reunion slash catch-up situation. And a celebration, too, for signing with Indigo yesterday."

It takes me long seconds to process the words, the majority of my thoughts still on a hamster wheel of how close I came to throwing my ethics out the window.

"Um, at your house?" I finally ask.

Wilder nods, a concerned crease forming between his brows. "Despite what just happened, a big part of why I came today is because I don't want you to think sex is all I want from you."

"I don't." My quick denial causes his brows to arch. Knowing that he's a second from once again proving how well he knows me, I lift a staying hand. "I'm not saying that to avoid confrontation. I really don't feel that way. Besides, if you only wanted sex, there are a million women out there who don't have our baggage."

His lips press together, then relax. "I like our baggage. It's a little beat up, sure. Covered in peeling stickers and dents. But the insides are irreplaceable. There's only one *you*. Only one *us*. If I could take you out on normal dates, I would in a heartbeat."

My insides melt. "You would?"

He nods solemnly, but there's a telling twinkle in his eye. "As long as it wasn't crowded. And there were no fluorescent lights anywhere. And we stayed within ten feet of an exit at all times. You know... normal date stuff."

A laugh burbles out of me and he grins. Almost as soon as it forms, his smile falls. He shifts toward me, the heat of his body curling against my front. *So close. Not close enough.* When I register the intensity in his eyes, my stomach does a backflip. My heart receives a similar memo, suddenly racing.

"Evangeline, I know it's been less than a week, but I need you to know—"

A knock on the door right beside my head makes me yelp and jerk forward. My forehead collides with Wilder's chin. We both curse.

Molly's laughing voice reaches our ears. "You guys all right? Sorry to kick you out, but April needs the room for her five o'clock lesson."

"Absolutely, sorry!" I say—too loudly based on Wilder's soft chuckle as he scoops up his guitar case. "Be right out!"

I scramble to grab my purse and water bottle, thankful for my habit of spending the last few minutes of each lesson having the student help me tidy the room. When I move to open the door, Wilder's fingers catch my wrist.

"Meet me back at your house." The low, firm tone sends a zinging shock through my body. My eyes fly to his. "We can leave your car there since it will be dark soon. I'll drive you home after dinner. I'm staying the night, by the way." He pauses for a quick breath. "Say 'Yes, Wilder.'"

The ache between my legs intensifies so fast it flirts with the border between desire and necessity. Saturday night plays behind my eyes. Behind *his* eyes, which watch me with penetrative focus.

A much older memory rises out of nowhere, playing from start to finish in seconds. I was six or seven. Wilder and I were caught outside in a spring downpour. My fault—I'd pestered him relentlessly to push me on the swings until his dad stepped in and told him to. Wilder was so annoyed with me that he pushed me too hard and high on purpose. Eventually I threw a fit and told him to go away.

He was halfway back to the house when the clouds opened and freezing rain poured down so fast and hard it soaked me in seconds. The sound was shocking. A vast, rushing roar that sent me stumbling away from the swings in terror—a terror that grew wings when I realized I couldn't see Wilder anymore. The house and pool had likewise disappeared. The swing set ten feet behind me was barely distinguishable behind undulating, liquid curtains.

Then the rain shifted to hail. Stinging bullets of ice

struck me all over, my sweater useless as a shield. In a mindless panic, I started screaming, running blindly toward where I thought the house was.

Wilder caught me, jerking me off my feet and hugging me so tightly I could feel his ribs beneath my cheek. He yelled about the pool and how I could have drowned, but I barely heard him because I was so *relieved*. Then he covered my head with his arms. For what felt like hours but was probably a handful of seconds, I trembled in a cocoon of his wet sweatshirt and steady heartbeat as the hail battered him.

I remember thinking the world was ending, but it was okay because we were together.

Looking up at him now, I feel it again—that the world around us is a roar. A never-ending storm. But I'm safe because we're together.

"Yes, Wilder," I whisper.

wilder

The sound that comes out of Evangeline on her first bite of the pasta dish Jax and Eddie prepared makes me want to throw her over my shoulder and run from the dining room, then come back and beat the shit out of my bandmates.

"This is delicious, you guys," she gushes, not noticing the sudden undercurrent at the table. Even Zander picks up on it, his eyes darting around in curiosity and speculation, lingering a bit too long on Evangeline. While it's ludicrous to be triggered by him —she doesn't have the hardware he prefers—it still pisses me off.

I glare across the table at Eddie, daring him to make the joke brewing in his laughing eyes. Lucky for him, he glances at me first. He wipes the smile off his face and lowers his head, shoving food in his mouth. *Smart man.*

Jax clears his throat, drawing my attention away from his brother. His eyes hold a mild rebuke—one I absolutely deserve. In spite of his long crush, Eddie took the news of Evangeline and me getting together with admirable maturity, even telling me he was glad we'd finally pulled our heads out of our asses. He's been nothing but supportive since, and he hasn't flirted with her once tonight. It's not his fault I feel like a powder keg rolling toward a bonfire.

I force myself to relax back into my chair, ignoring the way my skin crawls and itches. This dinner seemed like such a good idea when the guys proposed it. It didn't occur to me how difficult it would be to watch Eva, Jax, and Eddie pick up right where they left off three years ago. Their effortless, lighthearted friendship doesn't include me. It never did. I'm still the dark, cold planet orbiting light years away from their suns.

I don't know what I was thinking. That it would be different now? That I would be different? If anything, I'm *worse* now that Evangeline's mine. Every time I hear them laugh together, my fingers curl into a fist on my thigh and my teeth clench. My emotions are playing a manic game of tag and my body is no better: cold—hot —cold—hot.

My eyes keep finding the beers Eddie and Zander are nursing, both bottles still half-full. I don't understand how they can just sip them every once in a while. Why drink unless you want to get buzzed? No one loves the taste of beer that much.

Being sober fucking sucks.

I eventually take a bite of the pasta—it *is* fucking good—and decide then and there that I'm learning to cook. Someday, Evangeline will make those sounds for *my* food.

The faint fragrance of her shampoo envelops me as she leans over to murmur in my ear, "What's wrong?"

I'm a possessive, jealous fuck.

"Nothing," I whisper back, turning fast to catch her soft lips with mine. She jerks back, her already rosy cheeks darkening further as she faces her plate and scoops up more pasta.

Her embarrassment, her rejection, spreads ice through my chest. The crawling sensation under my skin worsens.

I grab my water glass and drain it, wishing it were alcohol.

"So, Eva," Jax says, his gaze flickering between us. "When are you and Lily heading into the studio?"

Evangeline answers haltingly at first but warms up as Jax guides the conversation into other topics. Eddie and Zander eventually join in, and the four of them chat easily as they eat. Evangeline is animated as she only is when she feels comfortable; there isn't even any awkwardness with Zander, the two of them spending a solid five minutes geeking out over some new keyboard that just hit the market.

No one tries to involve me. The part of me that's still rational knows they're not being rude. They simply know me. I'm not chatty, don't like being forced into conversations, and will only contribute if I feel like it. It should be a relief, but instead it stings in a way it never has before.

They know I'm not like them.

Not *normal*.

No wonder Evangeline was embarrassed when I kissed her in front of them.

The toxicity of my thoughts reaches dangerous levels, numbing the tips of my fingers and sending a snaking, burning sensation down my spine. Their voices become jarring. Dissonant.

I have to get out of here.

Grabbing my barely touched dinner, I stand fast and ignore the sudden silence as I collect their empty plates.

Evangeline scoots back her chair, but I shake my head, not looking at her. Afraid she'll see the monster in my eyes.

"I've got it."

As I walk into the kitchen, Eddie says something that makes Evangeline laugh softly, and I almost, *almost*, chuck the plates into the sink. Instead, I set them down gently, then grip the edge of the sink as hard as I can.

I can't fucking breathe.

Footsteps snap my head to the side. Jax turns the corner, the big salad bowl in his hands. He stops when he sees me, his expression twisting with concern.

"Take a minute," he says in a low voice. "I'll tell her you got a phone call or something."

My throat too tight to speak, I jerk my head in a nod. It takes a few seconds to convince my fingers to release the sink, then I flee into the back hallway. I ascend the stairs two at a time, but it still takes forever to reach the top.

A high-pitched whine fills my ears. I run the rest of the way to my bedroom. Inside, I shove the door closed right as my knees buckle.

I hit the floor hard and swing forward, my forehead smacking wood, my hands clenched in my hair.

Make it stop. Make it stop.

The Shadow's spikes close around me, sinking fast and deep. Before I'm fully aware of moving, I'm off the floor and stumbling into the bathroom. I rip open the cabinet beneath the sink and crouch to grab a plastic container full of first aid that my mom stuck in all the bathrooms when we moved in.

A strangled gasp escapes as I tear off the lid and dump the contents on the tile. My vision sparkling at the edges, I sift through the mess until I see it: a box of gauze. As I pick it up, something small and hard rattles in the bottom.

The instant relief I feel has me biting my cheek against a sob.

No, no, no.

Just one.

Don't do it.

No one will know.

You'll know.

You need this.

Feeling like a passenger in my body, I watch myself rip open the box and pull out the gauze to reveal the treasure at the bottom.

Two small, circular pills.

White noise fills my head.

I'm not shaking anymore.

The pills hit my palm.

I stare at them until my vision blurs.

Something wet hits my mouth.

I lick tears from my lips.

"No," I whisper. "Please."

Who I'm asking for help?

There's no help here.

Only the memory of Evangeline pulling away from me. Laughter around me, never touching me. Never mine. The cold dark. Her face wearing a thousand expressions across a lifetime. Lust and longing and hope and disgust and fear. Anger. *Hurt.*

River's resentment.

My parents' sad, worried eyes.

Shame. Guilt. Self-loathing.

It's too much.

It's all too fucking much.

Pointless.

Hopeless.

I lurch to my feet and turn on the tap, then toss the pills into my mouth and scoop a palmful of water to swallow them. Knowing what's coming relaxes muscles all over my body. I slump against the vanity and make the mistake of looking at my reflection.

"You made it fourteen days." I laugh, low and bitter, at the flushed, sweaty, tear-eyed man in the mirror. "You're pathetic. A coward and a failure. And you're a fucking drug addict."

Tears distort my sight.

The man in the mirror melts away to nothing.

evangeline

What if I told you

I tossed the match?

Would you keep me

Or throw me back?

It's been thirty minutes since Wilder disappeared, since Jax came back to the table with a smile that didn't reach his eyes and told me he had to take a call from their manager and would be back soon.

I'm not stupid.

There's no phone call.

I waited as long as I could, in case I was wrong, but finally asked for directions to Wilder's room. Now, as I walk down a hallway toward the closed door at the end, boulders of guilt knock together inside me.

I fucked up.

When he kissed me, I reacted badly. I should have fixed it immediately. I *knew* he was upset, that he felt rejected. But I couldn't bring myself to do anything about it. Instead, I let him quietly implode beside me and pretended I didn't see it.

As great as it was to see the guys and reconnect, the familiar dynamic triggered old, defensive behaviors for me. Namely, my habit of relying on Eddie and Jax to buffer me against Wilder during the final months of our tour, when I was falling apart while he lived his best rock star life. Never choosing me, *seeing me*, except when we were onstage.

But that's not true anymore. And if I believe what he's told me, it wasn't true then, either. He's always seen me. Wanted me like I wanted him. He was just afraid.

I hate that I hurt him, especially after all we've shared. I hate even more that a twisted part of me enjoyed the reversal of our former roles. The power I had over *him* this time.

The admittance makes me queasy.

Dinner was a bad idea. It was too soon, our relationship too new, the potholes of our past still littering our present road.

I stop outside his bedroom door but don't reach for the handle. Closing my eyes, I breathe slowly through my nose. It takes a solid thirty seconds for me to find the courage to open his door, and I almost lose it when I see how dark it is inside. The only light comes from the hallway and from behind the half-closed bathroom door.

A shiver races down my arms as my eyes dart around the large room. Slowly, my vision adjusts, bringing into focus a king-sized bed to my left. I can barely make out Wilder, his black-clad body and dark hair blending with the bedding.

Each step into the dark ratchets up my heart rate.

"Wilder? Are you awake?" My voice is small, compressed by guilt and nervousness.

He'll forgive me, won't he?

What if he doesn't?

Wilder shifts slightly, a heavy sigh reaching my ears. I push forward until I'm fully surrounded by shadow, until my knees hit the bed. Clutching the comforter, I shuffle around the side closest to him, stopping when I see his face. The barest light from the bathroom reveals his closed eyes, but I can't tell whether he's asleep or pretending because he doesn't want to see me.

"I'm sorry about earlier," I say, my voice wavering. "Actually, I'm sorry about the entire night. I was acting like an asshole. I... I think it was just weird, being around the guys after so long."

"It's fine, Fairy."

His voice is calm, his eyes remaining closed. A trickle of relief is sucked beneath the oil-slick of foreboding. Something isn't right.

"Can I turn on a light? So we can talk?"

There's a long pause during which I try and fail to tamp down my illogical fear response to the darkness around me, to his unnerving reaction. I glance at the bathroom, at the hallway, reassuring myself there are two points of light. Two paths to escape. But I don't want to escape this—him. So I ignore the tingling in my feet that urges me to run toward safety.

"Can we talk tomorrow?" he asks finally.

"Tomorrow?" I echo, pushing the word past a stab of pain in my chest.

His lashes flicker and part, eyes absorbing the shadows and appearing black as pitch. "Yeah. I guess barely sleeping the last couple of nights caught up with me. Can you ask Jax to take you home?"

The apathy in his voice raises the hair on the back of my neck. "I don't want to leave if you're mad at me, Wilder."

He reaches out, warm fingers covering mine where they still clench the comforter. Coaxing me to release the fabric, he pulls my hand to his mouth. Soft, warm lips press to my palm.

"I'm not mad," he murmurs, breath puffing against my skin. "I understand why you pulled away. It's okay. I'm just exhausted."

He kisses my hand one more time before releasing it and rolling onto his other side, dragging the comforter over his shoulder. I open my mouth, an offer to sleep here beading on my tongue, but it doesn't come.

If he wanted me to stay, he wouldn't have told me to have Jax drive me home. If he weren't mad, he would have tugged me onto the bed and into his arms. He would have turned on the lights for me.

He wants me to go.

And if I'm honest, I don't want to stay. Not in the dark—not even for him.

evangeline

"Earth to Eva."

I startle, my gaze snapping away from the kitchen window where I was watching two squirrels chase each other across my back fence. Seated across from me, Lily watches me with a furrowed brow. I don't know how long I was zoning out, but her laptop is closed, her headphones lowered around her neck.

"What's going on with you? You look like a zombie and your focus is shit."

I drag a hand through my hair, wincing when my fingers hit knots. "Sorry. I didn't sleep last night."

One of her dark eyebrows lifts. "Given that you don't have the glow of a marathon sex sesh, I'm going to assume insomnia?"

I nod, unable to articulate the complex truth. How

do I explain that I'm a grown woman terrified of the dark behind my own eyelids? That when I'm stressed, it gets worse. So bad I have to sleep with the overhead light on, which ends up being a snake eating its tail scenario—I need the light on to sleep but can't sleep because of the light.

The soft *clack* of headphones hitting the table pulls me out of my head again. I belatedly register the mix of sympathy and frustration on her face, but before I can think of a lie to defuse her worry, she asks, "Did something happen at dinner last night?"

Hot shame geysers through me. Avoiding her eyes, I study my hands. The sight of my ravaged cuticles makes me wince.

"If it's about Wilder, I promise I won't say 'I told you so' or anything like that. Believe it or not, I'm rooting for you two."

"Since when?" I ask, then shake my head quickly. "Sorry. You didn't deserve that."

"Eh, I probably did. I wasn't exactly Team Wilder at first but..." she trails off, color blooming on her cheeks. "Rye has told me a lot more about the bond between you guys, how you were as kids and stuff."

For the first time since getting home last night, the dense fog inside me clears a bit. I smirk. "Oh, really? Exactly how much are you guys talking?"

She palms her cheeks but not before I see them darken even further. "Pretty much constantly. Is that weird for you to hear? I've been afraid to talk about it, but I'm crushing hard. And he seems really into me, too. It's tripping me out. How is he a year younger than us and ten times more emotionally mature than every dude I've dated?"

I manage a laugh. "It's not weird for me. I saw this coming from a mile away."

She studies my face, her eyes hopeful and wary. "You're sure he's not bread-crumbing me?" she asks in a small voice. "Acting all perfect just to get in my pants and dump me after? I know he's been with a lot of girls."

"Definitely not. First of all, I'd kill him. Second, I've known him since we were both in diapers, so believe me when I say I've never seen him this into someone. He talks about you nonstop. You deserve someone like him, Lil. A genuinely good guy who's loyal, stable, and kind. It's true he's been a serial dater for a few years, but only because he's a hopeless romantic searching for The One. So if you aren't looking for anything serious, you need to tell him."

She nods quickly. "We've actually talked about that a little—what we're looking for—and we're on the same page. Now he just needs to ask me out and put us both out of our misery."

I sit back with a smile. "He'll crack before the end of the week. Probably on Friday once he sees your outfit for the showcase."

Happiness flashes across her face, then a speculative focus. "And you're sure the two of you don't have unresolved romantic feelings for each other that could potentially destroy all three of our lives in the distant future?"

I mimic gagging. "Absolutely sure. Someday I'll share with you the eight million reasons why, but we'll save that convo for your tenth wedding anniversary when it's too late for you to run away screaming."

She finally laughs, looking like a hundred-pound weight has come off her shoulders. "Okay. Thanks, Ev."

I nod at her laptop. "Where were we?"

She wags a finger at me. "Nice try. I spilled my guts, so now you have to. Quid pro quo or whatever."

I groan. "Can we not?"

Not to be deterred, Lily shifts her laptop aside and leans forward on her elbows. "You have to talk to someone. Unless you've decided to tell your mom what's going on?"

I shake my head.

With a self-satisfied smile, she sits back and crosses her arms over her chest. "Tell Dr. Aoki your troubles."

I make a face. "Ew."

She stares at me, and stares some more, until I heave a resigned sigh. As uncomfortable as it is for me to talk about my feelings to anyone—even my mom—I know I need to vent before I explode. Or, in my case, implode. Unfortunately the necessity doesn't mean the words come easily.

When the silence tiptoes into the Land of Uncomfortable, I finally blurt, "It's not you. This is really hard for me. Talking about feelings. Like I'm sweating right now."

She nods, her lips twitching.

I keep rambling, my gaze bouncing around the room. "I've always been this way. Reserved, I guess? It's not like my parents ever punished me for having feelings or talking about them."

My mind latches onto an old, old memory, and it ejects from my mouth. "Wilder has a great-aunt on his mom's side. Katherine. Growing up, I was super scared of her because she'd say weird stuff all the time. Predictions that always came true."

Lily's eyes widen. "Like what?"

"All sorts of shit. One year, she said it was going to be a white Christmas even though there was no snow in the forecast. It snowed Christmas Day." I smile at that memory, then shiver at the next one. "Another time, she told my parents that Hunter shouldn't climb on the play set in the Ashburn's backyard. They laughed it off because my brother has always been super athletic and had been crawling all over that thing since he could walk. Later that day, he slipped on wet leaves inside the playhouse at the top and fell out of it. He broke his arm and had a mild concussion."

"Whoa." Lily rubs the goosebumps on her arms. "That's trippy."

I nod. "Anyway, when I was around five, I was running in the Ashburns' backyard and tripped over a root. I hurt myself pretty bad. Scraped up my knees and face and was bleeding a lot. But I just sat there in a daze. Didn't scream or cry or anything.

"Katherine was the only one who saw me fall. She didn't ask if I was okay, just sat next to me and started talking. She told me about how when you build a dam on a river, you have to make sure there are outlets and spillways. If you don't, when there's a really bad storm, the dam will overflow and eventually crack. I had no clue why she was telling me this, obviously, but I finally started crying. She patted me on the head, helped me stand, and took me inside to my parents."

Lily whistles softly. "I need to meet this woman." She folds her hands beneath her chin and grins at me. "Is that your way of telling me I get to be your spillway?"

My lips tug upward. "I guess so. But I don't know where to start."

She hums in sympathy. "The last week has probably been super intense for you."

"It really has." I take a steadying breath, my eyes stinging. "I don't know what I'm doing, Lil. What a normal relationship looks like. The three guys I've dated since high school have either dumped or ghosted me after a few months. Now there's Wilder and this... this *thing* between us. It's so big and overwhelming. I feel like I'm going crazy."

My throat clogs. I blink fast as the burning in my eyes intensifies, spreading through my sinuses.

"Keep going."

The compassion in her voice opens another pressure valve, and my voice spills through it.

"He's said so many things I've always dreamed of hearing from him. It's been amazing. Healing. And it probably sounds naive, but he means every word. I've never felt so seen and heard, so accepted. Like even my weirdest quirks are somehow amazing to him."

Lily makes a small sound. "It doesn't sound naive, Ev. It sounds like he's in love with you."

Distantly, I recognize the words should make me feel something. Hope, maybe. But they don't penetrate.

"Maybe he is. Maybe I'm in love with him, too—

maybe I always have been. But can you love someone you don't really know?"

She frowns. "What do you mean?"

A few tears leak from my eyes, but my hands feel too heavy and numb to wipe them away.

"Wilder is like the deepest part of the ocean. Hidden depths upon hidden depths. There are parts of him I'm not sure he'll ever let me see, parts I don't even know if he *can* show me. But like I said, he's also opened up to me. I know he cares about me, wants to be with me. And the sex is unreal—literally unreal. I seriously thought penetrative orgasms and squirting were myths."

Her eyes widen comically. "Say *what*? Holy shit. How does it feel to be a chosen one?"

I laugh weakly. "Pretty awesome."

She sobers. "This feeling that you don't know him… it could be because of the time you spent apart. Maybe give yourself, and him, a break? It's going to take more than a few days to catch up on years." She pauses, her head tilting and a spark igniting in her dark eyes. "Or do you think he's lying to you about something?"

"No. I don't think so? Honestly, I don't know if any of what I'm feeling is real or if it's old fears sabotaging me. What if this distance I feel is all in my head? Am I'm expecting too much from him? Freaking out over nothing? Maybe I'm just an insecure idiot. Or maybe this proves that we're all wrong for each other. What if this is a giant mistake?"

I don't realize I'm crying in earnest until Lily yanks a napkin from the holder between us and hands it to me. I blow my nose loudly.

"It's been five days," I say through another sob. "This is crazy, right? What the fuck is happening to me? One second I'm fine, the next I'm freaking out."

Lily can't quite conceal her shock—she's never seen me lose it like this. "Shit, Ev. What the hell happened last night?"

I sniffle my way through a recounting of yesterday, from Wilder showing up at my work to my fuckup at dinner and what happened after. But I don't stop there, backtracking to tell her about not seeing him Sunday or Monday, the spotty texts, and how scared I was that he was getting ready to ghost me. How yo-yoing between emotional extremes has fucked up my sleep, my focus, and worst of all, my understanding of myself as a calm, rational person.

When I'm done, Lily doesn't immediately reply, her gaze on the table and her expression troubled. Knowing she won't sugarcoat her opinion, I try to prepare myself. A wasted effort, as I've barely stopped crying when she lifts her head.

"The way I see it, you have two options. Option one,

you believe his explanation for pulling away the last two days—however stupid it was—and you believe that last night he wasn't upset with you, just crazy tired. Option two, you drive yourself up the wall with various worst-case scenarios. I realize option two is kind of unavoidable given your history with him, but have you considered option one? Taking him at his word?"

"I—" I close my mouth and actually think about it. "I've been fixated on the fear that he's not being totally honest with me."

She nods in understanding. "He yanked you around for years, Eva. Of course it's going to take time to trust him. But trust is also a choice, you know? Either you push through your fear or you decide it's not worth it."

"It's worth it," I say quickly. "I *want* to trust him."

"Then give yourself some grace as you navigate this. He says he's all in and you believe that much, right?" I nod. "Maybe setting some boundaries would help, like telling him straight-up what you need to feel safe in the relationship—communication expectations, emotional transparency, et cetera."

I rub my face, groaning. "That's not too, I don't know, needy?"

Her lips purse. "Fuck that. There's a difference between neediness and communication of your needs, and any man who can't recognize the difference is a turd. Besides, this isn't a typical new relationship with a dude you met a week ago. Your baggage with Wilder comes with extra weight fees and carry-ons."

I snort, then grimace and blow my nose again. Calmness seeps through me, as well as heady gratitude for the woman across from me.

I give her a watery smile. "Thanks for being my spillway. You're an amazing woman and an incredible friend."

To my shock, tears fill her eyes. My jaw slack, I rise halfway from my chair. She waves me back down and grabs a napkin, then dabs it delicately beneath her eyes.

"Shut up. You're welcome. Ugh. I even forgive you for threatening my mascara with that warm and fuzzy shit."

The laugh bubbling in my throat chokes off when a key rattles in my front door. Lily swivels in her chair, frowning. "Please tell me that's not Rye. He can't see me almost crying until we've dated at least six months."

I snatch my phone and check the time; when I see it, the blood drains from my head. "Oh, fuck. When Wilder texted me this morning, I told him to come over at four. I completely lost track of time."

Lily's expression morphs from worried to horrified. "Go dunk your face in cold water," she hisses.

It's too late.

The door swings open on Wilder, his head bowed as

he tugs the key out of the lock. The sight of him makes my heart soar and my stomach plummet. He looks up and sees us in the kitchen.

"Hi. Sorry. I'm a few minutes early." He finally registers my tear-wrecked face and his eyes widen in alarm. "Evangeline?"

Lily stands and swiftly packs up her laptop, headphones, and phone. "Call me later," she whispers, then hurries toward the door. "Hey, Wilder. Good to see you. Coming to the Indigo showcase Friday night?"

Wilder, looking panicked and confused, moves out of her way. "Yes, I'll be there."

"Great," chirps Lily. "See you then!"

She slips past him and pulls the door closed.

wilder

The thump of the door closing behind Lily jolts me like an electric shock. I want to follow her almost as much as I want to scoop Evangeline into my arms and kiss every inch of her blotchy, tear-stained face. My feet are likewise conflicted, remaining glued to the floor.

What happened?

Is she going to dump me?

Is it over?

I know she wanted more from me last night—starting with a different reaction to her apology—but I couldn't give it to her. With my tolerance being almost nil from two weeks of abstinence, the Oxys took me the fuck out. Making my voice sound somewhat normal during our brief conversation was next-level difficult, and there was no way I could let her turn on a light. She would have taken one look at me and known I was loaded.

My anxiety climbs so high my voice shakes when I ask, "Is this about last night? I'm sorry, Fairy. I—"

"No," she says softly.

Instead of relaxing, my heart races even faster. I take a halting step toward her. "Then what's wrong? Did someone—is your family okay?"

She stands up fast. "No! I mean *yes*, everyone's fine." A brief, breathless laugh leaves her, and she rubs her already flushed face. She mumbles, "God, I wish you weren't seeing me like this. I'm a total mess."

I speak without thinking. "I love you messy."

Evangeline's head whips up, her eyes huge and unblinking. A second later, I realize what I said. But there's no panic.

Fuck it.

"I love you messy," I repeat as I cross the living room. My eyes absorb every inch of her: crazy hair in a listing bun, swollen eyes, baggy sweatpants, two different-colored socks, and an oversized green sweatshirt with a bleach stain on the hem and tear marks on the shoulders.

Her beauty is both suffocating and replenishing. I can't breathe—the only air I need is her.

Stopping a few feet away, I hold her gaze until I lose sight of everything else. Until there's nothing in the infinite span of the universe but us.

Her rapid breaths.

The fear and hope in her eyes.

My heart—her heart.

"I love every version of you, Evangeline. Happy, angry, stubborn, bossy, sad, tired, embarrassed, nervous... it doesn't matter. Whatever you are, I love it, because I'm hopelessly in love with you. I know my timing, as usual, is completely fucked, but it's the truth and I'm not going to cheapen it by pretending that was a slip of the tongue."

She trembles before me, eyes glassy with tears. I have no clue if she's about to say the words back to me or throw me out. In this moment, I don't care. Whatever she decides to do with my deformed heart, she deserves to know the truth inside it.

Her lips part on a swift inhale. Then she blinks several times and says the absolute last thing I expect to hear.

"I'm afraid of the dark."

I dig my nails into my palms so I don't reach for her. It's not the declaration of love I was hoping for, but I know how hard those words were to say. How vulnerable she feels right now.

"I know, baby."

"I'm not talking about a few nightlights." At my lifted brows, her lips twitch. "Okay, more than a few nightlights. But it's deeper than that. It's also about the people who are closest to me. That's why I asked you to turn on the light last night. I needed to see you, to talk to you, and when I couldn't... you became the dark I couldn't find my way out of."

There's no controlling my full-body recoil.

Evangeline gasps. "I'm sorry."

"It's okay," I croak.

She shakes her head and lurches forward, wrapping her arms tightly around my waist. I hold her close, hoping this isn't the last time she lets me.

"That came out totally wrong," she says against my chest. "I haven't slept and my thoughts are all jumbled. Last night was my fault, not yours. I'm sorry for hurting you at dinner." Tears thicken her voice. "You're not the dark I'm afraid of, okay? Not even close. If I'm afraid of anything, it's my own damn head."

I *am* the dark, though, even if she doesn't know it. But I'm also a selfish bastard who doesn't want to live without her light, so I cradle her to me. Soak in my relief and her radiance. Unable to let her go even if it ends up destroying us both.

"I'm sorry," I whisper into her hair. "I'm sorry, Fairy."

She squeezes me, then lifts her head. The redness has mostly faded from her cheeks, but the skin around her bloodshot eyes is still swollen, her eyelashes wet spikes.

I'm hurting her.

I need to save her.

I can't lose her.

"What are you thinking right now?" she asks softly.

I kiss her forehead before resting my chin on her soft hair and hugging her a little tighter.

Hating myself. Loving her.

"I was thinking about you getting lost in the woods when we were kids and wondering if that's when it started."

"I think so, yes. That's definitely my first memory of being afraid of the dark." She hums. "I've never forgotten that it was you who found me. You led me out."

I led you from one dark to another.

I can't keep you safe.

You shouldn't trust me.

All the words I can't say sit like shards of glass in my throat, but Evangeline doesn't notice. She ducks her head back into my chest, rubbing her cheek against me.

"I love you, too, Wilder. So much."

A glowing wave of warmth spreads through my

body. When it reaches the end of me and recedes, it leaves behind a melody. Exquisite and lovely and painful and haunting. Bright like her. Dark like me.

My heart's song as it becomes whole for the first time.

And then shatters.

CHAPTER TWENTY-EIGHT
evangeline

Pressure points thump-thumping

Beneath our fingertips

Liquid breath flowing between our lips

And yet we're still dying of thirst

Rye strides toward Lily and me with his signature grin. "Twenty minutes to go, ladies. How are we holding up?"

"Super great," Lily answers, the sarcasm in her voice as obvious as the appreciation in her eyes. Even though I'll never look at Rye like *that*, I have to admit he's extra-handsome tonight in a black button-down and slacks that actually fit his giant shoulders and mile-long legs.

When he finally drags his gaze away from Lily, who looks absolutely stunning in a silvery minidress, I ask, "Did you see him?"

My friends exchange a loaded glance that makes me want to knock their heads together. Then Rye shakes his head. "I might have missed him, though. It's crowded out there."

There is a massive tent in the backyard of the opulent mansion we've been sequestered in since our sound check an hour ago.

When our new manager reached out with the invitation for a private showcase, she definitely downplayed the event's magnitude. Instead of the intimate setting we imagined, there are at least a hundred people milling outside beneath string lights and space heaters. And not one of them looks like anyone we'd see at our usual shows. Instead of jeans and T-shirts, it's cocktail dresses, suits, and champagne flutes.

I've already talked Lily out of hyperventilating twice. My own pre-show jitters are muted, smothered by a different worry. All I can think about is Wilder, who said he'd come early to see me before the show.

I check my phone for the hundredth time, but there are no new messages after the one I sent him before we came inside.

> Text me when you get here and I'll send Rye to find you. Xo

While the downstairs suite offered for our use looks like it belongs in a five-star hotel, the cell service is shit. I have no idea if he's tried to call or text me back, and when I tried to sneak back outside, a harried woman wearing a headset all but shoved me back into our room.

"Did you try calling him?" asks Rye.

I bite my cheek so I don't snap at him.

"No service," Lily answers for me, "and no one we've asked knows the Wi-Fi password."

Rye shifts his weight. "If you want, I can look again. Not sure if I can make it back before you go on, though."

I shake my head and force a smile. "Don't worry about it. I'd rather you hang here. I'm sure Wilder is out there somewhere."

He promised.

I move to the nearest window and twitch aside the curtains, squinting through fading daylight at the tent. We're too far away for me to make out faces, but I don't see anyone with Wilder's distinctive height. Not even a flash of Eddie's neon-green hair, which would at least reassure me since the whole band is supposed to be here.

Trust him.

Closing my eyes tightly, I summon memories of the last two days, wrapping them around my heart like a shield. Wilder and I spent every spare minute together. Scattered between beautifully mundane activities like playing guitar, soaking in my hot tub, and his first charmingly disastrous attempt at making me dinner, we had frank conversations about what each of us needs to feel secure in our relationship.

While there were moments I could tell he was uncomfortable—namely when I told him I want to tell my parents about us—he didn't have a single panic attack.

And the last two *nights*... even thinking about them sends currents of heat through my body. I thought sex with him had been incredible before, but having him stare into my eyes and whisper he loves me while he moves inside me? I'm forever altered by it. He's always been a part of me, but now he's in every breath I take and every beat of my heart.

The final memory I summon, possibly the most profound one, is falling asleep in his arms late last night, only to realize this morning that I'd forgotten to turn on the main nightlight in my bedroom.

He'll be here.

After heaving a sigh that fogs the glass, I turn and

drop onto the couch beside my purse, tossing my useless phone into its depths.

"I need to, uh, use the restroom," Rye says, pivoting on his heel and heading into one of the adjacent bedrooms.

Lily sits next to me and hands me my giant bottle of water. I take it and fiddle with the cap as I stare sightlessly across the room.

"You good, Ev?"

Her nervous voice is a welcome gust of wind clearing my polluted thoughts. *God, I'm such an asshole.* I grab her bouncing knee, pressing down until it stills, and hold her gaze until the worry in her eyes shifts to relief.

"I'm good. All warmed up. You good?"

She nods. "I am now that your bossy-diva face is on."

I smirk. "Ready to explode some brains?"

A smile teases her burgundy-painted lips. "Hope they have a good cleaning service."

As my laughter fades, we hear voices in the hallway outside coming closer. Along with the confident tones of our new manager, Mallory Simmons, we recognize the rapid-fire speech of our equally new publicist, Anita Allman.

We make it to our feet right as the main door opens. Anita flies into the room first and beelines for us, her corkscrew blond curls bouncing around her head. Even though she's barely five feet tall, objectively cherubic in appearance, and has been nothing but sweet so far, Lily and I agree she's absolutely terrifying.

"Ladies!" she gushes, her hands fluttering around us. "Look at you two! Gorgeous, absolutely gorgeous. Aren't they gorgeous, Mallory? I can't wait to get you to my favorite stylist. He's going to have the best time elevating your look."

Feeling Lily tense beside me, I grab her hand and give it a reassuring squeeze. Anita doesn't notice or doesn't care about our discomfort, muttering to herself as she catalogues us from feet to hair like she's taking notes on everything we need to change about ourselves. Which she probably is.

I have a new appreciation for why Wilder always hated meetings with our publicist, whose focus was invariably on him while Eddie, Jax, and I were left mostly unscathed.

"They're gorgeous," agrees Mallory in a genuine but much more subdued tone as she approaches us. "Now give them some space, will you? Your crazy energy is the last thing they need right now, and I'd like a minute with our clients."

Anita giggles, unoffended, and spins around. She squeaks when she spots Rye reentering the room.

"Hello, there! And you are?" She barrels toward him and grabs his arm. "Is that a full bar? Oh my. I could use a drink, handsome. How about you?"

Rye throws us a *PleaseHelpMe* look as she tugs him toward the bar, but before either of us can react, Mallory captures our attention. "He'll survive," she says with a knowing smile. "I know Anita is intense, but I wouldn't have recommended her unless she was the best—and the best fit for your style. You'll get used to her. How are you feeling? Nervous?"

"A little," Lily says. "This isn't our usual crowd, that's for sure."

Mallory's dark eyes sparkle. "I know, but remember they're here for you, not the other way around."

"Who is *they*, exactly?" I ask. "We thought there'd be maybe a dozen people here."

Mallory chuckles and shakes her head but not in a patronizing way. Whereas Anita is a shark wearing the skin of an angel, Mallory *looks* like a shark but has the personality of a mellow, level-headed big sister. She also has a two-decade-long track record of managing successful pop artists and was recommended personally by Breaking Giants' manager, Phil, who's like a crotchety uncle to me.

"This is all Anita's doing," Mallory says, glancing toward the bar where the publicist is laughing hysterically at something Rye said. From the expression on his face, he didn't intend whatever it was to land as a joke.

"Not gonna lie, ladies," continues Mallory, "there are a lot of recognizable faces out there. Pretty much everyone who's anyone in the Seattle music industry is here, plus a handful of players from Los Angeles and New York. Producers, artists, journalists..." She trails off as she takes in our expressions.

"I'm gonna throw up," whispers Lily.

Despite my own queasiness, I pull her into a hug. "We've got this. It doesn't matter who they are. We're going to give them the exact same Glow we'd give a bunch of college kids at a house party. Okay?"

She nods against my shoulder. Behind her, Mallory mouths, "Sorry," right as Anita's high-pitched voice fills the suite.

"Just got the text, my gorgeous girls! It's showtime!"

I sigh into Lily's ear and mutter, "Guess we should've asked *her* for the Wi-Fi."

Like I hoped she would, she laughs.

evangeline

Lily and I stand hidden from view by a wall of curtains that leads directly to the temporary stage. A few seconds ago, the lights inside the tent dimmed and those rigged to scaffolding at each corner of the stage flared brightly.

The crowd is screaming.

Screaming.

Lily stares at the sky, fading white wisps on a canvas of deep blue. "What the fuck is happening right now?" she asks dazedly.

A hysterical giggle escapes me.

The stage lights lower and the noise from the crowd spikes even higher. From the cacophony comes a familiar whistle, piercing despite my earplugs. As soon as it tapers off, I hear another welcome sound: an obnoxious, warbling scream. Laughter mixes with the ongoing cheers.

"Jax and Eddie," I tell Lily, who returns my giddy grin.

A woman positioned a few feet away waves for our attention and holds up one finger. *One minute.* We nod and look back at the stage as a shadowed figure enters from the other side and walks to the central mic. There's a gentle hum of feedback before light rises on a man— not Cory Donovan, who we were told was introducing us.

This man is well over six feet tall and wears faded black jeans, scuffed combat boots, and a leather jacket. The chaotic waves of his hair gleam darkly beneath the spotlight. His hands in his pockets and his stance relaxed, he oozes confidence and charisma. Like he was born for the stage.

My shoulder knocks into Lily's as my knees turn rubbery.

Wilder's smooth, rich voice floats across the back- yard, quieting the crowd as effectively as a lullaby. "Hey, everyone. Believe it or not, for once I'm actually excited to be here with you fancy fucks."

As boisterous laughter fills the air, Lily grabs my arm and whispers, "Oh my God, I think I love him, too."

As the crowd's laughter fades, Wilder continues, "As

some of you are aware, I've known Eva my entire life. Our dads are in this little rock band called Breaking Giants." He pauses for another burst of cheers and applause. "And while I've only known Lily Aoki a short time, I know she's one in a million. How? Because Eva would settle for nothing less in a creative partnership and *she*, ladies and gentlemen, is absolutely one of a kind. These incredible women have more talent in their pinkie fingers than any of us can hope to claim in our lifetimes, and mark my words, tonight we'll be listening to the birth of a legend.

"Without further ado, allow me to welcome to the stage Eva Marie and Lily Aoki of Glow!"

I barely hear Lily's squeal of excitement over the roar from the tent. Feeling like I'm floating, I follow her onto the stage and move toward the man with a grin on his face, love in his eyes, and my guitar in his hands. He lowers the strap over my head, gives me a quick kiss on the cheek, and jogs offstage.

As I face the mic and the ecstatic crowd, I still feel him. Watching me, loving me, believing in me. It hits me suddenly that even when we were apart, he was never far away. And he never will be.

No matter where I go in life, he'll be there.

As constant as my shadow.

♫

AFTER THE SHOW, Mallory leads us back down the hallway toward our suite. Lily looks as blissed out as I feel, her eyes unfocused and a small, dreamy smile on her face. My entire body, toes to fingertips, buzzes like a live wire.

Mallory is talking, wisely directing her words to Rye. "Food will be waiting in the room. They'll have forty-five minutes or so to freshen up and relax before Anita drags them back outside to mingle. Make sure they hydrate, eat some protein, and go easy on alcohol. And make sure Eva takes a vocal nap." She hands him a sheet of paper as we near the suite. "Anita already went over this with them, but here's a list of ways they can respond to questions they don't want or know how to answer. Got it?"

"Yes, ma'am."

"Cute, but if you call me ma'am again I'll make you regret it."

Rye blanches. "Sorry. Never again."

"Good man."

Mallory gives Lily and me quick, tight hugs. "Phenomenal show, ladies. I'll see you soon." She strides back down the hallway, her shimmery halter dress swishing around her legs.

Rye ushers us inside the suite. "You two back on planet Earth yet?"

Lily giggles. "Nope—oh, chocolate!" She hurries to the table laden with food and grabs a plate.

Rye follows. "Protein first!"

"Pfft," she says, a brownie already passing her lips.

I laugh, which earns me a glare from Rye. "Vocal nap!"

I roll my eyes at his bossiness but mime zippering my lips, then kick off my Converse and head to the bar to switch on the electric teakettle. My throat feels okay but I know better than to push it, especially since the night is only half over and I have a lot of talking ahead of me. As the water heats, I grab a plate off the table and start loading it up.

"I feel drunk," mumbles Lily, this time around a hunk of cantaloupe. "Drunk off how surreal that was. Did you see that one guy tearing it up our entire set? He had to be my grandfather's age. And the woman who started crying during Eva's violin solo? I saw her in a movie trailer a few days ago."

Rye nods, chuckling. "My favorite part was when Eddie tried to start a mosh pit and security almost hauled him out."

Lily chokes on her cantaloupe and spits it out so she can laugh freely. "How did I miss that?"

I shrug, my eyes watering with the effort of not laughing.

"And then there was—" Rye stops suddenly when the suite door flies open. He grins. "Hey, man! How great was their set?"

Wilder's eyes find mine as the door swings closed. He stalks toward me. "It was great. I need to talk to Evangeline."

The heat in his eyes and the gravel in his voice make me gulp. My hand shakes on my plate. I squeeze my thighs together, the throb between them a sudden, steady drumbeat.

Lily cackles, grabbing Rye's arm in one hand and her plate of food in the other. "We're going to give you guys some alone time. Explore this castle a bit, maybe get into some trouble. Grab that bottle of sparkling water, Rye."

Rye frowns in bewilderment. "Huh? But—*oof*." He rubs his stomach where Lily landed a punch, then comprehension spreads on his face along with a ruddy hue. He grabs the bottle and a giant, wrapped sandwich. "Oh, um, for sure. We'll be back in ten minutes."

Wilder doesn't look at them as he says, "Make it twenty."

wilder

Evangeline squeaks as I lift her from the floor and guide her legs around my waist. The feel of her in my arms, warm and pliant, and the delicious, musky scent of her sweat make my mouth water. I want to lick every salty inch of her, but there's one spot in particular I'm dying to devour.

"Which one of these doors is a bedroom?" I ask roughly.

Arousal and alarm war in her eyes as she points a trembling finger. *Good.* It means she remembers the promise I made last week—the one I'm about to make good on.

I waste no time crossing the large living room and shouldering my way past a partially open door. A swift kick closes it behind us. Luckily, the lights are on, so I don't have to waste time searching for a switch. Striding to the giant bed, I tear back the gold-embroidered comforter and dump her on the sheets. Then I crawl over her on all fours, my eyes soaking in the feast beneath me. Beautiful, flushed face and eyes that haunt my dreams. Corseted breasts heaving against the long-sleeved mesh bodysuit beneath it. Miniskirt riding up with every restless swish of her legs in their artfully ripped black tights.

Fucking exquisite.

When I bend down and nuzzle my face into her neck to taste her drying sweat, her hips punch upward on a breathy moan.

"Wilder, wait. At least let me—" My palm over her mouth muffles the rest of her words.

The spark of indignation in her eyes brings a wicked grin to my lips. "No talking. If you want me to stop, you can smack my head. Better hit me hard, though, because I'll be drowning in your pussy."

Her pupils dilate, dainty nostrils flaring. I watch the war play out in her eyes—her need to have my face between her thighs battling with the bullshit societal conditioning telling her she should wash first. Like her sweat doesn't simply enhance her natural scent and make me fucking feral.

I drag my nose along hers and over one flushed cheek. "What's it gonna be, Fairy?" I croon. "Yes or no?"

She nods, a sharp jerk of her chin.

"Good answer."

Releasing her mouth, I drag my hand over her neck to her chest, where my fingers make quick work of the eye hooks of her corset. The stiff fabric sags open, revealing her bare breasts under soft, black mesh. Her nipples pebble beneath my gaze, the pale mounds jerking with her panting breaths. I flick one nipple, then the other, smirking when she slaps her hands over her mouth to trap the sound that wants to escape.

"Ever thought about piercing these?"

Her eyes throw sparks that make me chuckle and kiss her deep and sloppy and hard. When I come up for air, she looks dazed but still has the wherewithal to jab a finger at the watch on my wrist.

I cock an eyebrow. "You think I'll need more than a minute or two to have your cum all over my face?"

Embarrassment and lust turn her face bright red. Grinning, I resume my downward path, pausing on her chest until the transparent fabric shines wetly around her nipples and her fingers twist and clench in the sheets above her head. I move lower, and lower still, every stroke of my hands and graze of my tongue slowly overwhelming her brain until all she can do is *feel*.

When I find the edge of the bed, I pull her with me by the hips until my knees hit the floor. Without me asking, she spreads her legs, shimmying until her miniskirt is pooled around her waist.

"Such a good slut for me," I whisper.

She makes a small, desperate sound as I lean forward, pressing my nose to the juncture of her thighs and inhaling. *Goddamn.* My balls tighten and my patience evaporates. I grab the waistband of her tights and strip them off, then pull her thighs onto my shoulders.

"Fuck," I grunt as I lift her toward my face. "You have the prettiest, neediest pussy I've ever seen."

She's quivering ambrosia on my tongue. I savor every flavor and texture I can find with long, slow licks before finally giving her swollen clit the attention it deserves. Within seconds, her thighs begin to tremble around my head, her head thrashing from side to side. At the barest brush of my teeth, she explodes with a ragged cry, bucking against my face. Growling in satisfaction, I drive my tongue inside her to feel the fading contractions of her orgasm.

"Oh my God," she whispers, her muscles going limp.

I bite her labia—not hard, but hard enough to make her spasm. "Not my name, brat."

She yanks my face up by my hair, the burn on my

scalp transferring directly to my dick. When she sees my expression, the irritation on her face melts to surprise. Then intrigue.

I chuckle and wipe my hand over my mouth. "You can hurt me another time, Fairy. Right now you need to eat and drink some tea. Do you want to rinse off?"

Her expression softens and she nods. She releases my hair, her fingertips trailing over my cheek and passing, featherlight, across my lips. Her eyes flicker down to the bulge in my pants.

"Can I return the favor first?"

I shake my head, bending forward to give her pussy a final kiss that makes her twitch. "Later," I murmur, avoiding her probing eyes as I get to my feet. "I'll turn on the shower. Is that your bag in the corner?"

"Yeah. Thanks."

Pain pinches my chest at her small, disappointed voice, but I keep walking, grabbing her small duffel and heading into the bathroom. The room matches the suite's aesthetics, all white marble and gleaming gold accents. I crank the dial in the glass-walled shower, leaving my fingers under the flow as it heats up. My other hand lowers to my dick, adjusting it to a more comfortable position.

Do I want a blowjob from Evangeline? Abso-fucking-lutely. But I haven't let her go down on me. And I can't explain to her why because it will make me sound like a lunatic. While the thought of her mouth on me is one of my favorite fantasies, the idea of it happening in reality gives me an uneasy feeling. Like the act is beneath her or will diminish her somehow.

There's another reason, too—at least at the moment. Despite how hard I am, it will take more time than we have for me to climax. Which has absolutely nothing to do with her and everything to do with opiates.

Self-disgust curls through me.

"Did you get my text?"

At Evangeline's soft voice behind me, I wipe the scowl from my face and turn. My IQ drops a hundred points at the sight of her standing naked before me, her toes curling into a cream-colored bathmat as she spirals her hair into a bun and secures it.

Amusement brightens her eyes. "Hello?"

I don't lift my gaze from her body. Even her belly button is perfect. There are three small moles under her right breast that remind me of Orion's belt. I want to lick them. Map them. Make my own constellations on her body with bite marks.

She snaps her fingers in my face, her voice full of laughter as she says, "Focus, Wilder."

I finally lift my gaze and hear the question she asked. "I didn't get a text from you. Actually, I was going to ask you the same thing. I called a bunch when I got here, but you didn't answer, and some jerk security bro wouldn't let me in the house to look for you."

"There's no cell service in here." She smiles faintly, and the tension I didn't realize she was carrying vanishes. Unfortunately, that tension transfers right to me.

"You thought I wasn't coming?" I keep my voice light. *Even though I promised?*

"No, I knew you'd be here," she says quickly. Too quickly. "Your intro was a nice surprise, by the way. Thank you. I love you." Lifting to her toes, she gives me a kiss, then slips past me into the shower. "God, that feels good. Hey, when you make tea, can you use the sachets I brought in my purse? It's on the couch. Oh, and don't tell Rye I've been talking, okay? He'll be annoying about it."

I smile and nod like my gut isn't churning. Like she didn't just lie to me. Like I'm not the biggest hypocrite in the world.

The biggest liar of them all.

evangeline

After close to an hour of networking at Anita's side, meeting dozens of people whose names and faces all blur together, she finally releases us to mingle on our own. Lily immediately vanishes toward where we last saw Rye, leaving me standing alone at the end of a buffet table of picked-over hors d'oeuvres.

Exhaustion creeps over me as I scan the dwindling crowd for Wilder. I don't see him, which isn't much of a surprise. After Jax and Eddie left a little past ten, he probably found somewhere dark and quiet to chill until I'm ready to leave. I couldn't be more ready, but before setting us free, Anita politely ordered us to *make ourselves available* for another twenty minutes.

"You look like you could use this," says a voice to my right.

Forcing a pleasant expression onto my tired face, I turn to find a man holding two glasses of white wine, one of them extended my way. He's handsome in a men's-cologne-ad way, with light brown hair, an easy smile, and hazel eyes. The starched white collar of his dress shirt gapes open, framing a swath of tanned skin. Despite an air of casualness, he reeks of wealth, from his shoes and watch to the suit he's wearing, which fits too well for it not to be hand tailored. While he looks vaguely familiar, I'm positive Anita didn't introduce me to him tonight.

As good as a glass of wine sounds, and as much as he doesn't *look* like a creep, there's no way I'm taking an unsealed drink from a stranger.

"Thank you, but I'll pass." Mindful of the fact I have to play nice, I soften the rejection with a smile I hope looks real. "Wine will only put me to sleep at this point."

He nods sagely and sets the glasses on the buffet table. "Coffee then," he says, offering me his arm. "Shall we?"

Irritation flashes in me. My gaze flickers around us in a futile search for a reason to refuse and snags on Anita. She's standing about ten feet away and looking right at me. For a second, I think she's going to rescue me. Then she stabs a finger toward my companion and mouths, "Talk to him."

Damn. He's someone important, then.

Swallowing a sigh, I clasp the man's forearm. "Sounds great."

The expensive material of his suit tickles my fingertips as we walk toward the bar. This close, I can smell a light, expensive cologne. When his head dips toward mine, I fight the urge to pull away.

"It's torture, isn't it?" he asks in a soft, teasing voice. "Having to be polite to strange men?"

I'm so startled I almost trip. The arm under my hand flexes, warm fingers landing on mine to steady me. "Whoa there." He chuckles, the sound warm and infectious. Drawing to a stop, he looks down at me with an indecipherable expression. Something in the realm of sympathy.

"I promise not to ask you twenty invasive questions, give you my business card, or invite you to dinner. In fact, we don't even have to talk. I just know Anita. You had about thirty seconds before she sent someone far more annoying than me your way." He shrugs. "You've been going nonstop all night, and I figured you deserved a break."

I blame my tired brain for the fact I simply stare at him until he winks and draws me back into motion. At the bar, he releases my arm and orders two oat milk lattes, then chats with the bartender as she makes them.

Feeling both grateful and baffled to be ignored, I watch as he leans across the counter and whispers something that makes her blush. The sight of his cheeky grin—totally different from the polite smile he gave me—does what his words couldn't, allowing me to finally relax.

When he eventually turns and hands me a latte, I don't have to force my smile. "Thanks... I'm sorry. I don't know your name."

"Clay Eaton. Nice to meet you, Eva." He looks around us, then nods. "Follow me."

He leads me outside the tent to a cluster of empty teak chairs set around a low table, the area thankfully well lit. A patio heater radiates nearby, chasing away the chill. I settle in the chair closest to the heater, closing my eyes briefly in relief. When I open them, Clay gives me a knowing grin.

"Thanks again," I say haltingly. "My feet are killing me."

He nods and sips his drink, gaze moving from my face to roam the crowd remaining in the tent. I scan the crowd, too. But the person I'm looking for is nowhere to be seen.

"Anita's spying on us," murmurs Clay. "She's going to think I put that frown on your face. No, don't look for her. Pretend I said something funny. Or better yet, think about that grandpa's sick moves on the dance floor earlier." My soft laugh brings a satisfied smile to his face. "Knew that would work." He glances at the tent again. "Okay, we're in the clear."

I take a deeper drink of my latte, appreciating the creamy warmth and the faint bitterness of espresso, and try to relax. Easier said than done. Unlike me, Clay seems perfectly content sitting in silence with a complete stranger, his head tilted back and eyes closed.

When I catch a glimpse of Anita and Mallory staring in our direction, I'm almost relieved to have an excuse to socialize. "So did you order oat milk because you like it or because you know dairy messes with airways?"

His eyes open, humor creasing the corners. "The latter. Though I don't dislike it."

"Know a lot of singers?"

Another slight smile. "You could say that."

I tilt my head, my eyes narrowing at his evasiveness. "How do you know Anita, anyway?"

Expensive fabric whispers as he straightens. "Haven't you heard? If you throw stones at a publicist, nine out of ten times you'll hit an entertainment lawyer, too."

I blink in surprise, reassessing him. "An entertainment lawyer, huh?"

He grins. "You sound surprised."

"I am, a little. No offense, but I figured you were the son of an Indigo exec or some other industry bigwig."

His brows lift. "How so?"

Emboldened by the humor in his eyes, I wave vaguely at him. "All... that. The tailored suit. The shoes. Even the haircut is a tell. Plus, you can't be more than thirty."

He chuckles. "Well, I appreciate the compliment. Backhanded as it may be."

I grin back at him. "You're welcome."

His eyes lock on mine and his smile changes. With a spark of panic, I realize it's the same one he gave the bartender.

I blurt, "I'm not flirting with you!"

Clay laughs heartily. "Duly noted. For the record, I'm not flirting with you, either. I prefer women with fully developed frontal lobes."

I choke on laughter. "Rude."

His smile softens to a teasing curl. "That being said, if you're single at twenty-five, give me a call." My mouth drops, but he continues idly, "To answer your round-about question, I turn thirty in June and have been practicing for almost five years. I like to think I've carved my own success, but you got me on one count—Eaton and Associates is a family business. Full disclosure: I'm only here because I stole the invite from my much more successful father's desk."

"Ah," I say with an exaggerated nod. "Then you're a *fan*."

He laughs again. "I'll admit to being a Glow convert after tonight, but the theft was at my sister's behest. She's around here somewhere. Dark hair? Crazy vibes? Also lacking full brain development?"

I roll my eyes but can't help laughing. "Doesn't sound familiar. What's her name? I don't want to leave without meeting her."

Clay opens his mouth, but then his gaze lifts over my head and he closes it. A second later, a shadow falls over me and Wilder asks, "Evangeline? You ready to go?"

"Hi! Yes, absolutely." I jump to my feet and offer Clay an apologetic smile. "Sorry. You've been great company, but I'm wiped out."

He nods, smiling affably. "Completely understand."

Wilder's chest brushes my back, a hand curling around my waist and flattening over my stomach. While my body instantly lights up, my head tumbles with surprise. Neither of our families is here tonight, but there are still people around who *know* our families. Though we didn't discuss boundaries outright, I know it's why his kiss onstage was platonic and at least part of why we separated right when we came outside.

Maybe he's jealous, whispers a small, pleased voice inside me. I slap that voice into a mental closet.

"Clay," Wilder says stiffly.

Looking between them, my confusion spikes—they clearly know each other. Clay's expression is aloof, almost cold, his eyes flat and dark. He's like an entirely different man than the one I was laughing with a minute ago. A shiver rolls down my body.

"Wilder," he says as he stands. His eyes move to me and soften slightly. "Great meeting you, Eva. Have a good night."

My tongue tangles; by the time it unwinds, Clay has disappeared back into the tent. Wilder stares after him until I palm his face, directing his gaze to me.

"What was that about?"

He shakes his head. "Nothing."

I frown. "I don't know what kind of beef you guys have, but he was perfectly nice and didn't hit on me"—*overtly, at least*—"which puts him in a very small percentage of the men I spoke to tonight."

I don't mean the words as an accusation, but I feel him stiffen. Before I can clarify that I'm not upset he couldn't stay by my side, he envelops me in his arms and kisses my forehead. I inhale a midnight rainstorm wrapped in warm leather. My body instantly relaxes, and I muse that his touch is a drug. One I'm happily addicted to.

"Don't be fooled by his nice-guy act," he says after a moment. "Clay is a manipulative bastard just like his stepsister, who ambushed me ten minutes ago."

I lift my head. "Huh? Who's his stepsister?"

His jaw clenches and releases. "Kendra."

wilder

Fucking Kendra.

Evangeline probably thinks I was hiding out in the dark somewhere for the last hour of the party. I kind of was. But I was also watching her. The second I saw Clay heading toward her, I was moving in her direction. Which was when Kendra intercepted me.

I knew she was at the event, of course, having spotted her lurking toward the back of the crowd during Glow's set. As the only person scowling instead of enjoying the music, she was hard to miss. Clay stood beside her. While he, at least, was bobbing his head to the music, seeing all his creepy focus centered on Evangeline set off alarm bells. No doubt he was there because Kendra wanted him to use him to drive a wedge between Evangeline and me.

That part of her plan, at least, backfired before it even unfolded. I may have a reputation as the least social party guest in history, but a life on the sidelines has made me observant as hell. Clay has a well-established type: tall brunettes who resemble his stepsister—fucking *gag*—so I wasn't worried about him hitting on Evangeline with any real intent. I was worried even less about Evangeline falling for his charming facade, not with the taste of her still in my throat and her *I love yous* filling the cracks of my heart.

I was ready for Kendra when she slithered into my path. Now she regrets every moment of pseudo-intimacy between us, when chemically induced trust led her to show me her closet full of skeletons... among them the twisted bones of her relationship with her stepbrother and stepfather, as well as a graveyard full of their corrupt dealings. I let her say her piece, listened to all the usual threats wrapped in false affection, then made it clear if she ever goes through with anything, I'll use it all—every last dirty secret she shared—to ruin the reputation of her family.

Throwing her past vulnerabilities in her face didn't feel good, but it was necessary to quell her mistaken belief that she's the only one with leverage in our fucked-up association.

Kendra may have the ability to ruin my life—she

could tell the world I'm addicted to pain pills, break my family's heart, throw a wrench in Night Theory's success, *and* destroy my chance of happiness with Evangeline—but I hold an equal power.

At the end of the day, a rock musician addicted to drugs isn't nearly as sensational as the dirt I have on the Eatons.

And she knows it.

♫

IT ISN'T until we're back at Evangeline's house, showered and curled up on her couch with a movie on, that she asks the question I've been expecting and dreading.

She would have asked the second I dropped the bomb of who Clay's sister was on her, but before she could, Rye and Lily found us. The women couldn't leave before saying a round of goodbyes and thank yous. Then we had to collect their instruments and belongings from the suite and wait for a valet to bring our cars. By the time Evangeline was buckled into my passenger seat, she was half asleep, and within five minutes she was out.

Between the half-hour cat nap and a shower when we got home—during which me washing her hair turned into desperate, slippery sex—she's now sleepy but lucid. I've been pretending to watch the movie while counting down the final minutes of my reprieve.

"What did Kendra want?"

"To start a fight," I say with a sigh. "She thrives on stirring shit up and causing a scene. When I didn't take the bait, she gave up."

Even shittier than lying to Evangeline is the knowledge I brought tonight on myself. The only reason Kendra was at the showcase at all was because of me. Four days ago, I reached out to her under the pretense of clearing the air and apologizing for how abruptly I dumped her. The real reason, however, is currently buried in my sock drawer at home.

Because I'm a worthless addict.

I fucking *knew* it was a mistake to call Kendra, just like I knew she wouldn't believe me when I told her I didn't want anything from her but pills. In her messed-up head, we're perfect for each other. She doesn't see our relationship as having been toxic because she's never known anything else. But even knowing that talking to her would bite me in the ass, I hadn't been able to stop myself.

My dad's sobriety books say the first step to recovery is admitting you have a problem.

Bullshit.

The second I admitted it to myself, the line I've

balanced on for years disappeared. I've fallen to the bottom of a well I dug myself, and every pill I take drops another bucket of sludge over me. I'm going to drown in the poison of my own making; it's only a matter of time.

So far, I've been able to avoid appearing visibly high around Evangeline, but my willpower wanes every time I lose the daily battle with myself. Every time I tell her I have to go home for a bit, or run an errand that doesn't exist. Every time I lie to her and to Jax, who still thinks I'm doing a dry-ninety with him.

In the mere seconds of silence as I wait for Evangeline to speak, I see a future wherein every scrap of goodness in my life burns away. Because I'm too weak to stop lighting matches.

"Is that how you met her? At an industry event because her stepbrother and father are entertainment lawyers?"

Despite how little I want to talk about the Eatons, I'm relieved at the distraction from my thoughts.

"Stepfather," I say, struggling to keep the disgust out of my voice. "And yes. Conrad Eaton gets invitations to everything. He's the guy everyone hates to need."

"Huh. I'd never even heard of the Eatons until tonight."

I twirl a strand of her clean, damp hair around my finger. Focusing on physical sensations—the slight friction of individual hairs, the scent of her shampoo—I can almost, *almost*, ignore the burn beneath my skin.

"Consider yourself lucky."

She rubs her nose against my chest and sniffs me, an adorable habit that makes me feel like the luckiest asshole in the world. I doubt she even knows she does it, and I'll never draw attention to it for fear of her stopping.

"What's so bad about them?" she asks on a yawn.

I shift in discomfort. I don't want to lie, but I also don't want to give her nightmares.

"Wilder?"

Her voice is more alert, and I wince internally. "They do all the usual shit for artists—negotiating contracts, licensing, copyright issues—but they're also criminal defense attorneys."

Evangeline sits up and frowns at me. "You're being vague on purpose."

"Because I don't want to upset you." Her frown deepens, and I sigh in defeat. "Remember when we were looking for a lawyer to negotiate our contract with Indigo four years ago? Eaton and Associates came up as an option, and I asked my dad about them. He warned me off them pretty forcefully. He didn't tell me anything specific, but I've heard enough since then to figure out why. Conrad and Clay aren't known for their integrity."

Knowing she won't stop digging until I give her something concrete, I make myself continue.

"There's a reason I didn't want you anywhere near Michael Dresden. Why whenever we're in the same place, the guys and I keep a close eye on him. Last year, two women came forward with evidence he drugged and assaulted them. Within a month, the charges were dropped and both women *just so happened* to move out of state. Clay was his lawyer."

Her lovely face twists with dismay. "My God." She pauses, and I can almost feel her mind working. "Kendra told you that?"

I nod. Kendra told me more, too. Like how Clay sent private investigators to harass and bully the women until they folded and fled.

Evangeline tucks her head under my chin. "That's so horrible. I don't even know what to say."

"Say you'll stay away from that family."

She nods. "I can't believe Clay seemed so normal. What a creep."

She yawns again, so hugely her jaw cracks.

"Come on, Fairy. Let's get you to bed."

She hums in agreement but doesn't move.

Grabbing the remote, I turn off the movie we weren't watching, then help her to her feet. Eyes half-lidded, she sways until I wrap an arm around her waist. She melts against me with a sigh, nose buried in my shirt.

"I love you, Wilder," she mumbles. "I'm going to love you forever. Just like we promised."

The words hit like a gut punch, stealing my air. Tears burn my eyes. Another bucket of sludge hits my head, burying me in more darkness.

Addict.

Liar.

Loser.

"I love you, too," I choke out. "Forever."

evangeline

Despite having never painted toenails in his life, Wilder handles the tiny nail polish brush like he does chords on a guitar—with focus, confidence, and an annoying level of innate talent. He's almost done with a second coat of the dark, opalescent blue polish. A warm hand cradles my ankle, occasionally sliding up to massage my bare calf or squeeze in chastisement when I move.

Sunlight diffuses through the glass slider behind him, bringing out hints of umber in his dark hair. Outside, newborn leaves glisten on the trees and bushes in my backyard, the memory of winter fading more with each passing day. The daffodils are in full bloom, a river of white and yellow confetti along the fence.

Soft music plays around us. My Kindle sits forgotten

on my lap as I cradle a mug of coffee and watch the most incredible man I've ever known carefully paint my toenails. A man who spent yesterday afternoon helping me iron out lyrics and melodies for three new Glow songs, then insisted on cooking me dinner—which wasn't even burned—and having me for dessert. The same man who woke me up this morning with back-to-back orgasms. Who followed me into the shower because he has a thing for washing me. Who made me coffee before rummaging under my bathroom sink for acetone, cotton balls, and nail polish because he noticed my pedicure was chipping.

It's not even 10:00 a.m. and I want this every Sunday for the rest of my life. I want *him* for the rest of my life.

"Come to brunch today."

I don't know who's more surprised by my sudden words. We both freeze; his fingers briefly tighten on my foot, then relax. With a final swipe of blue on my pinkie toe, he caps the polish and sets it on the coffee table. As his eyes lift to mine, I brace for disappointment.

"Okay."

"I completely understand—wait, what?"

He smiles slightly, giving my ankle another squeeze before gently relocating my foot to the floor. "Okay, Evangeline. I'll go to brunch at your parents' house." He glances at his watch. "You normally leave around ten-thirty, right?"

I close my gaping mouth. "Really? You're really okay with coming?"

He gives me a dry look. "Am I excited to face your dad? Not even a little bit. But I don't want to keep our relationship a secret anymore. Not from your parents or the public. And if we don't do it now, I'm not sure when we'll be able to. The album drops in two weeks and we announce the tour two weeks after that. Our team thinks we'll sell out fast and they're already prepared to add dates on both ends. We could be on the road as early as the third week of May."

My ears ring. He might be gone before my birthday. "That's like... five weeks from now."

"I know. And we might be gone eight months." He cracks a smile that doesn't reach his eyes. "This probably wasn't the best time to start a relationship, was it?"

Eight months.

I have only myself to blame for the shock I'm feeling. I've purposely avoided thinking about how limited our time is before our careers pull us apart.

No more Sunday mornings. No more dreamless, deep sleep in his arms. No more forehead kisses or midnight whispers or watching him brush his teeth. Instead, he'll be on the road and performing almost every night. Surrounded by fans. By drugs and alcohol. *Women.* At the thought, a particularly vivid memory from our first tour makes me flinch.

Wilder snatches my mug and puts it on the table, then claims my hands between his. His worried eyes study my face.

"Once our schedules for the next year are in place, we'll find the time to see each other. There will be breaks on tour. I'll fly home or fly you to me." He swallows, fear brightening his eyes. "Tell me what's going on in your head. Are you... is it too much? Are you regretting—"

"No," I gasp out, shaking my head quickly. "I'm sorry. I'm being stupid. You're right. We'll figure it out. The band and tour need to be your priority, anyway."

I make to stand, to escape, but pressure on my hands holds me down. He scoots closer, lifting a palm to cup the side of my face. This close to him, my muscles can't help but relax. My mind, however, continues storming, screaming as it spirals toward the ground.

"Eyes on me, Fairy."

Unable to resist that deep, textured tone of command, my eyes immediately find his. The connection between us flares, obscuring the world.

"I love you," he says with quiet intensity. "Yes, the band is a priority, but you're equally important to me.

I'm not who I was three years ago. I'm not interested in partying anymore, and the only woman I want is you. I'm yours, okay? Only yours. I know it's going to be hard to trust me because of my past mistakes, but can you try? Can you let me prove I'm different now? That *we're* different?"

My mental descent slows. Stops. The storm inside me disperses so suddenly I feel dizzy.

"Yes," I whisper. "I trust you."

One cloud reforms, a dark smudge at the corner of my mind, but I keep its contents to myself.

Please don't break my heart.

CHAPTER THIRTY-FOUR

evangeline

This pressure on my bones

Reminds me of home

Where it was you and me

Together deep in the sea

Sealed by tides and seaweed dreams

But sometimes, oh sometimes

I missed the stars

ours later, Wilder and I return to my house. Neither of us spoke on the drive home, and we remain mute as we walk inside and sit on opposite ends of my couch. Quiet vibrates around us as he stares at the dark television screen and I gaze through the sliding door at a sky now clogged with gray.

"It could have been worse, right?"

His effort to lighten the mood falls short, his voice more solemn than sarcastic.

My stomach clenches, my voice emerging hoarse with agitation and lingering disbelief. "My dad wanted to drug test you."

He sighs. "He loves you and wants to protect you."

My teeth clench, catching the edge of my tongue. Copper skates over my tastebuds. Wilder reaches for my hand and threads our fingers together. Mine are freezing. So are his.

"Your grandparents like me—or at least don't hate me—and your mom hugged me when we left. Hunter and Josh were cool. It wasn't all bad." He pauses. "Your dad didn't make a scene or anything."

No, he waited until Wilder had graciously offered to clear the table and was alone in the kitchen before cornering him. Oblivious to the fact I'd followed him and heard everything.

I unclench my jaw. "What he said to you, accusing you of being high because you yawned a few times..." I drag my gaze from the stormy sky to his profile. His dark lashes are lowered halfway, his expression inscrutable.

"I honestly don't know how you stayed as calm as you did. I'm so sorry."

He shrugs a shoulder. "What you told me on the drive over helped. I kept reminding myself that his reaction wasn't about me but about shit from his past. His dad... my dad. I tried to put myself in his shoes."

The nape of my neck prickles, the ennui in his voice clashing with his words. Despite the contact of our hands, he feels a million miles away. *Is this a type of panic attack? A self-defense mechanism?*

I clear my throat. "I hope you know I don't expect you to follow through on what you told him. You absolutely do not have to take a drug test to appease my father."

He lifts my hand and places a soft kiss to my knuckles. His normally warm lips are cool. "I don't want to be the reason for a rift in your family. I'll take the test." He releases my fingers and shudders; goosebumps pepper the side of his neck. "I'm going to lie down for a bit, okay?"

"Sure," I whisper, but he's already walking toward my bedroom, his gait lacking its usual grace. The door swings half-closed behind him. I listen to the sounds of him undressing, then the familiar creak of my bed frame as his weight settles.

I'm suddenly exhausted, too. *Sad. Angry.* Tugging a blanket off the back of the couch, I curl up on my side. My dry, burning eyes fall closed, only to open a second later when, in that single moment of darkness, I realized Wilder didn't look me in the eye once since we left my parents.

Not once.

I sit up, shivering as the blanket falls to my lap. The living room is shadowed, the sky darker than it was minutes ago. Raindrops spatter against the deck. Several nightlights give off haloes against the walls, and I focus on their glow until the vise on my chest releases.

I drag in a loud, rasping breath.

"Evangeline?"

Wilder's voice kickstarts my already racing heart. I twist on the couch to see him standing in the bedroom doorway. One hand braced on the doorframe, naked except for boxer briefs. His face is shadowed, his tall, muscled frame outlined by a light in the bedroom.

My father's voice ricochets between us, eerie in its utter calm.

"Do you think I was born yesterday? You can't even look me in the eye, can you?"

I'm brittle, bubbling taffy stretched between loyalties. I have no idea what lies at my breaking point.

"Can I hold you?"

His voice is soft. Wavering with emotion.

Snap.

I leap up and rush into his open arms. His skin is feverish as he trembles and holds me so tightly it hurts. I hold him even tighter. My nails drive into the muscles of his back like I can open him up. Crawl inside him and expose his depths.

Even if I'm terrified of what I'll find.

wilder

After the close call at Evangeline's parents' house, I wrestle back some control over my using. Once again, music saves my ass; in this case, the two-week runway to the release of Night Theory's sophomore album, *Fatalism*.

The stakes have never been higher for me—for any of us—and miraculously, that sense of purpose quiets my demons. I find a sweet spot where my general anxiety is manageable and my mind stays more or less sharp. No more nodding off or spiraling into withdrawals.

My free time shrinks even more, but whatever I have is spent with Evangeline. Even if it means I'm crawling into her bed at three in the morning and waking her up four hours later with my tongue. No matter what, I see her every night and prioritize texting her consistently during the day. As the world around me whips into a surreal frenzy, she keeps me rooted.

She doesn't bring up the drug test, and I sure as hell don't. I barely have time to think, much less dwell on how deeply I hate who I've become.

Every day is rigidly scheduled and sometimes lasts twelve hours or more. Our manager, Mack Martinez, and publicist, Shelly Reeves, rule our lives via a shared calendar that links to alerts on our phones. The only consistency day to day are time blocks for rehearsing, chef-prepared meals, and forty-five minutes labeled *private time*. Eddie is convinced the latter is their way of managing us down to when we shit and shower.

As restrictive as our schedules are, aside from the occasional joke, none of us complain. It won't last forever, and we've been preparing for this for months. Years, really. We're also mature enough to understand our skills as musicians can only get us so far. Having grown up in the shadow of Breaking Giants, I'm especially aware that none of this would be happening without the dedication and tireless efforts of the people around us.

As Mack is fond of saying: "You make the cake, we serve it."

There are countless live streams. Radio and podcast

interviews. A performance on a local morning television show. Surprise pop-up concerts in parks that inadvertently close neighboring streets and earn us citations. Within days of sending advanced copies of *Fatalism* to industry professionals, Mack and Shelly are flooded with interview requests from all over the country and as far away as France and Japan.

One week from release, our final and most commercially viable single, "End Times," drops. The accompanying music video—a trippy, apocalyptic mini-film—explodes the internet. When our soft-merch store launches the same day, it sells out within an hour. Preorders for a special edition vinyl sell out as well, and preorders for the standard vinyl go through the roof.

Three days before release, the most storied music magazine of all time does a feature on us predicting at least one Grammy nomination this fall.

The final Friday of April, *Fatalism* releases to the world.

In lieu of a standard launch party—which I vetoed months ago as it's the stuff of my nightmares—Saturday night we perform a release concert at the only venue in Seattle that isn't a stadium.

Eight thousand screaming fans greet us and carry us through the best set of our lives. And when I follow my bandmates into the greenroom after the show and see Evangeline waiting for me?

I've never experienced a comparable joy.

In this moment, there's no darkness at all. Only the welcome weight of her body when she jumps into my arms with a happy squeal. The impact of my shoulder with the doorframe as I clip it rushing back out of the room. The knowing laughter and whistles from the guys and our crew. The heat of Evangeline's cheek as she presses it to mine, as she squeezes me tighter.

"You were amazing," she whispers against my ear.

"That was nothing compared to what I'm about to do to you," I murmur back.

In the smallest of the three dressing rooms, the door locked behind us, we're a storm of moving hands and sucking kisses and gasping groans. She undoes my belt, yanks my zipper down, and tugs my pants and underwear off my hips. I pull up her skirt and rip down her tights, then cup the wet heat between her legs. She wraps her hands around my dick and pumps me as I kiss my way from one side of her neck to the other.

"Wilder," she moans. "I need you."

"Such a slut for me," I rumble into her soft throat.

She squeezes my dick. I bite her neck in retaliation and grin when arousal soaks my hand. Sinking two fingers inside her, I pump them slowly. My thumb makes equally slow circles around her clit.

"I love your angry little growls," I say as I nip her earlobe. "Frustrated kitten, aren't you? You want something thicker? Harder? Faster?"

She growls louder. "I'm going to kill you if you don't fuck me right now."

Chuckling darkly, I pull my fingers from her body. Before she can protest, I spin her around and bend her over an empty catering table. The tights bunched above her boots have the happy consequence of keeping her legs together. Her perfect ass lifts, providing a mouthwatering view of her dripping pink center.

She wiggles teasingly—the resulting crack of my hand on one pale cheek is shockingly loud.

For a long second, she freezes. Then she moans and thrusts her ass back in the air. "Again."

"Fuck," I hiss, watching the shape of my hand form in red on her pale skin. "No more foreplay for you. Arms up. Grab the table."

She immediately seizes the edge above her head. I spank her other cheek. She yelps, then writhes. "Wilder. *Please.*"

I line myself up and press the head of my cock inside her. The angle and her bound legs make it an almost impossibly tight fit. By the time I'm a few inches inside, we're both panting.

Bending over her, I growl, "Give me your mouth."

She twists her head to meet my kiss, our tongues tangling, our breaths interspersed with moans and whispers of, "I love you."

I start rolling my hips, my rhythm controlled and agonizingly slow. Every inch of me her body accepts feels like both victory and surrender. As with every time I'm inside her, I imagine more of my soul sliding into her possession. When our bodies are finally flush, powerful shivers rack my spine. I fight to stay still, ignoring the hammering voice of my need. *Take. Possess. Defile. Mark.*

I focus instead on Evangeline. She's perfectly still, her breaths shallow, her eyes tightly closed. Her teeth press deeply into her bottom lip, her fingers bleached with tension where they grip the table.

I press a shaky kiss to her temple. "Do you want me to pull out? Make you come first?"

She shakes her head. I almost smile at her stubbornness.

"Just... talk to me," she whispers.

Warmth spirals in my chest. Angling my mouth to her ear, I whisper, "You're doing so good, taking me so deep. I'm unbelievably proud of you. I love you so, so much. Being inside you is the closest to peace I've ever known. Just breathe. That's it. Take all the time you need. Tell me when you're ready."

She gasps. "I'm ready."

My body shakes with soundless laughter. She trembles, her pussy contracting so hard I choke on a groan. "I'm not moving until you relax more, baby. Otherwise it's going to hurt."

"Wilder."

I lift my head. Her silver eye blinks. Sees through me. Unmakes me. Her perfect pink lips move, the words registering a second later.

"I want it to hurt."

Fire whips up my spine. Darkness eclipses my mind—not my Shadow, though. This darkness is sparkling. Full of light. Of *her*.

I run my tongue over my teeth. "Tap my thigh if—" I lose the ability to speak as she pulls herself forward and pushes back hard. Intense pleasure obliterates my hold on reason.

Her arms tense to repeat the movement, but before she can, I seize her hips and take over. I don't hold back. *Can't.* I thrust into her mercilessly. The table rocks. Grunts and gasps float atop the vicious slaps of our bodies. My gaze stays fixed on my glistening shaft as I pull out, on the singular pleasure of watching myself disappear back inside her.

All that truly matters are these moments of oneness with her.

Evangeline shatters with a breathy moan, pussy fluttering around my cock. *Not enough.* With a growl of determination, I change the angle of my hips so I'm driving downward. I know I've found the most sensitive spot inside her when she mewls in protest, fingernails scrambling on the table.

Through gritted teeth, I tell her, "If it's too much, you know how to make me stop. But if you don't tap out, you're coming again."

She curses me.

I grin as I spank her. "Now tell me the truth."

She sobs. "I l-love y-you."

"That's my girl."

Hyper focused on her body's cues, I carry her up the next peak. This time, her body seizes around my cock like she wants to break it off and keep it. This time, she screams my name as warmth gushes over my groin and drips down my thighs.

This time, I jump with her.

Seconds or minutes later, I regain consciousness after the most insane orgasm of my life. I have no idea how I managed to stay standing. My hands are planted to either side of her body, my arms trembling with strain. I heave air into my lungs. Sweat drips from my brow onto her black T-shirt.

Evangeline makes a soft sound of contentment.

In that moment, when I'm peaceful and sated and drunk off love, I make a mistake.

The biggest mistake of my life.

I whisper, "Come with me."

She yawns, then stiffens. "Oh God, we were so loud. Do you think people heard us?" She twists to look at me with wide eyes. "Can we sneak out a back door?"

She didn't hear what I said.

"Fairy."

She blinks. "Sorry, did you ask me something?"

I brush a strand of pale hair from her forehead. "Come with me. On tour."

Her brows furrow. "Huh?"

I trace the Cupid's bow of her upper lip. "Eight months, dozens of cities. It'll be amazing. We can even add encores of our old songs and perform together again. Say you'll come with me. Be with me."

She stares at me blankly for a beat, then pushes up from the table. "Let me up. Pull out of me right now, Wilder. *Now, now, now.*"

Her voice rises and sharpens with every word until she's yelling and shoving me back roughly.

Still half-delirious from performing for two hours and falling apart in bliss, I stumble backward, wincing as my body slips from her heat.

Evangeline jumps off the table and yanks her tights up her legs. She only glances at me once, hissing, "Put your dick away."

I fumble, pulling up my pants with numb fingers. Cold radiates down my body, wiping away my delusion. Revealing the wide-open darkness around me as I free-fall.

I try to say her name but nothing comes out.

She adjusts her miniskirt with jerky movements, muttering to herself. "History repeating itself. Unbeliev-able." Straightening, she smooths back hairs that escaped her ponytail. Her hands shake. A crystalline tear drips off her chin.

I gasp. "Wait—"

She whirls on me. I don't know what's worse, the fury on her face or the shattered look in her eyes.

"You're asking me to go on tour with Night Theory," she says in a freakishly calm voice. "To break Glow's *legally binding contract* with Indigo and drop my dream —Lily's dream—like it's trash?"

I fist my hair and shake my head. "No. Absolutely not. *Fuck.* I wasn't thinking, okay? It just came out. I swear!"

She scoffs. "That's almost worse. It means you *subconsciously* believe my dreams aren't as important as yours. That your needs and wants are superior. My feelings—my dreams—don't even matter to you. They never have."

"That's not what I said," I rasp, horrified. "I love you more than I've ever loved anything in my life. How—how could you even think that?"

Her lip quivers. For a second, I think she understands. Then her expression hardens. "I need to think. Don't follow me and don't come to my house."

No, no, no.

Black cracks spread from my edges, racing toward the center of my being. My lungs squeeze. Words jumble in my head and tangle in my throat as she walks past me to the door. In my stomach, a demon screams.

The Shadow smiles.

"I'll call you," she says softly. "Just... give me a little bit of time."

The door creaks twice. Open. Closed.

My legs give out and I slam to the floor.

White noise fills my head.

Static nothing.

I blink and Jax is grabbing my shoulders, his mouth moving.

I can't hear him.

I blink and streetlights pass outside car windows. Colorful streaks across a void.

I blink again and I'm sitting listlessly on my bed with a bottle of pills lying near my hip. My body tingles. Terror ices my mind. *How many did I take?* Shivering violently, it takes me three tries to open the bottle. I dump the remaining pills onto the comforter and count them.

My gasp of relief slices the silence.

Only three. You only took three.

Like the drug in my bloodstream was waiting for acknowledgment, intense heat spikes inside me. My muscles melt. My mind quiets. I barely manage to lift my legs onto the bed and pull the comforter over me before losing the ability to move.

I float on a warm sea. Lapping waves flush away my darkness. Drown my Shadow. Drown me.

I'm nothing.

No one.

Emptiness. Silence. *Peace.*

CHAPTER THIRTY-SIX
evangeline

Here is sucking empty

A slipping memory of your skin

Here are fingers curling inward

Seeking the source of sin

For the first time in my adult life, I lie my way out of Sunday brunch, texting my mom that I have food poisoning. When she immediately calls me, I don't answer.

> Can't talk. Puking

> Honey! 😟 do u need anything? Electrolytes? Saltine crackers?

I'm good.

Okay. I'm so sorry. Just say the word
and I'll be there

Thx momma. Love you

I put my phone on the nightstand and flop back on my bed, wishing I actually *were* sick and my mom could come over, rub my back, and tell me everything will be okay—and I was still young enough to believe her.

I wish, too, that I had the guts to tell her the truth. That I'm not the levelheaded, confident, responsible daughter she thinks I am. I'm an insecure mess who's afraid of the dark. Afraid of everything, including love.

Turning my head on the pillow, I suck in Wilder's fading scent.

Sometime during the night, while chugging tea and journaling with every light in the house on, the inferno of anger and betrayal in my chest cooled to embers of regret.

I can't stop thinking about what my reaction blinded me to in the moment. The soft, adoring expression on Wilder's face when he asked me to come with him. His boyish excitement at the idea of us performing together again. His confusion, horror, and impassioned apology after I flipped out.

He really did speak without thinking, the words coming straight from his heart. My reaction, on the other hand, came straight from the fear center of my brain. The part of me that refuses to let go of who he was and accept him for who he is now—*again*.

Wilder isn't the same man he was three years ago or even six years ago. Every day of the last month and especially the last two weeks, he's proven that fact. Despite his insane pre-launch schedule, I never once felt like an afterthought. He texted me constantly throughout the day: quick hellos, selfies and videos of him and the guys, annoyingly funny memes about Taurus women, unfinished song lyrics, X-rated promises... And every night, no matter how exhausted he was, he found his way into my arms.

He's changed.

I'm the one who's stayed the same.

How long will I make him suffer for my inability to let go of the past? How long before he decides he doesn't want to walk on eggshells anymore or deal with my overthinking, insecure, moody self?

I owe him an explanation. An apology.

We were already planning to spend the afternoon together, his first in weeks with nothing on the schedule.

I'll surprise him with coffee.

Or better yet, a burned bagel.

I'll tell him the truth—open up to him about my insecurities like he's opened up to me about his anxiety. We'll get over this speed bump like we have others. And someday, we'll have a smooth road to walk.

Smiling to myself, I push to my feet and head to my bathroom to do something about my frizzy hair and eye bags.

♪

A PAJAMA-CLAD Eddie answers the front door. Shoving the drink carrier and bag of bagels into his arms, I rush past him into the house. He blinks at me in wide-eyed surprise, green mohawk soft and flopping over his right ear.

"There's a coffee for each of you," I say as I face the mirror in the entryway and try to fix my hair after the wind massacred it on the walk up from the curb. "I already drank mine. Bagels are in the bag. I got a variety, so have whatever you want, but leave an Everything for Wilder, okay?"

Eddie makes a strangled sound.

"Eva?" Jax stops beside his brother, looking from his full arms to me. His mouth hangs open. "Did Wilder know you were coming over?"

"Nope. It's a surprise." I jerk my head toward Eddie.

"Coffee and bagels. Is Wilder still sleeping or something?"

Please tell me he's still in bed.

Jax clears his throat. "Actually, he, uh... He's not feeling great. Should I tell him to call you later?"

My hands still, then sink to my sides. A fluttering sensation takes up residence in my throat. I face the men, finally absorbing their expressions. Eddie is unusually pale. He swallows convulsively, his eyes flickering to his brother every few seconds. And Jax looks like I caught them burying a body.

I try to swallow and choke. Cough to clear my throat. Drag in air that *burns*.

Footsteps pound down the stairs at the back of the house. "Did I hear the doorbell?" calls Zander. "Please tell me it's my food and not another psycho ex-girlfriend."

My ears ring.

Eddie closes his eyes.

Jax flushes.

Zander appears in the hallway past the kitchen. When he sees me, his eyes bug out. "Oh, shit."

My vision distorts like I'm underwater.

"It's not what you think," Eddie says quickly.

My hearing wanes like someone cranked the world's volume down. All three men are talking, but their voices are muffled. *Wah-wahah-wahh.* I touch my ears, half-expecting to find them plugged. They're not.

Suddenly, my senses turn back on.

"Tell her, Jax," snaps Eddie.

"It's the right thing to do," murmurs Zander.

Jax drags a hand over buzzed blond hair, his heavy sigh the hissing descent of a guillotine. I lock my knees. My armpits prickle. Each of my short, fast breaths is sandpaper against the silence.

Jax takes a step toward me, eyes radiating sympathy.

"Just say it," I croak.

"He's not cheating on you. He's..."

The guillotine pauses.

"He's what?"

What the fuck could be worse than cheating on me?

His expression hardens with resolve. "You know what? Screw this. I'm done covering for him. Follow me, Eva. You deserve to know."

He turns and walks down the hallway toward the stairs. Muscle memory takes over, operating my body for me. Eddie gives me a wobbly smile as I pass him. Zander keeps his head down.

One step. Five steps. Ten. Down the hallway to the end.

Wilder's bedroom door is cracked. Voices come from inside. Kendra's. His.

Jax grabs my sweaty hand and pulls me to the wall beside the door.

"—really believed you'd snap out of it, Wild, but I'm done waiting. You have to choose. Me or her."

"Her."

Kendra laughs shortly. "What happens when she finds out, huh? You think Miss Perfect will accept this?" A weird, rattling sound follows.

Wilder sighs. "No, I don't."

A foot stomps. "Then why are you torturing yourself? Torturing me?"

"For the last time, this isn't about you. If you want out, fine. I'll find someone else."

She sniffles, her voice softening. "Do you really feel nothing for me?"

"I'm not doing this with you again. You don't love me, Kendra. You only think you do."

"Don't tell me how I feel!"

Wilder groans. "Just go."

"I was your girlfriend for over six months. I kept your secret and protected you from everyone trying to pull you down." She laughs again, low and caustic. "You think she'll protect you? Lie for you? No fucking way."

"This conversation is over."

There's a loud slap, then Kendra bursts into tears.

"I'm sorry. God, I'm sorry. I don't understand. Make it make sense, Wilder. Please."

"You'll never understand," he says tiredly.

There's a long pause.

"You're right," she finally says, her cutting tone disturbingly at odds with her tearful outcry of seconds ago. "I'll never understand you throwing me away for a snotty, virginal bitch who's *so fucking stupid* she can't tell you're a full-blown junkie. Find another supplier for your Oxy, Wilder. I'm done with you."

If he replies, I don't hear it over the high frequency sound of my heart being cleaved down the middle. My knees give out. Jax's arm bands around my waist, his quick reflexes all that save me from hitting the floor.

The bedroom door swings open and Kendra strides out. She jerks to a stop at the sight of us, her mascara-ringed eyes widening with shock. Just as fast, they narrow, gleaming. A slow, vindictive smile curves her lips.

"Whoopsie," she whispers.

Flipping long, dark hair over a shoulder, she sashays down the hallway and out of sight.

Full-blown junkie.

My dad was right. And Kendra was right, too—I'm so fucking stupid. My hands curl into fists. Dimly, I register pain signals as my nails cut into my palms.

I defended him to my parents, to Lily. Spent weeks suffocating my own instincts in order to trust him. Tormented myself with self-doubts. Convinced myself I was the problem.

Nothing was real.

"Do you want me to stay?" Jax murmurs.

I shake my head and straighten. His arm falls away as I face the open doorway. The curtains in Wilder's bedroom are pulled aside. Sunlight fills the room, but I don't see or feel it. I'm a vortex of dark, bitter cold. But I'm not afraid.

I *embrace* the dark.

I walk a few steps into the room and stop. Wilder sits at the foot of the bed, his elbows on his knees and his head in his hands. He rocks slowly back and forth, fingers clenching and unclenching in his hair. He looks like he's in pain.

I feel nothing.

"Kendra, I told you—" He looks up and gasps. The blood drains from his face, turning his golden skin sallow. One cheek stays slightly red from Kendra's slap.

I wish she'd punched him. Broken his perfect nose or split his perfect lips.

Now that my denial has been stripped away, I see the signs clearly. Both in the present and in retrospect. Eyes that are more brown than green and slightly glazed.

Eyelids a touch too heavy. Pupils that are either extremely constricted or huge. Right now, they're far too dilated for the brightness in the room. Sweat beads on his forehead. Goosebumps coat his neck and bare, trembling arms.

A word comes to me: *dopesick.*

He's withdrawing and needs a fix.

Bile coats my throat, my body clenching against an overwhelming feeling of violation. All the times he was inside me, told me he loved me, while I had no idea he was high. Sudden bouts of sleepiness blamed on his schedule. Random errands and not answering his phone. Not looking me in the eye. Manipulating me into thinking he'd changed, that he had no secrets from me. Encouraging my vulnerability while he lied.

Lied.

Lied.

Wilder stands. A small prescription bottle rolls across where he was sitting, and he shifts to block my sight of it. "This isn't what it looks like," he says weakly.

"Don't bother." My voice is empty. As cold as the endless dark inside me. "I heard everything."

"Fairy, please. Let me explain."

"I'm not your Fairy. I'm not your *anything*. We. Are. Done."

His chest convulses. "Please," he whispers. "I'll go to rehab. Right now—today. I can fix this. I can change."

Cracks spread through my frozen core, but it's not sympathy that fractures me.

It's rage.

"I don't care what you do," I snarl. "I'll never forgive you or trust you again. Do you hear me? We're through. You've lied to me for weeks, but the worst thing you did was make me believe you loved—" Stabbing pain in my chest takes my voice. My vision blurs with tears.

He moves toward me. I scramble backward and collide with the doorframe. "Stay the fuck away from me."

Features contorting, he falls to his knees. "I d-do love you, Evangeline," he says through wracking sobs. "More than anything. P-please, please don't leave me."

"This isn't love, Wilder. This is manipulation. You only love yourself and whatever's in that bottle on the bed. You *disgust* me. I hate you. I fucking hate you!"

I don't realize I'm shouting until gentle hands capture my shoulders from behind and Jax says, "Hey, it's okay. Let's go."

He pulls me out of the room and down the hallway.

Behind us is a guttural scream.

I feel nothing.

evangeline

Neither Lily nor Rye are answering their phones. Since Rye's house is closest, I drive there first. Slowly. Carefully. Every few seconds, my hands convulse on the steering wheel. I take deep, even breaths and blink rapidly to keep tears from obscuring my vision.

I slow outside Rye's house and see Lily's car in the driveway.

I drive past without stopping.

Familiar roads lead to the highway. I merge into traffic. Stay in the slow lane. Exit. Three turns. Six stoplights. A winding road.

I finally park. Turn off the car. Leave my keys, my purse. Stumble up a path to the front door and ring the doorbell.

Footsteps approach.

Wood swings inward.
Blue eyes widen.
"Eva? What's wrong?"
"D-daddy."
He catches me as I fall.
As I break.

wilder

My dad finds me curled in a fetal position on the floor of my bedroom, the bottle of pills clutched in my hand and my phone discarded next to me.

He drops to his knees and lifts me into a tight embrace. Like he can keep me from falling apart.

But he can't. I've lost too many pieces.

"I've got you, Wilder. I'm here. How many pills did you take?"

Words come in stutters between gasping sobs. "N-none, but I was going to t-take them all. I-I lost her. Oh, fuck, I lost Evangeline. F-forever. I can't—don't want to live without her. H-help me, Dad. Please help me. I'm so sorry."

He pulls back to grip my face in his hands. Tears

track down his cheeks. Golden eyes, bright and determined, stare into mine.

"Listen to me, son. I know it seems impossible right now, but I promise it's going to be okay. You never have to feel this way again. Drop the bottle. Let it go."

My fingers spasm and open.

♫

THE FOLLOWING days are a blur of pain over a soundtrack of misery.

My mother singing, her voice cracking every other word. My sisters crying outside my childhood bedroom. Strong, calloused hands moving my sweat-soaked body. Cold porcelain under my cheek. Cramping muscles and my teeth chattering so hard I bite through my tongue. Hot compresses and showers. Fresh sheets soaked again in minutes.

Fire inside me. Burning hotter and hotter. Melting away my sanity.

Make it stop.

Just make it stop.

Agonizing need. Yelling and begging and screaming. Pounding on a locked door.

Let me out. Out. Out.

Falling. Convulsing. Blood in my mouth.

Blacking out.

A clinical touch and unfamiliar voice.

"Whatever he told you... these are severe withdrawals. Blood pressure... dangerous..."

Hands holding me down as I writhe.

The pinch of a needle.

Darkness again.

Everywhere.

♪

KATHERINE'S VOICE in my ear—maybe in my head.

"Find the light, Wilder."

wilder

I'm surrounded by light so bright my eyes water uncontrollably. But I don't think this is what Katherine meant.

This light is from a merciless sun beating down on the California desert. Directly in front of me sprawls a single-story building of darkly reflective glass and beige stucco. My apparent home for the next ninety days.

My body is feeble, my head spiky static, my heart a chasm. The last two weeks are a grainy smear of ash and fire, the flight and car ride here a blur, the goodbye to my parents a few minutes ago almost forgotten.

I don't know if I'm lucid or in the grip of an endless nightmare.

A man stands just outside the entrance. He's wearing

a suit but doesn't look stiff, and he has pale, intelligent blue eyes. There's no pity in them. No judgment, either. Just calm assurance and a hint of anticipation, like he knows something I don't and looks forward to sharing it with me.

"Welcome to Oasis, Wilder. My name is Dr. Chastain." With a soft smile, he gestures toward the door. "Ready?"

My sweaty fingers clench around the strap of my duffel bag.

Am I ready?

Yes.

No.

Maybe?

Fuck it.

I force my weak legs to carry me forward. "Yeah, Doc. I'm ready for air conditioning." I eye his dark suit. "How are you not boiling right now?"

He chuckles. "I'm used to it."

As he opens the door, cool air rushes out. Goosebumps roll over my damp, pallid skin. I manage two more steps, but my body jerks to a stop on the threshold.

I'm suspended between light and shadow, between the toxic, clinging webs of the past and the vast, terrifying unknown.

"Do you need help?" asks a low, kind voice.

My chin jerks. A hand settles on my shoulder. "One step at a time, Wilder. Together."

Deep in my darkness, a small, fragile light flickers to life.

And we walk inside.

transition

transition : a rhythmic or melodic interlude between

sections of a song

Life is a series of crossroads. Most of them we don't even notice and have no quantifiable effect on our lives. What we eat for a meal. What clothes we wear on any given day. If we answer a call from an unknown number or not.

Other crossroads are more obvious—they're the big life decisions. We fret over all the possible repercussions or rewards that await us depending on which direction we take.

But whether a crossroads is obvious or not, it still matters. Little ones can become life-altering. Decisions that seem momentous in the moment can shrink in importance as time passes and our perspective shifts.

Our choices, big and small, define us. Shape us and heal us.

They break us, too.

In the brief month Wilder and I were together, I faced hundreds of crossroads. Most of them only obvious in hindsight.

When I said yes to us that first night. When I swore to never regret him. When I promised to love him forever. Each kiss. Touch. Smile. The choice to trust and hope.

Every time I believed his lies... and the lies I spoke believing they were truth.

I once thought falling in love with Wilder would destroy me. I was right and also wrong. In a strange way, I'm grateful for what happened.

By embracing darkness, I lost my fear of it. I'm finally safe.

Nothing can touch me now.

- Journal of Eva Sullivan

Lyrics of "End Times" by Theory

Album: *Fatalism*

Bells were ringing at the end of time

The sky was on fire but you were mine

Ashes on our tongues, in our lungs

But you were mine

This story's ending already told

Stamped, sealed, sold

Beautiful by design

You were mine

Mine at the end of time

Close your eyes now, baby

and remember the color of mine

the first and last time

you told me you loved me

Beautiful by design

(Beautiful by design)

You were mine at the end of time

♪

Thank you so much for reading! Evangeline and Wilder's story concludes in *A Perfect Song Duet: Last Chorus.*

stay connected

www.lmhalloran.com
lm@lmhalloran.com

playlist

"Can't Get You Out of My Head"—Johnny Goth

"You Broke Me First"—Tate McRae

"buzzkill"—MOTHICA

"Girls Like You"—The Naked And Famous

"Wasted Youth"—goddard, Cat Burns

"War"—Chance Peña

"Darkside"—grandson

"Oxytocin"—Chandler Leighton

"Your Touch"—Foreign Air

"My Perfection"—Tokyo Project

"Toxic"—Omido, Rich Jansen

and more…

BREAKING GIANTS

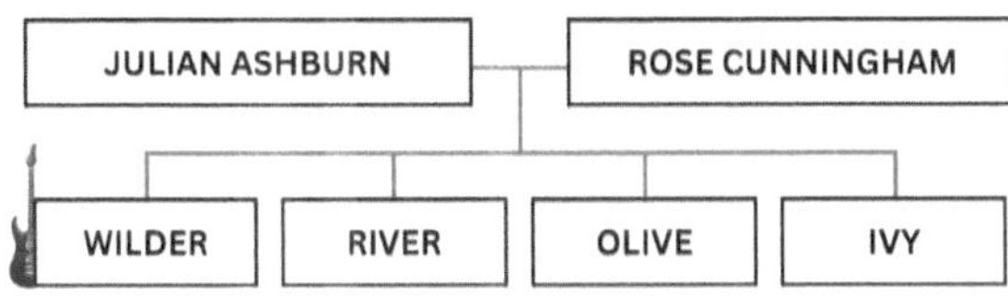

BREAKING SILENCE

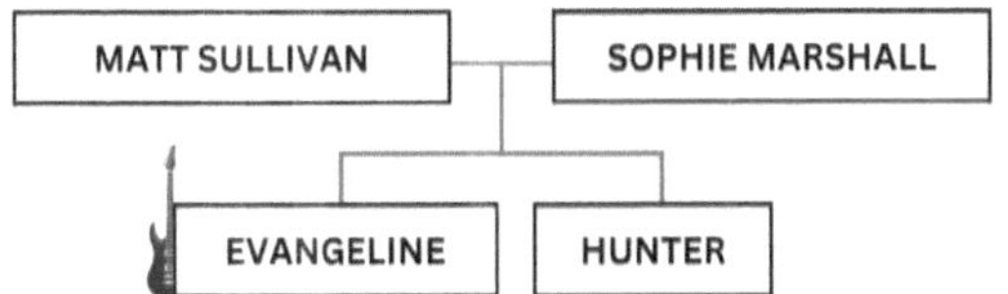

OTHER BAND MEMBERS

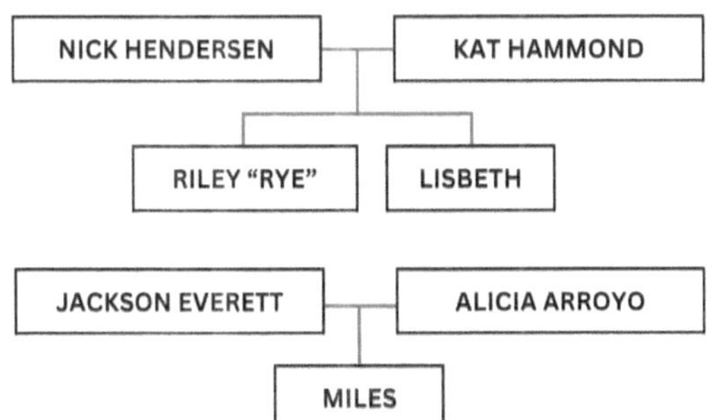

afterword

To those of you who've been in the pit of despair and clawed your way into the light of recovery, my hat is off to you. And if you or someone you love is still suffering, here are some resources:

National Drug Helpline
1-844-289-0879

Suicide & Crisis Lifeline
Dial 988

Substance Abuse and Mental Health Services
Administration (SAMHSA)
1-800-662-HELP

There are many paths to sobriety. What works for one person might not work for another. It doesn't matter *how* you get there, just that you do—one second, one hour, one day at a time.

My email is always open as well.

lm@lmhalloran.com

My brain is jello and my heart is in ribbons, but before I hibernate for a bit, I want to sprinkle some gratitude.

To the readers who heard I was diving back into excruciating angst and said BRING IT, *thank you.* Because of your excitement and support, I felt brave enough to lean into a very personal, emotional territory that I've skirted around before but never fully committed to. So thank you for trusting me with your tender hearts, for embracing flawed characters in romance, and for leaning in with me.

Shan, you absolute goddess, thanks for reading the very first draft of this book and giving me the best possible feedback: "I want to smack them both and then immediately cuddle them."

If you can relate, then just know it's food for my angsty soul and exactly what I was aiming for.

Sorrynotsorry.

To my alpha/beta readers: Heather, Danielle, Michelle, Jessie, Jaime, Amanda, Jen, and Dawn. I appreciate your feedback, encouragement, and sharp eyes more than you'll ever know.

To Emily A. Lawrence, Editor Extraordinaire, thanks for tirelessly fixing the same issues for almost eight years. I hope you know you'll never get rid of me (and that I'll probably never capitalize Mom correctly).

To Shauna and Becca at The Author Agency and every ARC reader and blogger who took a chance on this duet—you have my deepest gratitude.

Lauren, Emily, Brit, Nichole, and Shan: thanks for keeping me sane in the group chats.

To my bff/lifewife/braintwin, Lacee. Thank you for twenty years of showing up, midnight drives to the desert, breaking plates in parking lots (don't worry, we cleaned up after ourselves), questionable crafts, check-in times, survival modes, window-rattling bass, unflinching honesty, and unconditional love. You are the bravest, strongest person I know. This world became a home when I found you in it.

Finally, to my lighthouse, Dave, and to my sun + moon + stars, Stella, thank you both for your endless support and love, and for reminding me daily that I have a beautiful life to live outside my head.

Until next time.

xo,

Laura

When not writing or reading, the author can be found daydreaming or trying to keep up with her daughter. Some of her favorite things are puzzles, podcasts, and small dogs that resemble Ewoks.

Home is the Pacific Northwest.

lmhalloran.com